ISBN: 978-0-578-88251-2
Burgundy & Brown's
The Executives -
Book one of the Her Knight In All Of His Honor series…(three women separately meet powerful Grayson & Gannon men.)

Written By: Lawana Dinkins
Publisher: Lawana Dinkins
Book Covers For The Executives Designed By: Lawana Dinkins
This book is a work of fiction. Herein are names, occurrences and characters which are products of the author's imagination.

While this book may resemble real names, real individuals, and real-life situations, it was in no way created to represent the lives of **ANY** one person, solitaire or collectively, living or deceased, any business entity or business otherwise functional or non-functional.

This book may resemble or hold the same names as other fictional characters, identical fictional occurrences, locations, or same subject matter of other books created by other authors under their own individual talents for their own works, fictional and non-fictional, this book has no ties to such. By no means was this book created based on continuity from other books (fictional or non-fictional) of other authors, neither was it created to represent any other form of collaborative efforts.
For other information regarding this book and
Burgundy & Brown please visit the website @
burgundyandbrownportfolio.com

Burgundy & Brown

Her Knight In All Of His Honor

First Printed: September 2012 in the United States of America

About The Book & Its Author

Although this publication is the first of many romance novels to be published by Lawana Dinkins, the joy of writing is not brand new to the Self Publisher.

Over the years life's situations slowly stirred me away from one of my most cherished hobbies. It wasn't until a great associate of mine (he knows who he is) told me I should become a writer. No, I mean really write. Although he probably knew I would eventually do so, I'm sure he didn't know I would end up writing a fictional romance novel. I am grateful for his kind words, and I define those very words as the ones which gave me an additional tap on my shoulder. Those words encouraged me to join the hands of my creativity with those of not just readers but fans of fictional love stories who can enjoy and understand fiction as only being a source of great entertainment and imagination.

Again, From The Author – On a personal level, first and foremost incredulous thanks will always be in order for my creator, the one up above who loves me the most. The rest I'll keep to myself because he prefers it to be that way.
Thanks! -
This writing experience was absolutely wonderful. This book is my first idea/work to be published in this capacity, and I'm looking forward to sharing many more books with my current fans as well as new fans.

More from the author- I give much thanks to several individuals, for no matter the circumstances I faced, be it personal or from a standpoint of business, each of them continued to cheer for me regardless of the least and ample opinions held by others. With or without setbacks, each of my supporters knew I would get the job done. Thank goodness I realized it too, for success begins from within. Names were intentionally omitted because their hearts will tell it all.

To the readers of this book-
People who know me pretty well will agree I can t- a- l- k! Initially, I felt as though I did a little too much talking, forgetting to let the voices of my characters speak. Then again, I believe I did those same characters and the book itself adequate justice. As you read this book from start to its completion, I hope you will enjoy following my every thought, my every word and those of my characters.

Keep checking the website of Burgundy & Brown often.

Burgundy & Brown's
The Executives
Her Knight In All Of His Honor

Published in 2012
Burgundy & Brown and the B & B logo are registered.

Ephesians Ch 5 vs 20
Giving thanks always for all things unto God and the Father in the name of our Lord Jesus Christ

Fictional idea and characters created & developed by:
Lawana Dinkins

Publisher: Lawana Dinkins

The Executives
Her Knight In All Of His Honor was
Created, Written & Edited By:
Lawana Dinkins

THE EXECUTIVES
HER KNIGHT IN ALL OF HIS HONOR

By

LAWANA DINKINS

Prologue

"Yes Mr. Scranton, you'll have the updated memo on your desk by noon time on Tuesday of next week."

Claude cleverly lied as his assistant Maureen entered the conference room to retrieve her executive folder.

"Don't worry about it," said a confident voice on the other end of the sleek device, "everything is under control. I've never let you down before, have I?"

Maureen began to exit the oversized room. Claude rose then proceeded to follow her. Hoping to discourage any furthered invitations, with his cell still to his good ear, Claude reached and immediately closed the conference room door behind her while almost simultaneously adjusting the cedar wood blinds for increased privacy.

"That remains to be seen-" the voice on the other end of the receiver interrupted Claude.

"And I won't! So just relax!"

"Relax!" Claude countered in an angry whisper, "are you out of your....," appearing to be embarrassed by his own outburst Claude pauses, his eyes wander the room before his frustrated voice lit into the person on the other end of the line, "are you out of your mind? this has gone for too long as it is. Look, just be careful please, and keep my name out of it," Claude pleaded before nervously flipping his cell phone shut against the bone of his waist.

His years as an overzealous competitor had finally succeeded in making a villain out of him. For months, he's been on pins and needles while covering his tracks with lies, unsurprisingly exceptional ones.

Periodically, Claude assumed the position of 'acting' CEO whenever Jim Grainger, the CEO of Stone and Nichols was consumed with other things such as recovering from surgeries, extended business trips, vacations with family and projects due to company expansion. Unknown to Jim, inside corruption is becoming more prominent, a corruption capable of destroying the building blocks of his beloved and impressive legacy.

Chapter 1

The Executives

Oh! There she is. Cadrin Porter, corporate publicist for the daring elite. Along the paths of lessons learned and those where opportunity shouted the loudest, Cadrin began rising through the ranks of public service. Her famed interest was to one day in some capacity represent corporate leaders. She finally got her chance to do just that. She was volunteering and had been running late for an appointment when she was sidetracked by the approach of the Director of Administration who asked her if she would be interested in working within the field of public service. Unaware the studios volunteer already held ownership of a degree in Public Relations, she was delighted to learn of Cadrin's credentials. The gig presented to her by the Director of Administration was a small one, offering her work here and there along with trusty perks. Attending networking events for budding entrepreneurs are prudent in Chicago. Often and at no charge, Cadrin would attend some of the life changing events.

Through networking with others whose careers were near the heart of her own dreams had finally given her the confidence to begin her own PR business; to serve the corporate elite.

Every hour she spent in her office had become another steppingstone towards her becoming self insured. Frequently the call of duty took her to the conference rooms of clients and gave to her countless public appearances. There's no doubt that right now she is living her dream. What's the feeling it gives to her? For a now five-year-old company, well, the feeling is better than nice. Her obviously wealthy clients either gravitated to trouble or it to them. Whether or not they were at fault for their misfortune, they entrusted her to unravel mishaps and spread her wit over their good name. It was unbelievable. Some of their own self afflictions could place them into much more impressive ridicule than any grueling competitive outsider could have thrown at them. However, there are still some out there who would like to give it their best shot.

There he stands. His name is Andrew Weston, he's of Lox Gable. Andrew and his Executive Director of Marketing, Nick casually standing underneath an enormous chandelier inside of a crowded ballroom of the Acapella Chicago Water Tower drinking from flutes of champagne. Cadrin had been invited there by her client to help celebrate the results of her outstanding dedication. He'd told her the celebration was for her, but she knew it was solely for the clout of Lox Gable.

The beat of the room had a flair going on about it which fondly reminded her of a high-end wedding reception. Andrew is good at a lot of things and how to throw a good party is one of them. The talk around the after five clock said Andrew is understandably known for glitzy gatherings. Cadrin had heard right. The only things the event is missing is a fancy wedding cake and of course the bride and groom.

Now Andrew is no fool, he didn't take the monetary measures of his company for granted, not for a second. His hired party planners are suave in their field. They worked to no end to ensure him an almost exact replica of a bank breaking affair at almost half the cost.

Supplying Andrew's company with the recognition it needs had been a relatively easy task for Cadrin. Under the diagnosis of her client, she had conquered the world. And didn't she? Money in some fashion or another makes the world go round, then back again and again...she's standing amid proof and Andrew couldn't have found himself in higher approval of her efforts. Because of her exemplary leadership, his bank account hadn't suffered not one bit.

Andrew's request had been somewhat rather odd in the beginning. It was mid afternoon when Cadrin had just begun to sit down alone in front of a movie when her home phone ranged. An associate now turned a good friend of hers had called her up during a commercial break telling her she should quickly tune into the Corporate Networking channel. The channel highlighted the corners of Chief Executive and Financial Officers. Andrew's company was up next. Roslyn thought Cadrin should check out Andrew's personality to determine for herself where it came to rest when it settled down to the vision of his corporation. She thought maybe Cadrin wouldn't mind her credentials being found in his rolodex. From the moment the two met, Roslyn always had a substantive look out. While she didn't make Cadrin's career, the two leads she gave to her within the five-year stint made Cadrin's resume much more impressive.

Roslyn is the former assistant to a prior client of Cadrin's. Her genuine friendship towards the corporate publicist is remarkable.

Cadrin and Roslyn rarely disagree about anything. They always discuss topics others are reluctant to share due to personal reasons. Like Roslyn, Cadrin knew how and when to respond and when to be quiet and listen. So, the two of them clicked immediately. Cadrin's admissions were always followed by "you know that's right girl," from Roslyn and a, "call me later!" Listening to Roslyn discuss Andrew, Cadrin decided to pause the movie that had been playing before she'd answered Roslyn's call. Immediately, she engaged the programming her friend called her about. Still holding the phone so she could hear Roslyn rant and rave over Andrew, Cadrin pulled her bare feet up onto the couch, her eyes studied, deciphered and widened at the jargon of the cool natured mogul.

Andrew demonstrated a respectable no-nonsense tenure about himself which for Cadrin was without a doubt, refreshing. She often found herself tuning up the not so cool behaviors of a few of her prior clients who meant well, but all in all did more harm than good to their corporate visions.

"He's rather good. Isn't he?" Cadrin remembered her friend saying to her.

"So far so good, he is all that," Cadrin said to her. Although she didn't skip to another station, Cadrin still kept a hold of the remote just in case she needed a quick out.

Andrew had been in the process of restructuring his million-dollar company. He had a high interest to appeal to a totally different support base, stating he wants everyone around the world wearing his brand.

Continuing to stare at the screen, at the corner of her mouth Cadrin gently bit the tip of her index finger appearing as if she could see herself working on the behalf of Andrew and his company. In her opinion, Andrew appeared easy to work along side of. She smiled at what she envisioned. She continued to listen. He was already utilizing one of her favorite rules of thumb, "*In order to get more and better work done you need the right people on board.*" After Cadrin got an earful of how certain other practices within Andrew's company operated, it was the very next day she went online to research several pieces of literature like News Week and The Wall Street Journal to gain more insight on Lox Gable.

Cadrin was somewhat hesitant to submit her credentials to his office. Having been impressed with her contributions, her clients had always sought her out except those two who happily obtained her contact information thanks to Roslyn being on the look out. Many times, Cadrin had been unaware her friend was or had been on the hunt.

Mulling over the impressive segment on Andrew's company she'd heard the day before, Cadrin figured by now his desk had probably become flooded with business cards attached to flawless resumes. *"One more wouldn't hurt."* That thought provided Cadrin with the courage she needed.

Dressed in light weight jogging pants and an oversized t-shirt, Cadrin slid onto her feet a pair of flip flops. After arriving at the nearest post office, she prepared her resume to arrive on Andrew's desk the next day. If she wound up not getting the gig, she didn't doubt her bank account would still see her well beyond the months ahead.

Sighing, Cadrin hoped she hadn't been too formal or pushy by adding delivery confirmation to accompany her resume. Nonetheless, Andrew was extremely impressed with her thoroughness. By the end of the week, Cadrin's fax machine was printing out information in support of an interview at Lox Gable.

The approach of a server dressed in black and white attire brought her back from memory lane.

"You should try one of the hors d'oeuvres, Ms. Porter," the server offered after noticing the adhesive name tag situated onto Cadrin's silver beaded and sequined pullover style black tunic with handkerchief hem.

"I might as well," she thought to herself. Reaching for one of the pin wheels of specialty meats and cheese wrapped in

baked dough, Cadrin thanked the server before biting into it. She thought the taste would have been bland if it were not for the tanginess of the salami and cheese.

"Ah Cadrin, there you are. You've been all over the place this evening, haven't you?" Andrew's comment sounds more like a jubilant affirmation rather than a question.

"No, I..."

Nick barely touched her elbow. Cadrin didn't have the chance to answer him. The next face she sees holds a look of hope and anxiousness. His expression sings, "Please say you'll have a drink with me later," the silent yet eager plea came from Henry Brown.

"Here, I'd like you to meet a colleague of ours; well, we love to call him that. Anyway, this gentleman right here is none other than Henry Brown. He is a long-time supporter of Lox Gable."

Henry is obviously extremely interested in meeting Cadrin. No matter how innocently Nick attempted to alter the situation, Cadrin knows a push off when she sees one. Henry is about two inches taller than her five feet three-inch frame. He reached out to shake her hand. Cadrin could tell from the way Henry's knees buckled, he is a man who is heavy on his feet. There definitely will not be any dancing tonight. He's a touch on the stout side and has beaming eyes which never stopped glaring at her since the moment of their introduction. Cadrin knows if she doesn't find an excuse, Henry will be difficult to avoid for the remainder of the function.

Cadrin listened, nodding every so often in response to the small talk the gentlemen are trading back and forth amongst the three of them. Henry is probably a nice guy, and he likes what he sees each time he looks at Cadrin. However, she isn't captivated by him. Her father always told her she has the right to extend reciprocated measures to whichever guy she chooses, and she exercises every bit of such information to its fullest.

Sending a man mixed signals is not her style, so like any good Public Relations expert she separated herself from Henry's company.

"Listen gentlemen, I hope the both of you will excuse me for a little while. I see some old colleagues over there who looks as though they are about to leave. I'd like to get a word in to them before they head for the door. Please excuse me," making her way to the other side of the room, Cadrin hopes her expression didn't portray what she's really feeling.

"Sure thing Cadrin," Nick assured her.

Henry offered her nothing except a wide grin.

"Whew that was easy. Once Nick settles down, I hope he won't be offended when I fail to return," she muttered to herself.

Nothing is more boring to her than a man who repeatedly dishes out his achievements, one after the other without giving any attention to her own. Luck isn't on her side when it comes to men. The ones she's interested in are even tougher for her to figure out. When the majority looks at her, they make her feel as though they see nothing other than a pretty little trophy to sit next to their notoriety. Then there are the other men who she erroneously finds to be as equally intriguing. Unfortunately, they are also the ones who would engage her in conversation to only have their arms folded for the duration. They appeared to size her up as if scolding her for her solid up bringing.

Cadrin is the real deal, and it had become obvious to her they were probably looking for plain old dominance. They quickly realized she wasn't having any of that.

Maybe it is her outstanding career or her solid up bringing which turned them away. Whatever the case, they always ended up commending her for her achievements and wished her much continued success. It was probably for the best they decided against her, if only Kirk had done the same.

Although Cadrin wants a committed relationship, it's difficult for her to obtain such. Her solidarity helped her to become a pro in proving to others she doesn't need any man. Nights like this constantly put her solidarity to the test. Confidently, Cadrin holds her chin high as she passes by men whose lady is either holding his hand or have their arm locked at his elbow. She had to admit at times it's painful to be in attendance anywhere where love seemed to take over the room. It had taken her a while to get over her observations, putting them aside once she finally realized everything isn't always what they seem to be. There may be bliss in public but trouble at home. In any case, who's to say her feelings of loneliness wouldn't return.

Kirk was the last man she dated. She believed him to be the exception to the rule of stay away from Cadrin Porter. From the moment they met, she realized a budding relationship was promising. And she had been right, right up to the point of realizing Kirk was not the man whom she thought him to be. Having taken its course rather smoothly over time, without urgency a relationship developed between the two of them.

After two months into the wonderful place they'd built for themselves, the whispers had begun.

Ultimately, she and Kirk became ridiculed. Aside from small PR gigs, Kirk was Director of Communications for Lynn Fields, the same company which had brought Cadrin onboard as their PR.

Kirk's male colleagues were a bowl of pudding whenever Cadrin came near them, frankly their constant notice of her pissed Kirk off.

To this day, Cadrin remains amazed at how their obvious attraction for her succeeded in setting Kirk off in such a bad way. During an out of state function one of their leaders made a flirtatious comment towards Cadrin in the presence of her former beau. He wasn't aware Kirk had been privately fuming for months.

Not being able to take anymore, Kirk lit into him. His growl had been responsible for the CEO of Lynn Fields to get wind of his and Cadrin's union. Further, the CEO threatened to wave red flags under the noses of any of Cadrin's future clients. Kirk? well, he nearly lost his job for his ruffling of the chairman, and for the choice words he dealt him.

Cadrin and the company's CEO exchanged heated words. To current date, Cadrin has reason to believe the pissed CEO had chosen to turn her head on the matter, ready to mind her own business. So she hopes.

Cadrin left the men standing where they were and made her way over to a man and woman. She figured the woman is probably the man's date for the evening. Walking over to them, Cadrin took in a deep breath. Upon reaching them, she put on a healthy smile. As she exchanged hand shakes, smiles and general conversation with Mr. and Mrs. Let Us Rescue You, she looked back at Henry. She's thankful the nice couple didn't want to run her away. Periodically, Cadrin ushered them around the room just to walk and talk whenever she noticed Henry smiling at her from across the floor.

On Andrew's thanks and last well wishes to the crowd, Cadrin made an expeditious exit for the corridor.

Chapter 2

The Executives

Awakening to a windy and rainy Chicago morning, Cadrin Porter lie in her queen-sized bed gliding a fan of fingers over the two hundred and fifty thread count sheets. Not a lint ball to be stroked and that's just the way she likes it. She deserves and wants nothing but the best but nothing too frilly. Frilly just isn't her style.

She had been awakened by an annoying sound. It's her business line. The ringing of her cell phone is more than just an announcement. At four in the morning the sound is more like a piercing to the ear drums of the noteworthy perfectionist. Still in twilight, clumsily she searches the nightstand attempting to locate her cell. Opening it, she spoke with a not here almost there greeting.

"Ca- Cadrin Porter."

"Ms. Porter, this is Catherine from Cannon and Langerfeld. I know we weren't supposed to meet until near the end of the month to iron out the details regarding that key prospect…well, I was hoping we would be able to meet this morning for an early breakfast, just to get a jump start on things due to a new and pressing situation. Just a few moments ago, I received a major fax informing me of what I hope will not prove to be a derailment. It's very detrimental we speak about this situation, very soon and in person."

"Good morning, Catherine," having listened to the flow of Catherine's words, Cadrin suspects her client probably had been up for at least an hour before phoning. In sleep driven rebuttal, Cadrin closes her eyes. Catherine had given no previous thoughts to the hour neither the fact her publicist may not be an early riser.

"I apologize for the hour, how silly of me to have disturbed you. Our current situation requires our immediate attention before I meet with the Advertising and Marketing Executives at ten thirty this morning, you see."

After mentally reviewing the poignant annunciations delivered by her client, Cadrin pined at the thought of having to abandon the comforts of her ensemble of linen, The Signature Series. Again, what she wants seems to
be unimportant in business and relationships alike. But she likes the challenge, that is at least when it comes to business. What she also wants is for her clients to behave themselves and stop pricking over her suggestions and give to her their total trust. She often reminded them they inquired upon her expertise for a reason.

"Alright, how does seven thirty sound?"

"Perfect," Catherine agreed.

The call ended with Cadrin rolling lazily to the opposite side of her bed. Before long she was up, ready, and driving to the café arriving just in time to smoothly maneuver her cobalt Lexus between a bread delivery truck and delayed construction.

"Good morning, Catherine. How are you?"
they shook hands.

"What's so urgent?"

"It's our prospect. They are refusing to come aboard if we do not increase our numbers by one hundred and fifty percent.

They want to bring on their sister company. According to them, it's a company which will significantly benefit through joint measures, but only if our project is outstandingly successful is when they'll consider us. Cadrin, I just don't get it. Why don't their sister company go it alone if our project is more useful to them?" replied Catherine.

"It's all about positioning," Cadrin explained before taking a sip of milk from the medium sized glass before her.

Catherine proceeded.

"If we can not achieve those types of results, they will seek other opportunities and we can't very well shove those numbers at'em without having substantive details and the labor to accompany them."

Catherine began to finish her breakfast.

Just as Cadrin had concluded on the ride to the café in which no one could ever recall its name, she knew Catherine's dilemma is calling for some quick revisions and fast. The two mind boggled individuals continued to chat in between bites of scrambled eggs and buttered croissants.

"Oh no, I swear it. Where does the time go?" Catherine began to throw a small fit while taking notice of the hour on her wristwatch. Acknowledging Catherine to be in a great big hurry, Cadrin quickly brushes the crumbs from her fingers before shaking the hand of her client.

"Tell the team I'm fully aware of the issue at hand, I'll be getting to work on a solution for you right away."

Catherine nodded as she rose from the table. Before she exited the café, she tried to leave in Cadrin's care a binder containing info on their prospect's sister company, but Cadrin already had such an aide at home.

After the meeting's conclusion, Cadrin sat alone at the squared and cozy table. She knows what several hours of the day will now call for, her undivided attention. Cadrin's time will be mostly devoted to revising her initial strategy for Cannon and Langerfeld, leaving her no time to prepare the full course home cooked meal she'd hoped for. Mouth watering aromas coming from her kitchen isn't going to happen, at least not today. As health conscious as possible, Cadrin ordered take-out and headed for home.

Chapter Three

The Executives

The steady drying of the roadway prompted Cadrin to take the interstate home. Once merging into the flow, she popped in the cd of a soulful male artist then selected her favorite number. As the melodies surrounds the leather interior, she presses the repeat button.

"You never can get enough of this one."

Cadrin began to sway her head to the rhythms of the talented and soulful artist. She presses the power-controlled buttons allowing the rain induced air to whisk through. Turning the volume up a few notches, she began to take in her surroundings. She thought it best to implement cruise control just to keep her heavy foot in check. During breakfast, Cadrin could see the apprehension in Catherine's eyes as they continued their conversation on how to lead Cannon and Langerfeld to bigger and better accomplishments. Although Catherine didn't allow the words to escape her lips, she's counting on her publicist to save the day, and Cadrin knows it.

Reluctantly, Cadrin wished she hadn't promised Catherine she would get to work so soon on the revision for Cannon and Langerfeld. She's exhausted. She can't remember the last time she'd gotten a good night's sleep. Since things pertaining to Lox Gable had been just about to end, she'd taken on Cannon and Langerfeld as an additional client. Big mistake. Before she would realize just how great of an impact the workload of Cannon and Langerfeld were to have on her agility, her responsibilities had begun to spill over from one conference room into another. The only real time of leisure she had to come her way in months had been the after five affair put on by Andrew. Sad to say, the event didn't award her anywhere near the amount of free time she needs for regrouping.

Just seconds away from dropping everything to the floor, Cadrin entered her home's foyer.

"Home finally."

Cadrin tightened her grip on her armload of materials and dinner. Never in her professional career had she brought home nagging issues in the form of a huge three ring binder filled to the max, compliments of her client. She'd already composed a binder relating to Catherine's prospect. No matter though, Cadrin appreciated the extra input.

She kicked off her shoes and went for the couch. With dinner on the sofa table, she began to smooth her hand over the drops of rain which had vastly dotted the vinyl covering of Catherine's jam-packed notebook of information. Thanks to her client she had gotten up early that morning, and now that she's back at home, she can hardly keep her eyes open.

With a dampened hand she grabs the ringing phone from its base. Tiresomely, she carries the phone into the kitchen along with her take-out.

"This is Cadrin."

"That's classic of you. I'm not surprised at all."

"What? Who is this?" upon answering the phone she remembered she noticed the number belongs to an out-of-town area code. She then quickly recognized the smooth tone as belonging to Kirk Phillips.

"Is that the way you're answering your home phone nowadays? That can only mean one thing."

"And what's that?"

"All work and zero play."

Cadrin doesn't have time for this. Kirk is the last male she expected to call her up. She hadn't spoken to her ex-significant other for two years. As a matter of fact, his phone call is only two weeks shy of the anniversary his temper almost got them fired from Lynn Fields. Through her nostrils, Cadrin unintentionally blew a force of wind into the phone.

"You hate talking to me that much? I mean for real; it has only been two decades. I'm a nice guy, honest I am. I hope you still remember such."

Kirk could always get a laugh out of her.

"I love to hear such sound from you, it's sweet."

In a hurry Cadrin gathered her composure. "*How dare he call,*" she complained of him. All the apologies in the world from Kirk are not enough to get her to forget he almost cost her of her employment and maybe to this day, her career.

"For your information, I get just enough time for play. If anyone other than my clients know how I feel about my work, it should be you."

"You're right about that. The way I recall it, there were many nights of midnight oil, candles lit in our background, and I was the one with the candles."

Yes, she remembered those late nights and early mornings very well. Those cherished moments had been enjoyed by both. Now beyond Lynn Fields, they had found comfort in having gone their separate ways, but the damage had already been done.

"You sound incredibly good for an old guy. It has only been two years since we last spoke~" she commented as though they'd seen each other just yesterday, "is there a reason you called?"

"Yes, there is. I just wanted to say hello and~"

"Hello, Kirk. Are you back with Lynn Fields and company?"

Kirk cracks a smile at her joke. The 'company' was in reference to the foundation of his reason for having left Lynn Fields.

"And how did you learn how to reach me?"

Cadrin thought he needed some help in explaining why he is on the other end of her phone line. Of all his exes, she is sure right now he should be speaking with any one of them, but he is on the other end of her line.

"No, I'm not, I'm happy to say. And I got your number from Nadine. She said the two of you talk every now and then. What about you? Are you working right now?"

"Yes, I am. And I'm looking at some of it right now," she said while eyeing the binder she left over on the couch's cushion.

"Still bringing work home, that's a good girl."

"Was there some other reason you called, Kirk?"

"Uh, no. It has been a while since we last spoke. I just wanted to hear your voice."

She smiled but this time she kept her joy to herself.

"So, what about you Kirk? How many clients are you working for?" fond conversations of how working in public relations never lacked a dull moment between the two. That's what brought them together in the first place. And such relationship is what he wants back in his life.

"Though it has been a month since I've landed a client, I'm still active. I needed the rest so I'm not complaining."

Silence fiddled its way to Cadrin's nerve endings. The anguish she feels tells her exactly why he'd called. He wants to rekindle what they had once shared. But it is what she doesn't know that's getting ready to shock her.

"Cadrin, my girl is engaged to be married….to me."

Stunned, Cadrin couldn't speak for a moment.

"You're engaged? Wow this is…a surprise. Well, that's wonderful Kirk." Why does she feel like she had lost him, twice? "How long have the two of you been engaged?"

"She's been wearing the ring for a couple of weeks."

"Sounds like your bride to be swept you off your feet."

Kirk, her former lover is surprised to learn she is taking his news as well as she is. *They* were in love once.

"Cadrin, I'm glad to hear you sound so genuine. I don't know why I expected anything less of you. I don't mean that in a bad way. This is big news."

"Well, I mean it. I really am happy for you, Kirk."

"Thanks." He paused. "There is another reason why I called you." Now nothing other than silence is on the line. Kirk hoped she would take the lead but this time she didn't cut him off. He's determined to get his feelings across, and if doing so is going to make him look like a fool, he will own up to being such fool on today.

"Cadrin, I need to know if you still feel the same way for me as you once had, the way you did in the days of Lynn Fields."

"For goodness's sake Kirk, you're getting married."

"I know and how do you really feel about that?"

"I told you I'm happy for you. I really mean it."

"Yes and telling me you're happy for me really didn't answer my question."

"Kirk, please."

"Okay, let me be more direct. I need to know if you still love me." Silence again on their lines. He began again. "Cadrin I still love you, I never stopped." Silence is destined to stay apart of their conversation.

"Make it easier, this is the worst…"

"If you still love me like I suspect you still do, just say the words. I love my fiancée but if there is a chance for us, I need to know. It won't be easy, but I will not move forward with my engagement." Cadrin's expression did an ohhhh.

"Kirk, I'm not trying to get you to end things with your fiancée."

"Will you answer my question, please?" She knows she should have ended the call long ago, then she probably would have ended up calling him right back. She had been doing so well in getting on with her life and her career, now this.

"Kirk, I never said I didn't love you. We both know the reason why we ended our relationship. You thought I was being overbearing and you refused to sign up for anger management. Did you ever enroll?" she kept on, "just because we are not together anymore doesn't mean there's no problem."

"I'll answer your question only if you can find it in your heart to answer my question first?"

"Yes, Kirk, I still love you."

He smiled to himself. His joy faded once she changed her tune on him.

"We went our separate ways for a reason. I'm not going to ruin your engagement. Now will you answer my question?"

"No, I haven't followed up with beginning any classes. My control issues concerning my anger are not as bad as you think they are."

"It was bad enough for you to leave Lynn Fields."

"I left for you. To remain there would have caused more than enough trouble for you. I knew if I left, Lynn Fields would keep you on. There was no point in you being at a disadvantage because I wasn't able to refrain from knocking the hell out of that guy for constantly coming on to you."

Silence found its place back on the line.

"What about the man at the restaurant? Kirk, you cursed him out just for briefly staring at me. After you left Lynn Fields, the CEO and I had a blow out about our differences in opinion over the whole thing. End result, she said if she were to ever again get wind of another interoffice or some other work-related romance involving me, she would make strong efforts in any way she could to inform a present or future client of mine of the relationship I had with you while working on the behalf of her company."

"What did she have to say regarding me?"

"Nothing. If she had, I would have stopped at nothing to warn you."

"I appreciate the concern." Silence again. "So where do we go from here?"

"We go back to the place where we were before you called. I'll get to the platter waiting on me and then back to my revision for a current client of mine. And you? You will probably get back to the new lady in your life. Although I will forever be grateful to you our separation was not totally about saving my career, it was also about you. You said you left Lynn Fields for me. Now you should go sign up for those classes. You really should do that for your wife to be."

Cadrin heard a loud sigh come from Kirk.

"You always did drive a tight bargain, that's one of the things about you I fell in love with." Silence.

"It's getting late, Kirk. We should go ahead and say good-bye."

"Is that your way of offering me fortitude, even if it is only for an ounce of what we had?"

"Kirk, will you promise me you will take good care of yourself?" Cadrin fought to hold back her tears, she had no idea she could be so strong. She honestly believed Kirk was 'the one.' They ended up having more strength than the tie which had pulled them together.

"I promise. But will you be okay?"

"All is well here, Kirk…bye."

Cadrin slowly moved the phone away from her ear; it remained close enough for her to hear him say to her soul, "Wait! Before you leave me, if I had said yes that I had gone to anger management, whether it was the truth or you ended up finding out it wasn't doing me any good if I had gone, or I had lied about going altogether, would we be an item once again?"

Through stinging tears, she said, "Kirk, I can read you like a book."

"I'll take that as a yes and a no. I love you Cadrin."

"Kirk."

"I know. I'm getting married. But if I can't admit my love for you to anyone especially you, in my book my inability to speak those words would project I never loved you in the first place."

"I agree, Kirk."

See why they had been together? Although things didn't work out for them, each brought to the table the same understanding of the other.

"By the way, the number I'm calling you from is my personal line. If you find you need someone to talk to, I hope you'll call me."

She paused.

"Good-bye, Kirk."

The call ended.

Finally, after removing all thoughts of Kirk, Cadrin was halfway through the binder when she decided to take a break or at least what she considers to be one for the moment. With her legal pad in hand, she paces back and forth concentrating as if her intentions are to present her presentation directly to Cannon and Langerfeld's potential partner. She hates last minute revisions. Such untimely occurrences continue to prove to be just the fuel she needs to stay ahead within her profession. In the end, again the compromises she deals with proves her to be worth her salt, crediting her with many accolades of recognition. Once completing the pages of the binder, she began her revision. Three days later, she gave her presentation a format suitable for the ears of Catherine as well as her group of marketing and advertising execs.

"Hold it please!" Cadrin yelled. The closing elevator doors were brought to a halt by Katie who is one of the one hundred and forty employees of Cannon and Langerfeld. She and Cadrin always exchange conversation whenever they got the chance. Cadrin doesn't mind talking with her about current events and anything of reason which relates to her job as a corporate publicist.

"Ms. Porter, it's great to see you again," Katie is always so formal. Cadrin translated Katie's salutation to be out of respect for her professional status. Hopelessly, Cadrin wishes the building's occupants wouldn't be so formal. Then again, she did work her butt off to gain and maintain her status, so she dismissed the thoughts of any downgrades.

"You're here to meet with Catherine Schofield, right?"

"Yes, I am."

Katie pressed the appropriate button on Cadrin's behalf. The doors of the elevator opened onto the building's twelfth floor.

"You remember how to find her office, it's just down the hall," Katie pointed eastward, "take the first right, another right and then left," Katie finished with a smile.

"Yes, I remember. Thanks Katie. It's great seeing and talking with you again, too."

As Cadrin walks down the corridor on her way to Catherine's office, she finds herself to be greeted with fresh air. A trip to the twelfth floor is always an exhilarating one. The newness of the air awakens her senses along with the scent of freshly baked pastries which frequents the executive offices around eight a.m. each morning. Cadrin had been anticipating their meeting for weeks as did Catherine.

Cadrin took in a deep breath as she walks down the carpeted hall. She's dressed to leave a memorable impression. She hopes her presentation will do the same. From her wardrobe she selected a gray skirt suit, silk white blouse and gold accessories. As she approaches Catherine's office, she overhears a raspy and down-home southern tone giving clear details on the day's agenda.

Giving notice to Cadrin's presence Catherine whispers, "Come on in."

Cadrin entered the nice sized office, taking a seat on the other side of Catherine's mahogany desk.

"I hope I'm not interrupting," Cadrin responded in like manner, "I have a copy of the presentation. We can go over it together before we meet with the execs."

Anxious to learn of Cadrin's solution, Catherine quickly ended the call. Cadrin passes to her a copy of the revised presentation. Catherine carefully scanned the connotations which were presented to her. She slowly flipped one page after another.

"I am extremely impressed. This is great stuff. You really did your homework. The team is waiting. Why don't we make our way to the conference room?" said Catherine.

The team consists of marketing and advertising personnel. They each sit around the large oval table waiting for Cadrin and Catherine to enter the conference room. Their facial expressions already spoke total objection. Eight years ago, such realizations would have sent Cadrin home with an excuse. Now, she is more confident than ever leaving the nonsense where it belongs. Outside.

They each take their designated seat, immediately they began exchanging small talk with the other occupants. A few minutes would past before their chatter became minimized due to the execs' shuffling of their own papers.

The team looks on as Cadrin began to look over her notes as well.

"Are we all ready?" asked Catherine.

Cadrin nods yes as she watches Catherine rise to address the room.

"I'd like to thank each of you for again putting aside the necessary time to meet with myself and Ms. Cadrin Porter. I'm sure each of you are aware of the new challenges we're facing regarding our potential partner. Because of these new developments, I have sought additional help from our publicist. Her insight has identified and developed detailed strategies to aide us in accomplishing the goal at hand. With that, Ms. Porter would like to bring those strategies to our attention. And please, if anyone has any questions regarding these solutions, please hold such questions until the floor opens," Catherine took her seat.

Catherine's introductions always make Cadrin feel like royalty. With a smile, Cadrin proceeded to distribute each member of the team a folder which holds their own copy of her presentation. She began by explaining in detail how the company can achieve an increase in revenue mainly through philanthropic endeavors, domestic, and international.

"Philanthropic acts are an obvious plus with any prospective business partner," said one of the unimpressed attendants. As Cadrin continued in voicing steps on how to execute such endeavors, and where the importance of such will lay when it comes to their potential supporter, her nay sayer leaned to one side, cocked his head and bit the pen he's holding. Finally, he nods his head in approval of her solution.

The team members listen intently as they follow her page for page. Cadrin continued to provide insight as she begins to pace slowly about the floor. She always speaks with greater assurance when she does this. At the close of the meeting, the team members and Catherine were highly satisfied and eager to implement the loads of information presented to them. Also satisfied with the outcome is Spencer Youngerman. He began walking towards Cadrin.

"*Oh God, here he comes. Not today Spencer.*" For what seemed like an eternity, Spencer tried to be the man in Cadrin's life, but she turned him down each time. He isn't her type anyway.

"Well, Cadrin it looks like you're placing Cannon and Langerfeld on the road to greater financial success. Even after the project's completion, your insights will allow us to see exponential results in other areas of the company. It looks like someone has a bonus check in the mail," Spencer applauded her.

Pleased with her compliments, Cadrin turned to witness another thumbs up from across the room. It came from Ed who is consumed with scarping down a cream cheese bagel.

Two months later Cannon and Langerfeld turned their prospect into a business partner, twice. And they owe all their thanks to one Cadrin Porter.

Chapter Four

The Executives

"**H**ello, sir. May I help you?" the lobby receptionist of Stone and Nichols rose to her feet, her action emulating that of a drill sergeant. The only difference is the fact of her being dressed just like a perfect little display placed behind a store front window. For some unsuspecting visitors, her strong personality is very intimidating.

"Yes," the courier referred to the name and title on the gold envelope, "I have a delivery for the CEO of Stone and Nichols, Jim Grainger."

"I'll take that," Ms. Flanagan, the lobby receptionist said.

"Ma'am, as lovely of a woman you are, I would love nothing more than to hand this over to you. Fact being, I have strict orders forbidding me to deliver this packaging to no one other than the CEO, I'm afraid I won't be able to oblige you."

"Non-employees are not allowed to the Director's floor," said Ms. Flanagan. She busied herself in stepping around to the other side of her desk to confront the courier, face- to- face.

"Ma'am, I have my orders. If we can reach Mr. Grainger by phone, I'm sure we can clear all this up, right away."

After a miniseries of disapproving facial expressions, Ms. Victoria Flanagan withdrew an outstretched arm and proceeded to reach Jim by phone. She exudes a no-nonsense aura. But today she is no match for the courier. He had been looking for laughs through his own mischievous ways.

"Grainger here," said Jim.

"Mr. Grainger, I do apologize for disturbing you. There's a young man here, a courier who is insisting he personally deliver to you a package of some sort," her tone straddled professionalism, holding on to the brink of shameful strong arming. The harshness of her eyes sent choice words the courier's way.

"I've been expecting him, please escort him up."

Earlier, Jim received a phone call from his portfolio manager who is vacationing in Del Rio. The call concerns a pending loan packet from one of the many financial institutions which assisted Stone and Nichols in gaining presence across the globe. The bank's loan officer uncovered unexplainable material which raised his immediate concern.

The courier waited in silence as the elevator drew upon the fourteenth floor. He soon grew tired of the only noise heard, humming by one of the other occupants of the elevator.

"Wow, I've never been to a secured floor before, hadn't been on the job long," the courier tried to impose a light conversation on a bitter situation."

"Um humph," Ms. Flanagan gave an under-breath reply. At their stop, she and the courier exited the elevator, heading in Jim's direction. The CEO would have looked like Saint Nick if it hadn't been for his grey pin striped suit.

"I'm Jim Grainger, CEO of Stone and Nichols."

The courier quickly recognized Jim and handed to him the clip board to initial and sign his signature on several x indicated areas. After having complied with the courier's directions, Jim was awarded the package.

"Why would a two point five-million-dollar loan be taken out on a project which was cancelled month's ago?" wondered Jim as he hands the courier back the felt tip pen.

Feeling as though her authority had been literally trotted upon, Ms. Flanagan exemplified a dignified huff as she spun on the heel of her shoe and began to escort the attractive gentleman back to the first floor of Stone and Nichols.

"This way please," she dryly said to him.

Paying no attention to Ms. Flanagan's obvious lack of approval when it came to the ways of the provoking courier, Jim walked back to his office trying to make sense of the findings uncovered by the loan officer. Had he previously overlooked it? Or maybe the unexplained sum is due to enormous miscalculations by the bank. But why had no one contacted him before now?

Jim's portfolio manager informed the loan officer to keep quiet as the findings could possibly tarnish the reputation of Stone and Nichols.

Several media crew members overwhelm the entrance to Stone and Nichols. Reporters, cameras and microphones are everywhere. Somehow the media received information from an unknown source explaining the development company is involved in some sort of a scandal.

Unaware of why so much chaos had been beckoned to the premises of his company, Jim apprehensively exits the limo. As soon as his foot contacted the sidewalk, a reporter and a camera operator from a local Chicago news station brought Jim center stage.

"Mr. Grainger, can you tell us why Johnson Everdeen has named Stone and Nichols as a defendant in a lawsuit with two point five million dollars at the base?" shouted one of the reporters.

Shaken by the civilian's allegations, Jim tried to avoid the microphones, and the embarrassing multitude of questions by attempting to put some distance between himself and the visitors. No such luck. The reputation of Stone and Nichols is in disarray and dwindling fast. Without a word, Jim broke through the circle of reporters before running up the steps and into the building. Quickly, he heads for an elevator.

"Mr. Grainger! Mr. Grainger! I tried to forewarn you of the press, but there was no answer. I left several messages!" professed Victoria Flanagan.

Earlier, Jim had enjoyed the luxuries of a steam sauna and failed to respond to his buzzing cell phone.

Through the gap of the closing doors of the elevator, Jim yells back to her, "No one from the outside gets to the secured floor or anywhere else in this building, not without me knowing about it first!"

"Yes! I understand!" confirmed Victoria as she leaned over the desk's counter for hopes of stealing a full image of the frightened mogul before the doors of the elevator were to fully come together.

Everything is falling apart. On the way to his office, Jim felt as though the walls of the corridor were closing in on him. The reputation of his corporation is now under a microscope and Jim knows he needs to seek the kind of support which will block the blows of destruction. Otherwise, the company's public image will be shattered.

Three weeks would past before Stone and Nichols sought the expertise of publicist, Cadrin Porter. Coming to the aid of a million-dollar corporation, Cadrin classified Jim's call as the perfect opportunity she needs to expand her credentials. Stone and Nichols will be her seventh high profiled client and she's not in favor of passing up the opportunity.

Cadrin always lacked outside interference when dealing with the woes of her clients. She's devoted in catering to their every beck and call: Countless meetings, unscheduled meetings, The Early Show. Whatever the day orders, she's ready to meet it face- to- face and toe-to- toe. But on this particular day, the order of business will invite to her world everything but the usual.

"Another shot of white wine, Mr. Grayson?"

"No thank you. The first time around was plenty."

The flight attendant nodded. She proceeded to being an aide to the other members in first class.

Vance Grayson leans his toned back up against the airline seat. Checking the hour on the face of his wristwatch, he apprehensively relaxes his shoulders against the seat before turning off the overhead lighting above his head. Smiling at one of the flight attendants, Vance closes his eyes. For the remainder of his flight, he spent some of his time thinking about what one of his colleagues, Harper St. John had said to him about mediating over cases in Chicago. Harper had been through three cases there himself. Each time he thought things were working out in his client's favor, he ended up prolonging his residency within the city. Strangely enough, Vance's recollection told him Harper may be onto something. For whatever his optimism is worth, he hopes Harper's interpretation of a Chicago case is way off base when it comes to this one.

After Vance had closed his eyes, an older lady seated across the aisle from him leaned over her arm rest to get a better look of him. In approval of what she saw, she smiled.

Vance's looks are astonishingly pleasing to the female eye. He exudes a professional and dignified tenure; the man is not categorized as average. His features are captivating. His golden-brown complexion is smooth and produces definition. His lips showcase a slight of curve to the upper, with a dimple resting at each corner, a third can be seen as it attempts to play hide and go seek from beneath the glistening slick black hairs of his thinly coated, and slightly chiseled chin. Women from all walks of life pursues him. He has the looks of a Romeo. Refreshingly, his mannerisms show the opposite.

Vance's plane came in for landing just as he began putting away a Black Enterprise magazine which he had read before taking a peaceful nap. Inside the airport he involuntarily gained the gazing eyes of almost every woman who crosses his path, the young as well as the matured.

"Pardon me, Sir. I'm so sorry. Please forgive me, they all look just about alike," she said. A female traveler purposely retrieved Vance's luggage while at baggage claim. He'd been busy fumbling with his itinerary as he'd aimlessly reached for his luggage. She was abrupt enough to allow his hand the convenience of briefly encountering her own. During an encounter such as this one is almost customary each time he's out in public. For him, it's sort of a relief on the days when they don't seem to notice him as much.

"Thank you for picking it up for me. I hope it wasn't too heavy for you," he playfully joked while flashing that brilliant smile of his.

Obviously turned on, the woman grabbed her own luggage and walked away displaying half capped excitement.

Outside the Chicago airport a limo awaits Vance's arrival. Carmichael's secretary single handedly made such arrangement including Vance's stay at an upscale corporate apartment where he will reside during his stay in Chicago. With a situation of this magnitude, both parties can only estimate how long he will be in the Windy City.

Vance browses around the limo's compartments. Its interior smells like it's fresh off the assembly line or just maintained with a special grade of chemicals not available to the general public. Disturbing his intake of the limo's compartments, Vance's cell phone ranged. He immediately recognized the number on the lighted display.

"Hey bro, what's up?" Vance said.

"Vance, hey man. Has your flight landed?"

"Yeah, I arrived about twenty minutes ago."

"Where are you living?"

"While I'm in town I'll be residing at a corporate apartment located within one of the newest developments near the downtown area."

"Yeah, I know the area. We'll hook up, browse the town or maybe I should call Gwyneth to let her know you are back in town. She's been asking about you."

"Whoa, Mr. Match-Maker will you make me a wreck? I am not interested in that woman. She's a snob. There is no chemistry between us whatsoever," Vance offered while scooping ice into a glass tumbler.

"Are you trying to say you're seeing-?"

"And besides, I'm not here for that. This time it is about business only, and oh! of course, I'll be spending some time with my little brother."

"Ha ha, that's funny Mr. Attorney Man."

Even though Vance is unable to give his brother any specifics on when they will catch up, it is great for him to be within such proximity of his youngest sibling. Although he isn't so little anymore, Troy never could avoid such small term of endearment. He is a looker that's for sure, but he's no comparison to his big brother.

After Vance concluded a sketchy breakdown of the activities he and his client will undergo on tomorrow, he'd finally arrived at his home away from home. Vance isn't the type to accept lavish perks. But when it comes to where he will rest, he never hesitates to indulge the offer. His clients always came through, paying for some of the finest hotel accommodations or lodging situated onto private property nestled in the hills of cities like Atlanta and Gatlinburg.

Once Vance arrived on Secretariat Lane, he was led to the door of the corporate apartment by the driver of the limousine. The limo driver unlocks the door. He handed to Vance the keys, leaving him there to look around the place he will refer to as home probably for the next month or so.

Vance pushes the door open to discover a spaciously furnished room. Easily, he located a light switch on the wall next to the entrance.

"Ahh, Johnson Everdeen did not disappoint," Vance commented. He stood behind the closed door examining the room's layout. It's roomy with a vaulted ceiling, crown molding and the furnishing is a mix of traditional and contemporized décor which speaks bachelor.

Pleased with what he is seeing so far, Vance sat his belongings in the center of the room. Leaving the luggage there, he began walking slowly towards the hall while glancing at the neat little kitchen. Faint lighting is there, too. Still looking around the room, Vance went ahead and made his way down the moderate hallway which gathers a hint of lighting, thanks to the opened blinds of a nearby window. He then entered the only bedroom there. It's nice he thought. Actually, relaxing was his choice of word.

"Everdeen has truly got class," nodding repeatedly, Vance proceeds to make his way back to the living room hitting the light switch to its on position before exiting the large oasis he will call his bedroom. Almost back in the living room, it is from the hall where his eyes made contact with a complimentary golden tray of plastic wrapped treats. Earlier, on his way down the hall he remembered hearing a bulb pop. Looking up at the rack to see a row of bulbs over his head, Vance removed his cell from his waist. He found a step ladder of which he only needs two steps of it to help him change the blown bulb. He 'climbed' off the ladder and laughed only a little while looking around the room as he began recalling the rest of the place he'd seen just minutes ago. There is absolutely nothing else his home away from home needs for the space claims perfection. Okay, he's not royalty, but that's how most of his clients treats him. He doesn't mind their honor. Neither does he mind the times when they are subtle for his paychecks are quite representative of fame.

Chapter 5

The Executives

The next day Vance met with Johnson Everdeen, and the remaining legal supporters to review the documents they will utilize to build a strong case against Stone and Nichols.

Once the meeting concluded, Vance realized he is famished. There had been no time for a fulfilling breakfast at home, so he's left with the only remedy of filling his belly; to endure a continental spread consisting only of croissants, doughnuts and fruit provided by his client. Later, with the iridescent taste of grits and salmon croquettes on his lips, he instructed the limo driver to stop by Claudia's, a soul food restaurant better loved for serving breakfast around the clock. While enjoying the down-home cooking, Vance notices a streamer gliding across the bottom of the televised programming. The ridiculing comments of people passing by the counter where he's eating stole his attention away from the bit of heaven on his plate. The news on the flat screen television involves information implicating the legal matters of Stone and Nichols. Vance only shook his head at their remarks.

After finishing his meal, he decided to instruct the limo driver to drop him back off at the corporate apartment. He had already shared one of his choices in dining and sees no need to share the fact he wishes to catch up with his brother, Troy.

The hot shower Vance took did wonders for his aches and pains. Feeling rejuvenated is what it will take to perhaps win a bowling match against Troy. Troy does have a right to brag. Vance never heard tell of his sibling losing more than two matches. Vance must admit it; his brother is pretty darn good at the sport. After his shower, Vance put on a pair of jeans; the laid-back approach is his favorite when he's not on business. To compliment his dungarees, he selected a comfortable long-sleeved light blue buttoned down collar shirt. Grabbing his cell phone from the granite countertop, he presses the appropriate speed dial digit.

"Hey man, you got some time for your one and only big brother? I thought we'd bowl and continue to catch up while at the lanes."

"Yeah, it's been a while since I've schooled you at the lanes."

"Ha. Ha. That's cocky. The looser buys the winner a beer," said Vance.

"Yeah, I prefer imported myself."

"Oh, is that right? Just come with some money in your pocket little bro." The two laughed and continued to tease each other with boastful bouts as Vance waited for a cab which he will take to the car renters.

Once the cab reached the lot of luxury vehicles, Vance climbed out and immediately began to walk the parking lot checking out the rides available.

"Now is the time to test this baby out."

After finalizing the documentation with signatures and the funds to back it, Vance returned to his vehicle of choice, a Lincoln MKS. Hearing a call come into his cell, Vance feels his plans with his brother are about to come to an abrupt halt. Johnson Everdeen is scheduled to come face- to- face with Stone and Nichols thanks to their shrewd publicist, Pete Monahan.

Without Carmichael's approval, Pete secretly orchestrated a wave of media attention onto the premises of Stone and Nichols. This is twice the development company is delivered unwanted attention. Over the phone, Vance apologized to his brother, asking for a rain check before starting up the car's engine.

Driving every bit of sixty-five miles per hour, he returned to the corporate apartment where he changed clothes before heading to Stone and Nichols.

After arriving at the million-dollar company reclad in his tailor-made suit, white shirt, and cuff links he wore earlier, Vance quickly exited the vehicle. Due to the chaos, he had no choice other than to man his way through the crowd. It's characteristic of Monahan, Johnson Everdeen's PR, to pull a move such as this one. His rhetorical action is his signature in dismantling the opposition. Vance is well aware of his practice. Because of Pete's 'expertise' in public relations, Carmichael is forced to look like the bad guy in front of the spectators.

Once Vance's vision located his client, from a distance Carmichael shrugged his shoulders. He walked briskly towards Vance.

"Vance, I apologize. I didn't do this," Carmichael spoke of the hail of reporters and their media gear which has been left to sprawl over the pavement appearing as if they had been forgotten.

"Monahan took my statements out of context," Carmichael explained. But Vance already knows what is going on here. He certainly knew Monahan would try to place Carmichael at fault for any mishaps which will take place on today. This day isn't Vance's first run in with the 'publicist.'

Vance and Carmichael made their way to the huddle of Everdeen supporters. Vance quickly took the lead without any overbearing remarks.

Opposite them, Jim Grainger is visibly and understandably disturbed by the entire ordeal.

"Jim, pull yourself together. It's just an attempt to rattle you. You gotta remain calm about this. It's just an attempt to rattle you," Jim's lawyer repeated with anxiety.

"We'll handle everything. Ms. Porter and I will rectify this brief nonsense," said Jim's lawyer.

Dodging the press would have implicated probable guilt for sure, so Jim took Cadrin's advice and allowed the reporters to remain and build center stage on the courtyard of Stone and Nichols, away from the street. Tension is mounting and tempers are on the verge of erupting.

Jim's lawyer gave an opening statement regarding the allegations brought against Stone and Nichols. While Jim had been out of the country Claude had begun work on taking out a two point five-billion-dollar loan in the name of Stone and Nichols to gain notoriety in the world of development using Johnson Everdeen as a cover.

Both moguls stand on separate and raised platforms preparing to formally address the public.

Standing alongside Jim's lawyer, Cadrin stepped in closer, ready for her turn to address the spectators.

"Ladies and Gentlemen, I am Cadrin Porter, PR on the behalf of Stone and Nichols. Through all of this, my client will continue to exude the same respectful demeanor which his company is built upon with due respect not only towards the community, but also to former and present industry partners as he combats these hideous allegations."

Jim stands with tension; his gaze looks every spectator in their accusing eyes. Several of them didn't blink. From every angle, all focus seems to be incredulously on him.

"*Why aren't they preoccupied with the crew from Everdeen?"* Jim wonders. *"The Everdeen CEO is young, frisky and capable if need be of rebuilding his company from scratch. Still young enough to see it make a good name for itself all over again."* It is shocking to him, the pending lawsuit. Carmichael could have threatened to take any big timer to court but he didn't. He chose to take a legal stand against an innocent and almost fragile human being, Jim thought. Fragile is how Jim feels on most days.

In Jim's opinion, this press conference is just absolutely ridiculous. *"How dare he*, Jim continues to criticize, "*shame on him for picking a legal fight with…me. I hope to one day sell my beloved company to not only the highest, but to the most respectable bidder."* That is what's to be left of it if Carmichael gets his day in court.

The entire set up of media gear in front of Jim's eyes provoked sweat to wash the palms of his hands. At Cadrin's conclusion, on cue Jim used the seams of his trousers to soak up the embarrassing moisture accumulating on his hands.

On the left side of the Stone and Nichols huddle stands Carmichael and company ready to intervene. Shouts tumble from their side, coming from Pete Monahan.

"Will Stone and Nichols swindle them out of two point five billion dollars, too? They'd better hold onto their franks!" Before Cadrin knew it, Jim lost his composer, stampeding across the gap which separates the two parties. His lawyer as well as Cadrin, quickly followed suit. Jim grabbed Monahan by his lapel and began to furiously shake the man.

"Jim, wait a minute! Cut it out!" yelled Jim's lawyer.

"Jim! Your reputation!" shouted Cadrin. "He's not worth it!" she continues.

"Wanna bet," Jim said through gritted teeth. It's true enough Jim is headed over the hill. Okay he is over it, but he still has a lot of fight left in him. The attention of the media caused him to become backed into a corner of sheer embarrassment. Thanks to his present situation, he believes his employees and closest colleagues now believe terrible, and other untrue things about him because of all this. From this point, he believes everything he executes or try to execute will be tripled guessed. The fading trust and respect from those closest to him will slowly discredit him. Because of their mounting fear, Stone and Nichols will surely suffer. Not if Cadrin has her say in the matter.

Monahan's comment caught everyone off guard.

By this time punches are being thrown. Vance nearly lost his jacket in the tussle. Just as Monahan reared back with his fist in attempt to strike Jim, the outside v of his arm grazed the side of Cadrin's jaw line. She stumbled. Quickly coming to her aide, Vance places Monahan in a Full Nelson, a wrestling technique used to completely restrain an opponent. While Monahan tries to free himself from confinement, Vance stares directly into the eyes of Cadrin.

"Are you alright?" Vance yelled through the commotion.

"No! My client! Jim! Jim!" In a form fitting knee length skirt, Cadrin frantically kneels to help bring Jim back to his feet.

Again, Jim fell to the ground. Through the bustle, he was helped to his feet by his lawyer and Cadrin before his hired helpers ushered him away from the chaos.

Realizing Pete won't do any more harm, Vance released the Full Nelson. In a matter of minutes, the scene at Stone and Nichols graduated from sweltering tension to destruction.

Minutes later, Vance tries to scan the crowd in search of Cadrin while attending to the needs of Johnson Everdeen. But amid the chaos, he'd lost her.

After the remainder of the excitement subsided, Vance busied himself helping the news crew and the reporters in cleaning up the aftermath.

"Vance, I apologize for the abruption created by my publicist. I didn't anticipate on that kind of unprovoked behavior out of him, especially in a setting like this one. I hope his actions haven't cost me a new attorney. I assure you I was clueless of this arrangement involving the press. Once I received his call, I had no choice but to show up, or have the thing proceed without me."

"Carmichael it's not your fault. I'm very aware of how Monahan conducts business. You're not the first to be blindsided by him."

"I had no idea he would take such a cheap shot especially this early on. If he does anything remotely close to what he demonstrated here today, he'll be dismissed."

"I'm glad to hear that. We can't afford to continue experiencing today's event," stated Vance.

Carmichael agreed as he helped Vance gather up an overturned podium.

Even though it is late, the bowling alley is beginning to bring in its bulk of patrons. Vance thought it might be possible to cash in the rain check. However, the tension he'd previously gotten rid of found its way back to his shoulders. The pain is more agonizing than before. On his drive back to the apartment, he couldn't help questioning himself. "Where is she? Was she injured?" he tried going against his inquisitive nature by reminding himself he's in Chicago on business, and not by any means there to be captivated or even intrigued by one Cadrin Porter.

"Pull it together man. Let it go. You've got bigger matters to attend to. Besides, a woman that attractive, hmm. Surely, she is involved with a man who adores her," he said aloud, again speaking to no one or nothing except the sound of rainwater spinning from underneath the tires of vehicles as they travel to and from the parking lot of his residence.

Once Vance was done rationalizing his decision as to why he should forget about Cadrin, he got out of the car and headed for the door of his residence. Entering the large room, Vance took off his jacket. He couldn't help rehashing his inner argument. His subconscious countered. "*Why do you care who she's seeing?*" that's an incredibly good question. It's one he dares not answer. He can just see himself now trying to explain things to Troy. If his brother found out he's willing to go against the demands of his own professional duties to take up time with a lovely distraction, he will never live it down. For him, the will to do exactly that came suddenly. It is an act which has no shame in letting him know his heart requires something his duties as a corporate attorney can't solely give to him. He fails to get the sexiness and seriousness of the look in Cadrin's eyes out of his mind as she'd knelt to help Jim. He remembered how nice her skirt held the curves of her hips while she helped the old guy back to his feet. The spritz of sweat in her t-zone brightened her face's complexion, setting off a sexy glow about her features. He still wonders if she has any idea of how tantalizing she looked to him.

He hated she saw him at his worst. Maybe she thought the moment was probably one of his finest. He hoped keeping Monahan in that Full Nelson while she helped get her client out of harms way was a good look on him. Even if he hadn't been intrigued by her, he would have responded to the situation the exact way he had. In her mind, he hoped the inset of him is golden.

Before preparing for bed, Vance checked his messages. There is only one to be heard. Troy had given him a call to find out if he could get tickets to the next Johnson Everdeen showdown. Exhausted, Vance only gave a tiresome half chuckle at the foolishness of his brother. Before retiring for the night, Vance took on the role of Monahan and convinced Carmichael it will be best and without any delay to address the public as any reasonable effort to combat any negative assumptions against the multi-billion-dollar investment corporation should be next on his to do list.

The event at Stone and Nichols is all over now. Thankful, Vance folded back the covers on his bed before falling across the mattress. Now lying across the king-sized bed and underneath the covers, Vance lay silently asleep. After a while he began to toss and turn. The covers of the bed began to shift over his body. Slowly, Vance rolls onto his right side. The skin of his chest and stomach began to become dampened with his body's perspiration which handsomely accentuates the toned muscles underneath. He can feel the trickle of cool water as it cascades down the center of his shirtless back. Doting persistent paths of discomfort which are determined to hone his still tense neck and shoulders, her gentle caresses comfort him. His senses begin to become overwhelmed, eagerly developing a mutual dialect with the comforting strokes delivered by the beauty he unexpectedly came eye to eye with only hours ago. Rudely, the sound of a car's horn awakens him. Feeling the perspiration on his stomach reminded him of the water he felt rolling down the middle of his back. Yes, it had only been a dream.

"Damn it," he said before again falling off to sleep.

Chapter 6

The Executives

Vance spent nearly half the morning trying to figure out why he's so angry with the fact his early morning romp had only been a dream. Or maybe, his anger is due to the fact against his better wishes, Cadrin is becoming a permanent fixture within his mind. Even though he thought he'd succeeded in putting his feelings in check, his subconscious state of mind had other plans. To say it's factual he doesn't desire to be involved with a woman is inaccurate. As an attorney, his responsibilities regarding his clients especially those like Johnson Everdeen are a big deal to him. Getting romantically involved with anyone especially someone from the opposing side, he's aware of how the notion will aggravate his credibility.

After a quick shower, Vance dressed in a pair of semi loose fitting cotton and polyester draw string slacks. Shirtless, he made his way to the kitchen where he retrieved a skillet from the rack above the stainless-steel stove. From behind the double doors of the refrigerator he selected the ingredients for a cheese omelet grabbing four eggs, green onions, red bell pepper, mushrooms, ground sausage and a bag of cheese, three shredded. After chopping the vegetables, he added each to a bowl where he combined them with the egg mixture, a sprinkle of salt and four dashes of black pepper flakes. Separately, he prepared the sausage. Once the meat was browned, he garnished the egg mixture with it. He watched the omelet begin to form in the hot skillet as delicious aromas fill the air. Once breakfast was ready, Vance slid a perfect omelet onto a round china plate. Taking a seat at the bar, Vance picks up the remote and presses its power button. He hoped he wouldn't catch a repeat of yesterday's event on the morning news. While watching the news, every so often he took big bites of the sausage and cheese omelet. Ready to phone his client, he brushed his hands of crumbs then lowered the television's volume. During his conversation, Vance's back remained turned, allowing him to miss the highlights of yesterday's indignant event.

"Good afternoon, Ms. Williams. Will Carmichael arrive soon?" Vance asked.

"Please call me, Delia. He should arrive in about thirty minutes or sooner. He asked me to apologize to you for his tardiness."

"Thank you, Ms. Williams."

She shook her head at him.

"Delia," she said with a flirtatiously induced tone.

Vance could see the movement of her tongue as she'd hung onto her name.

"I'd prefer, Ms. Williams. But if you insist then I guess it is Delia," Vance said. He stood back from the desk to take full account of her persistence. Even though he thinks Delia is attractive, she's not his taste neither is her act of forwardness.

Delia is pleased she got her way. However, something in Vance's tone informed her she really hadn't made it to first base. Today is Vance's second visit to Johnson Everdeen, it is also the third time he overstepped her flirt filled ways.

Thirty minutes passed and Vance still casually strides around the enormous lobby waiting on Carmichael, periodically glancing at his timepiece then at Delia. Carmichael's arrival time is now further delayed more than either he, she or Vance had expected, so Vance decided to continue his wait outside in the car. It was a move he hoped would deter Delia from dishing out another advance.

Fifteen minutes later, a red Miata swept past Vance's car swiftly pulling into the space marked CEO. Seeing Carmichael had finally arrived, Vance got out of the car and waited on the sidewalk for Carmichael to join him.

"Please excuse my tardiness, it was family oriented. Thanks for waiting." The two men walked side by side, stride after stride looking like a pair of photogenic male print models working on a corporate ad. Beaming with joy, Delia is quite appreciative of Vance's return. It isn't customary for a man whom she adores to fail in expressing his mutual interest in her. Every moment Vance is in her presence, he continues to show her he is the opposite of what she is accustomed to. There is no letting him get away in it. She knows she must step up her game.

Vance needed more details on the business ventures of his client. After the chain of events at the press conference, he wants to avoid as many surprises as he possibly can. From Carmichael's office they discuss Jim Grainger as Vance began to take notes.

"You mentioned to me there was a potential business deal between your company and Jim Grainger's. Just how long was your association with Stone and Nichols before naming Jim in your pending legal suit? Have the two of you had any major disagreements from the past or experienced anything out of the ordinary?" Upon hearing Carmichael's chair as it gave way; Vance looked up from his notes. He glanced up to see his client finish his recline. Carmichael is leaned back in his ergonomic black leather chair. He'd propped his legs atop the glass of his desk and crossed one shoe over the other.

"Umm," he took a few seconds, "I've been an associate of Jim's for just a little over three years. Vance, as far as disagreements there's nothing to note for the present," he thought to himself for a few more seconds, "now, wait a minute. There was somewhat of a disagreement about a year ago."

"A disagreement, what disagreement?" said Vance. Vance prepared himself to tentatively engage an explanation. He doesn't know where Carmichael is headed, but he hopes his client's answer will be one bold enough to hold its weight in court.

"Jim Grainger approached me with an offer to partner in a business deal presented to him concerning a revitalization project. It was a piece of developmental property. There was an upscale multi unit high rise in the making. It was quite a lucrative opportunity. I was all for it until my lawyer at the time pointed out clauses within the agreement which were not all that favorable to Johnson Everdeen. To say the least, I informed Jim I decided to turn down the opportunity. Of course, he tried to convince me in seeing the collaborative benefits. I informed him the offering party would have to modify the documentation before I would attempt any reconsideration to partner with him. Once Jim told me of their refusal, it was in such second he'd failed in any hopes of possibly securing Johnson Everdeen as a partner. He was really counting on my company's involvement. That about sums it up."

Stone and Nichols had never been dished negative publicity in the past. Jim's company is honorable as it is built on integrity. That's why Vance or Carmichael for that matter can't understand why Jim would pull such a move. Nonetheless, Carmichael sees motive.

After the meeting, Vance headed back to the corporate apartment to change his attire. He was finally awarded some time to spend with his brother, Troy.

Mimicking the speed of light, the black and gray swirled ball hurls down the lane toward eight pins, knocking down each.

"Strike!" yelled Vance after watching the pins fall, placing him in the lead, but he probably won't stay there for long. Now the final game is being played and Vance is getting closer to buying that mug of imported beer for Troy.

Sure enough, it was after the last game had been played when Vance ordered Troy a glass of Flat Tire Ale, a draft from Rome.

Although Troy made fun of his brother's client, his curiosity regarding the pending lawsuit remained high. Troy didn't want to come off as nosy. But after Vance's vague details on his ride from the airport, he needed insight. Some insight is better than none, but he is dealing with Vance.

"On the way here, again you were tight lipped about your client's recent troubles. Are things still out of sort, or are you guys on the way to recovery? Well, I mean aside from the lawsuit."

Taking another barbequed wing from the foil lined basket, Vance finally began to speak.

"That outburst from my client's publicist was unexpected. Later that evening, my client called a brief meeting to formally express his disapproval regarding Monahan's behavior. If he acts a fool again, he'll be dismissed, per Carmichael. And if Carmichael doesn't keep his word, he'll be looking for a new attorney because I'll quit," Vance's response wasn't exactly what Troy was expecting to hear. However, he wasn't surprised at all. He knows his brother has a lot of integrity and is very sharp aside from and within his profession. He also knows his sibling will refuse to further build his credentials with ingredients less than complimentary of his own morale.

Vance was on his second order of seasoned fries when he and Troy were approached by two young and attractive ladies who only moments ago indiscreetly eyed Vance and Troy from afar. Having to build only an inkling of courage, the women approached the bar where the brothers are sitting.

"Hi, I'm Victoria."

"Hello, I'm April."

"Are the two of you brothers?" asked Victoria after discovering neither man wears a wedding ring. She thinks their resembling features are striking.

"Yes, we are," responded Troy.

"I'm Troy and Mr. Don right here is my brother, Vance."

The ladies look the brothers over again.

"How would the two of you like to bowl a few rounds with us?" asked Victoria while April looked in the opposite direction, she's busy sizing up Vance.

"Your friend doesn't talk much, does she?" said Vance.

"I talk," the woman responded. "The losers will buy the winners a wing basket, and we hope the conversation is free," touted April. "Do we have a deal?" she asked.

Vance is hesitant. Getting a look at Troy, he sees his brother is all for it. After a few rounds of tied games, they sat around the bar enjoying wing baskets. The brothers almost let them win but thanks to April's sharp tongue from earlier, they'd changed their minds, but her sass didn't cancel out their snack. The evening wore to a close with April offering Vance her contact number so they could keep in touch. He declined her offer.

Claude is on the verge of being found out. He knows he must do something and do it fast because if he doesn't, he knows it will only be a matter of time before Jim or his group of supporters will finally realize he's the one responsible for the public embarrassment Stone and Nichols is currently undergoing. Quinton assured Claude under the watchfulness of his eye that everything will be okay. Due to one of Jim's business trips, Claude had been again appointed to finalize loose details which also includes the failed business proposal between Stone and Nichols and Everdeen. Claude had taken such misfortune to be the perfect cover he needs to aide a trail of deceit, with Quinton's help of course. With all the lies the two of them are telling, who knows what else the two will further conjure up to deter any suspicions against them.

Cadrin heard a car pull up in front of her door's walkway. She walked over to the window to see Roslyn retrieve several bags from the passenger's side of the vehicle. During the week, Roslyn received several calls from Cadrin. Due to Roslyn's equally busy schedule, Cadrin had no choice other than to make good use of voice mail. In one of the messages she'd left for her friend, Cadrin said everything is okay in the best chipper tone she could deliver. On the last message

Cadrin broke down. She began to mentally recite it. "*Roslyn, I've never been so humiliated in my life. I blame myself for convincing my client to agree to the terms of the very company wanting to sue him for millions. A meeting like that was way too soon... I never should have allowed it.*"

Roslyn wanted to cheer up her friend as soon as she possibly could.

"Roslyn, you didn't have to come by. What's all this?" she said holding the door open for her.

"Remember the catering event for the daycare I told you about?"

"Yeah," Cadrin said.

"Well, it just so happens a set of twins within the bunch is having a birthday party, and you my best buddy is going to help me fill gift bags."

"Fill gift bags?"

"Yes. Thirty," Roslyn huffed as she placed the bundle of bags onto the middle of the family room's floor.

"The daycare's owner and the mother of the twins thinks it will be a good idea for the other kids to be able to take a little bit of the party home with them. I have bubbles, stickers, miniature boxes of candy, balloons, plus the kind you can put water in."

"That's so sweet, Roslyn. They are going to love you."

"I hope so," she and Cadrin took a seat among the bags of goodies. They began to build an assembly line of gifts.

"While we work like little elves here you want to talk about the message you left for me the other day?"

"What message was that?" Cadrin coyly stated.

"No. Come on now. You know, the one about you questioning your own capability of whether you are a great public relations expert. You blamed yourself for the mess which happened at Stone and Nichols in the presence of the media."

"Oh, that message," Cadrin casually acknowledged. She paused. Depressingly, Cadrin dropped an unused water balloon into one of the shiny blue gift bags. "Go ahead Roslyn. Tell me what you really think." For a moment, the room was silent. "Okay, if you won't say it, I will."

Roslyn maintains her silence.

"I caused my client public humiliation. He endured unwanted attention, hurtful remarks and got his ass whipped. I mean who else does he have to blame? He's blaming me."

"Cadrin, you did what you believed was the right thing to do. You didn't just get in the mix of PR yesterday nor can you allow an unforeseen incident to hinder you. And besides, it's all a part of the business. Right? I'm sure your client was aware of the fact he needed to make a public appearance, just like he knows he needs a great publicist. Has he blamed you for anything that happened?"

"No. Not yet."

"Well, if he hasn't by now, he probably won't."

Cadrin inhaled. Exhaling slowly, bit by bit she released the built-up tension which formerly owned her sound judgment.

"I guess you're right, Roslyn. Until recently, I had only heard tell of that kind of a disaster."

"Everything will be fine, you'll see. Helping others is one of the things you do best."

Chapter 7

The Executives

Today, now a week later along with the return of Cadrin's confidence is again in full swing. After her talk with Roslyn, she began to see the brighter side of her newest challenge. Presently, the overall public characterization of Stone and Nichols is not synonymous with disaster. Second, she knows she will always have Roslyn's positive thoughts. Third, Jim didn't dismiss her. Fourth, he didn't reprimand her. Fifth, is the point of no return; she didn't come this far in her profession to quit now, and most of all she received a fax from Jim's secretary, Maureen. The documentation is an itinerary outlining Jim's schedule. Cadrin is to meet with him at Stone and Nichols for a strategy meeting. She can't blame him. She totally understands his concern.

After the meeting concluded, Cadrin caught the elevator to the building's third floor. She promised Maureen during her next visit she wouldn't dare leave the building without first trying the chicken parmesan prepared in creamy pasta sauce simmered in white wine.

The Vintage is an independently owned and operated restaurant located within the million-dollar company. Every Wednesday after hours, the venue host wine tastings for the building's employees. Such a gesture didn't go unnoticed but today is Thursday, *"maybe next week,"* Cadrin thought as she continue to wait at the venue's entrance.

Cadrin was finally seated in a quiet corner where she placed her order over instrumentals softly playing in the background. The aura of the restaurant makes Cadrin feel as though she had been unexpectedly swept off her feet. The room's décor is of black, gold and a hue of brown. She also notices how attractively the soft lighting plays against the flat gold dinnerware and against the black tablecloths they are placed upon. The fact windows lack in existence doesn't matter, as brown curtains cover the areas which represents where windows would have been employed producing even more intimate offerings.

About ten minutes later, Cadrin's entrée of chicken parmesan hails from a gold server.

"Be careful. The sauce may still be a little hot," spoke a polite and considerate server, "If I'm correct please do inform me of your findings, I'll be sure to personally see to it you receive an exact and speedy replacement."

"Thank you for being so kind. I'll be careful."

Smiling, the server took a step backwards, turned and walked away leaving Cadrin to her meal.

Vance's highly inquisitive nature evident from his childhood years sent him on a quest to Stone and Nichols. Something about the allegations against Jim Grainger doesn't make sense to him. Nonetheless, he fully intends to uphold his duties as Johnson Everdeen's legal counsel. But he can't ignore the fact the fraudulent bill just doesn't fit a man like Jim Grainger.

Vance entered the Stone and Nichols building. He figured by walking around in observance of its atmosphere and the attitudes within, he would be provided with some level of confirmation which will denounce Jim's 'bad boy' character. He would be gracious for anything and will remain leery of taking anything negative he might learn to the bank.

Once Vance successfully reached the third floor, his sense of smell and taste became pleasantly enticed by the aromas which fills the air-conditioned corridor.

"Excuse me, Sir. Is there a restaurant on this floor?"

"Yes, only one of the best," replied a medium height gentleman.

"Just down the hall, make a right and you'll find Vintage."

Vance quickly came upon the upscale restaurant. The closer he became to the dining area soft music began to dance about his ears and stronger hunger pangs about his stomach. As soon as he'd approached the restaurant's doorway, he immediately became impressed by the woman he sees sitting in a nestled corner of the venue. *"Cadrin Porter."* From the center of the room to each corner of the restaurant, square tables are draped with black tablecloths. One lit candle from each table intricately shows off each designated space. Ceiling fans gently spin around, the light wind coming from them gives the entire room a cooling feel of an evening outdoors. Like an anticipating and lonely bachelor, Vance stands patiently at the door until acknowledged.

"Good afternoon, sir," the maître d' said. "Will you be dining alone?"

"Yes. *Maybe I won't be if luck is on my side*."

With a cloth draped over her arm, the maître d' began to seat Vance. Vance's boldness caused him to forget where he is. He's about to become immobile and hopes no one will recognize him as a supporter of Johnson Everdeen. He quickly gave the room a glance over hoping to find perfect seclusion. Eager, Vance couldn't wait a second longer. *"What the hell,* I apologize ma'am, I do see my party after all," he said looking in Cadrin's direction.

"Then I'll show you to your table, Sir." Vance followed the maitre d' over to the table which Cadrin occupies.

Resembling the look of a child whose hand was just caught in the cookie jar, a wide - eyed Cadrin fails to clearly think as she watches a hunk of a man act as though he is going to approach her table. Although she's shocked, she loves every minute.

"Hello, Cadrin."

Reacting to the husky yet tenured male voice, her curiosity is now more prevalent, responding with hesitancy and a mix of curiosity.

"Hello. Yes, I'm Cadrin Porter and you are?"

Is his cover blown? Surely, he isn't going to lie to the woman whom he can't get off his mind. Will he lie to the woman who he has many questions about? Will he lie to the woman who unknowingly made her way into his heart and his dreams?

"I'm Grayson," taken by her beauty he shyly laughs at himself.

"I apologize. It's Vance. Vance Grayson."

He offered her his hand for a shake, gently enclosing her small hand within his large grasp. She smiled at the stranger who is still standing.

"I recognized you as I was about to be seated," he said giving gesture in the direction opposite to them.

"I remembered you from the press conference held here just a few weeks ago. Are you alright?"

"Excuse me?" answered Cadrin.

"Are you alright? Were you alright?" his heart rate increased,

"When the fight broke out you were sort of struck in the process. The more I thought about it the more I believed you didn't realize you were hit."

At that moment, Cadrin realized she recognizes him too. How could she forget? She loved his disposition and the way he'd managed it. She ended up becoming so consumed with her attempts to rescue Jim, she didn't acknowledge the man who came to her aide. Let alone, her attraction to him.

"Smooth skin, passionate eyes. The way his upper lip meets the lower, positioned as if he was getting ready to whisper my name, "Look at the way his neat hairline accentuates his features, the way his--"

"Ms. Porter. Do you remember being hit at all?"

"What? What were you saying?"

Feeling insignificant, Vance is now embarrassed for having approached her. Her mind is obviously elsewhere, and he believes her distraction has nothing to do with him. Feeling no reason to ponder there any longer, he's now ready to go on about his business.

"I apologize for disturbing your meal," he began to walk away from her. His long strides quickly placed him out of her reach. Even though she realized she had made a careless mistake, she dared not to separate herself from her chair to chase after him like a lust struck fool. Him leaving the restaurant? It isn't going to happen, so she softly and though purposefully beckoned after him.

"Would you like to sit down?"

From what seems like a short distance in his world, Vance turns to face her.

"I beg your pardon?" He said with his hand placed over the lapel of his jacket.

"Please sit down," she pointed to the back of the empty chair across from her plate.

Vance returned to the table, more than willingly he took his seat. He's cool yet unprepared for her sudden change for good manners. His heartbeat is rapid, his palms began to moisten.

"*What type of questions will she ask me? Now that I've given her my name, it makes no sense for me to conceal the fact I am an attorney. But whose attorney is the question. Maybe she didn't notice me standing with the Everdeen crew.*"

If he kept that bit of information to himself, the media would scream liar. If Troy tuned in, he surely knew she'd caught the replay. He's almost certain she did, and he knows there's almost no chance he is going to let her out of his sight again. Maybe she did see the replay and will use it to test him.

"Yes, I remember you as well. You're on the Johnson Everdeen team of supporters. You were the only one over there towering above everyone else. I was a little preoccupied with my client, he was a nervous wreck. I'm sure you and everyone else realized such a thing."

Vance stared at the beautiful eyes which seem to be able to see straight through him.

"Why would you be here of all places? You are one of the Johnson Everdeen supporters, right?" she probed.

Vance just kept staring at her beautiful brown eyes, imagining his lips tenderly teasing and passionately caressing hers. He thinks she has the sweetest aura about herself. The sexiness in her confidence messed with his mind, had him wanting to ask for a private booth so he could verbally learn all there is to know about the woman sitting across from him.

While Cadrin mentally tossed negative explanations back and forth as to why he's there with her, Vance was awarded some time to confidently respond. He wanted to tell her anything but the truth. The weight of the whole matter would not sustain a lie. He's afraid of the ramifications the truth can bring.

"Yes, I am. I guess you can say I wanted to get a feel for the place."

"I don't understand. A feel for this place?" she questioned.

"Just what are you saying, Vance?"

Quickly think, Vance!

"It's something I always do; you know, checking out the defendant's territory. It's sort of like a pet peeve of mine."

She didn't totally believe him, so she took his answer to be just what it was. A response.

The waiter returned delivering a menu to Vance who hoped his answer is believable enough to protect his seat from being revoked. When he wasn't eyeing Cadrin, he noticed her meal looks delicious. So, upon the next return of the waiter, he ordered what she's having. Cadrin realized any specifics regarding his role within Johnson Everdeen hadn't been offered.

"I apologize. Earlier you mentioned something about me being hit."

Vance cleared his throat.

"Yes, I did. You were struck by Pete Monahan after the fight broke out between himself and Jim Grainger."

Cadrin shook her head.

"Please forgive me for being so rude. I owe you an apology. Now that you've mentioned it, I do remember being ruffled a bit. You came to my rescue. Thank you, Vance."

"You're welcome."

"So, what type of support are you providing Johnson Everdeen?"

Only a bit nervous he said, "Now that's no fair," he countered, smiling at her. I haven't asked you what's your role here at Stone and Nichols," he said as he gently leaned forward displaying more charm as he gently swirls wine round about his glass. To be charming is in his nature. He hopes for the sake of consolation, it will only exemplify his remark wasn't intended to be rude. Amidst the bliss there is a tug of war going on.

"That is true, Vance. You didn't have to ask a question of which you already know the answer to. At the press conference, I introduced myself as PR. And while Stone and Nichols is the subject matter at hand, surely you know my client is innocent, right?"

If it weren't for the spark in her eyes, he would have thought her to be the rudest woman he has ever encountered. Sexy or not, he doesn't like where the conversation is heading.

"Man, you have got to change this conversation quick. "Who wouldn't want to promote their client's innocence?" he said.

Vance knows Cadrin is getting on the defensive. The daunting trouble of their clients proves to be unavoidable. Nonetheless, Vance wants to see her again away from the demands their profession entails. To ensure such a thing can happen, he figures it isn't a good idea to inform her of his professional status when it comes down to Johnson Everdeen.

"Do you eat here often?" he inquired.

"It just so happens today is the first day. I heard some great things about it and decided to finally check it out."

"Ahh, there we go. We are on friendly ground now," I'm glad you chose today," he told her.

She only smiled at him. She's still having trouble figuring out his true agenda for being on the premises of Stone and Nichols.

The next day Cadrin dibbled and dabbled over the prior woes of her previous clients, it's her way of staying ahead of the game. She revisited manuscripts which she familiarized herself with some years ago. She wanted to find anything which could be beneficial in being the final glue in holding everything together. The troubles of Stone and Nichols are without a doubt on a much different level when compared to her former clients. With such thought, she remembered a rule of thumb shared by one of her PR professors. The professor's voice sound just as real to her today as it had been that day in class.

"No matter how bad or how foreign the challenge may be, you must accept what you have been given, then work at making those who bring about negativity and other complexities into understanding your creative way of thinking is better than any set back they can throw at you," she could still hear him say. Now more than ever she knows what he was trying to get into her mind and into the minds of her classmates. On that note, she put away her manuscripts, choosing instead to meditate on the information neatly inscribed on the back of a business card.

"*It was nice chatting with you. Vance Grayson.*" His gesture was followed by his home number. She began to speak aloud. "Vance Grayson." Cadrin all but figured him to be a liar. It's obvious to her he hid his true reason for being at Stone and Nichols the other day. Skeptical, she placed the card back onto the table. Standing in the middle of the room Cadrin looks around. Everything is neat and in its proper place as they usually are, so she decided she will do a little dusting.

"Alright, let's see now, where should I begin, surely there is an accumulation of dust in here somewhere."

She went to a hall closet, retrieved a duster, cloth, and Windex. Standing before a curio where little keepsakes are on display, she began to remove each before freeing every glass shelf of dust. Once she finished buffing each delicate item, she carefully returned each one back behind the wood and glass door of the curio, to again sit on the now polished glass. Once she realized she'd forgotten to buff one other item sitting way back against the wall of the display, she frowned.

"Look at this. I haven't held this little charm in years," she said of a porcelain dolphin duo. It had been given to her by Louis, a former boyfriend. Unfortunately, the keepsake brought back bad memories of their time together. He told her the gift symbolized free spirits going after their dreams in life, their place in the world. "Hhmp, I went after mine and finally began my own PR business. And he certainly went after his, chasing after every set of curvaceous hips which had come his way including my own," she spoke aloud. The second woman she'd caught him with was the event she needed to see. She told herself she'd had enough of Louis and was finally ready to let him go.

"He swore to me it would never happen again. He lied. He lied more than I was willing to admit at the time," Cadrin heard herself reliving the not-so-great side of Louis. The gift does have some good meaning behind it. Therefore, she released the tight grip. Gently, she placed it back on the shelf amongst the other keepsakes.

"So far, all I've done today is revisit the past. I might as well have been sitting at somebody's conference table," she mused. Cadrin glanced in the direction of the card which holds Vance's contact number on the back of it. Today is a good day to get to know him better. Maybe she would even find out what he is hiding.

"Hmm," work she thought.

Cadrin walked back over to the card, picked it up and began to dial the set of numbers only to stop on the last digit. She pressed the phones off button. Is she crazy? No. Maybe she is desperate. No matter the category, she did fess up to one thing and that is her attraction to Vance Grayson.

After vacuuming every carpeted room in her house, Cadrin left for a trip to the market. Afterwards, she returned home with the best-looking vegetables she could find along with other items she ended up trading half of her grocery list for. She hated to admit it. The entire time she shopped, she couldn't get Vance Grayson off her mind. All at once he had been such a liar and managed to be charming in doing so.

Despite whatever it is he's concealing, for the way he'd carried himself left her curious as well as strangely impressed. Therefore, she found herself wondering what is behind those dignified dimples resting at each corner of his lips. She refused to give in to her feelings. To no surprise, just like a great conversationalist she ended up talking herself out of giving him a call.

Keeping toned is a Saturday birth right for Vance and Troy. In their line of work an attractive physical appearance breathes strong influence into every aspect of their professions.

"Alright Troy, I'll talk to you later," Vance got into his car and tossed his gym bag towards the passenger seat. He just sat there for a moment. The last time he returned home there still was no call from Cadrin.

"*What did I do to make her not want to contact me? Bad luck has it, she doesn't trust me.*"

He started the engine. Prying into Vance's love life, Troy knocked on the car's window. It's Saturday night and the fellas always have something planned. Vance really did want a night out on the town but....

"Are you coming with me and some of the fellas tonight? We're going over to Mike and Pamela's to catch some classic moments in sports by some of the greatest."

Vance lowered the power-controlled window.

"I don't know, maybe."

"If you change your mind here are the directions just in case I'm already there," Troy handed to him a folded map quest print out.

"Thanks man," Vance said to his brother.

Vance entered the upscale apartment. For the life of him he could not forget Cadrin's look of apprehension out of his mind.

"Have I messed up?" Realizing he probably couldn't have handled the situation any better than what he'd demonstrated, Vance removed all negative thoughts from his head while he checked his messages.

There weren't any. Does he have the right to be puzzled? There is a bottom line to the situation. He lied to her, sort of. His excuse for being at Stone and Nichols was credible. But he failed to disclose his professional status, neither did he disclose the fact he represents the company who may cost her client his livelihood.

Vance is appreciative of the time alone. The solidarity gives him a chance to clear his mind. He's disappointed in himself for not telling her the full truth. Everything he picked up, a cup, the remote, he placed them all down with a thud. He knows tearing up the place by throwing an adult sized tantrum is not going to fix his situation; so, he seated himself on the middle of the couch, relaxing his back up against the large pillows behind his back. Slowly bringing both of his hands up to his face, he froze for a moment. It's more than obvious to him he and Cadrin displayed insurmountable chemistry during their dinner. Not even the relic of awkward moments had been able to destroy the fair between them. She is different. She isn't like so many other women he'd met. After those women got the opportunity to know him, they had the gumption to nice nastily scold him for his present and intact morals. And because of his unique points of view, the women from his past hadn't been able to embrace the key notes which made him into the man he will forever be. It's thoughts such as those which allow him hope when it comes to Cadrin Porter.

Chapter 8

The Executives

It had been an especially stressful night, but Vance managed to turn in around twelve a.m. The hour is a much later time than what he is used to. Before he did so, he realized he didn't re-inform Carmichael of his prior obligation back in Maryland. Right away, he phoned his client's cell.

"Carmichael," answered Vance's client.

Vance laughed.

"You sound exhausted. I can tell you're still at the office."

Before Vance's call went through, Carmichael and his secretary had just finished going over his shareholders list. The rhetorical questions had begun. Answers are needed. A meeting with them will surely reserve a week's worth of his time and Vance's.

"Yeah, I'm just about to head home."

"Don't stomp around there on the count of me," Vance joked.

"You don't have to tell me twice," Carmichael joked back.

"Listen, since a ruckus hadn't been brewing or anything, I just wanted to inform you I'm going to proceed with the prior obligation I mentioned to you prior to leaving for Chicago. It'll be brief, so don't worry. I'll be back here in Chicago in a couple of days. You have my contact information if any new problems occur. If I need to return sooner, I'll take the next flight out."

"I have it. You have a safe trip, enjoy your family and let me know if she's beautiful," he said of the reporter.

"Thank you, I will. And who said the reporter is a woman?"

"I could hear it in your voice. The reporter you're going to meet with is a woman, right? I'll bet she is a real looker."

"To be honest, we've never met. We've only spoken over the phone. I haven't had the time to look for an online photo of her. However, I am aware of the magazine she writes for."

"Ah, so the reporter you'll be spending some time with is a woman."

"Yes, I am meeting with a woman. I'm doing an interview for a magazine she works for. The meeting is only about my interview, nothing else."

"Alright have it your way," Carmichael laughed. Vance laughed back and said, "Just make sure Delia doesn't know how to find me."

Both men laughed aloud.

Vance is scheduled for an interview with a contributing writer for an upscale urban magazine based out of Maryland. The contributing editor offered to meet Vance in Chicago, but he wanted to personally check in with his parents. He failed to often communicate with them by phone since he'd been here in Chicago. He knows he will hear about that later. Although his parents are aware of his interview, they are clueless regarding when and where it will take place. Vance's surprise visit will make for an unsuspecting and wonderful surprise for them and his sister, Avionne.

After exiting the limo, Vance entered the airport. After locating his gate, he patiently waited in line behind a woman who is angry over the declination of an upgrade from coach to first class. Her pouting lips, furrows across her forehead, *"Anger in a woman is the last thing I want to witness."* Her behavior suggested to him the kind of rage he would have to endure if Cadrin ever came to learn of his role within Everdeen. He had her. He just didn't know it yet. The increasing desire she has for him just isn't going away.

"I have got to stop thinking about her; I can't give a decent interview side-tracked."

"Next please," said the man standing behind the ticket counter of Southwest airlines.

"Yes, I have a round trip flight to Maryland. It'll be under the name of Vance Grayson."

After several repetitive punches to the keyboard, Vance was awarded clearance. He had about a forty-five-minute wait before boarding his flight.

Vance wondered what type of questions the interviewer will ask of him. Just to break the ice, the editor wanted to email a list of sample questions to help prepare him. Since the offerings came without certainties, he declined the offer. In his line of work uncertainties come hand in hand. Over the phone, the reporter agreed not to ask him anything in relation to private matters. She was even asked to refrain from discussing anything specifically relating to his previous and present clients. Vance expects her to stay true to her word. If she doesn't, knowing Vance he will probably walk out on the interview.

Hearing an announcement for his flight, Vance stood and made his way to board. Hours later his plane touched down in Maryland. It was there he'd made his way to the front of the airport where he hailed a cab. On the cab ride to his parents', Vance knew his focus should have been on seeing his family. But getting Cadrin off his mind just seems downright impossible.

"You give the directions and I'll make sure you arrive safely."

"Thank you, Sir. I will."

Vance arrived at the home of his parents around two in the afternoon. Taking in its architectural design, there is no doubt his parents are proud of their investment. From the quiet road, the exterior of the Victorian styled all brick home resembles the cozy look of velvet. Two oversized stone planters sit on their own corner of the porch where four columns attractively bestow the home's entry. Its roof mimics that of saved pages found inside of a publication, showing off four deep and prominent inward folds. Two large oaks amply shade better than half of the family's back yard. The breath-taking home of fourteen rooms including an ample sunroom are surrounded by well manicured lush greenery with a fair number of small trees partially lining the home's side parameters. The lovely structure is the second home to be owned by Brian and Constance Grayson. Vance is the couple's first offspring to be put through college with the wealth of real estate generated from the first property owned by his parents. Brian and Constance were blessed enough to have put all three of their children through four years of college, still having enough revenue to state a substantial claim to a five-bedroom, three bath dwelling they'd called their first home. The couple discovered and fell in love with their present dwelling before their youngest graduated from college. Although it had been two years after graduating college before moving into a home of her own merits, Avionne is their only offspring who has really lived there. Her brothers Vance and Troy respectively, were already out and about discovering some of their own treasures in life.

By the time the cab stopped on the half circle of his parents' driveway, Vance's hunger pangs became more evident. Before he left O'Hare International, he had only a cup of coffee and not much else, but he dares not tell such to Mrs. Grayson. With his luggage in tow, he exited the cab on the curve of the driveway while holding a huge grin on his face. His mom had her back turned and failed to see or hear the car as it pulled up. Their next-door neighbor, Mrs. Arthur Harrison noticed Vance first and waved to him. *"Some things never change,"* he reflected. She was dutifully manipulating her yard's sprinkler heads. Often, Vance believed Mrs. Harrison's concern for the lawn is just her way of having fun; over there running about the lawn and getting soaked. He waved backed to her. His mother turned around.

"Oh, my Lord! Vance you're back from Chicago!"

He bent down to hug his mother.

"Hey Mom, how are you! I missed you, too. I'm back only for a couple of days. I have an interview for the magazine I was telling you guys about. After that's done, I'll be on my way back to Chicago. It's going to be a while before all of that is over with."

"It sounds serious, I heard~"

The case is the last thing Vance wants to discuss.

"Yeah, suspicious is more like it."

"But you will come home every so often. You will do that won't you?"

"Every chance I get, Mom."

Seeing the cab driver is in a hurry to leave, Vance quickly paid the cabby his fee.

"Thank you, Sir," the cab driver said as he pocketed the money before leaving the residence.

"Where's Dad?" Vance said as he grabbed the remainder of his belongings bringing them into the home's main foyer.

"Your father went to the market to buy some dinner rolls and sugar."

"What! Awl, Mom," Vance exclaimed with disbelief. "Ma, please don't tell me you're not baking from scratch anymore."

She laughed.

"Is somebody trying to say he misses my baked breads?"

Vance fell to his knees, "Please say it's not so. Please," he begged.

"Mama wouldn't dare baby."

Playful moments are always welcomed in the Grayson household, warm moments for sure.

"Boy get up here and hug your Mama."

Vance stood before bending down to give his mother another hug. He was ready to break contact before his hunger pangs had the chance to inform his mom he'd consumed much of nothing for breakfast that morning.

"I got tired of that hot oven and was ready to get out of the kitchen. I still ended up out in the garden in the heat. Don't you laugh at your mother."

He smiled instead.

"Your father said he would go and get rolls to go along with dinner. He should be back in a few minutes."

"I knew I smelled something delicious when I got out of the cab."

On his way to the kitchen, Vance walked that walk which just about every woman on earth will run to any outlet to see for herself. Troy has the same sexy and unique walk as well. It is a gift from Brian's bloodline. In the kitchen is where Vance found barbequed beef ribs covered in foil, baked macaroni and cheese, a pot of cabbage and collards, brown rice, and two apple pies made from scratch for dessert.

"So, how's my other baby?"

"Troy, Vance answered while looking for something to help him take a slice of pie, "that rascal's great, he sent his love."

"One of these days I'm going to get the both of you here together. Your schedules or so off beat. How do you two have time to dat~"

"Mom, where's Avionne?" he didn't want to explain again to his mother why he isn't seeing anyone. She always tries to get information out of him about his love life, telling him that's what moms are supposed to do.

"She's still at work. She was promoted to Executive Coordinator. Ooh, no I didn't!"

"What's wrong Ma?"

"I wasn't supposed to say anything, she wanted to tell you about it herself. So, you my hungry son, remember you haven't heard a word about it."

Vance blushed as he finished scarping down a healthy slice of home baked apple pie.

Brian arrived back home from the market just in time to hear the table being set for dinner. It is undeniable who Vance takes his height and looks after. Mrs. Grayson is a little below average height and attractive herself. Mr. Grayson is a tower as though Vance and still in rather good shape for an older gentleman.

Vance was about to call out to his father when Connie shook her head. Smiling she pointed to the kitchen's offset. Vance got her message. He quietly steps around a corner. His gut burns with laughter.

"I'm in here honey," Connie called out to her husband.

Brian sees their gorgeous dining table is set for three. Shaking his head, Vance's dad stands at the dining room's entry.

"Hi honey, go get washed up, dinner is ready."

"Okay," Brian had begun to place the grocery bag onto the granite countertop when he was interrupted. He can't take his eyes off the third and full place setting.

"Oh, honey is Avionne stopping by after work?"

"No, but I just feel it. One of those boys will get here before dinner is over."

"Constance, stop that. You don't know. You set the table for three? Connieee…" his words were dry, sinking into depression as if his wife is getting ready to be committed.

Vance couldn't take it anymore. The kitchen walls would not be able to conceal his laughter. He stepped into the kitchen from the small though elegant foyer.

"Vance!"

"Hey Pops!" Vance said as he greeted his father with a big hug.

"Well, well, well, Constance will you look at this sly devil," he said of their oldest son, still holding the bag with the rolls and sugar in it. The two men air boxed each other laughing as they threw short jabs and hooks into the air, bobbing and weaving around in circles. After the mocked match, they hugged again.

"Give me my pack of sugar and rolls before you have another trip to the market," Constance said with a wink at Brian who failed to place the grocery bag onto the counter. Brian released the plastic bag and kissed his wife on her cheek.

"When did you get here?" Brian asked now turning his attention back to Vance.

"About thirty minutes ago."

"Did Troy come with you?"

"No, but he sent his love to all of you. He had to remain in Chicago to give a tour to a group of perspective buyers. If he closes the deal, twenty grand is in it for him."

"Yeah, and a thousand has got my name on it,"

Brian said of a loan he'd given to Troy.

Troy saw firsthand from Brian and Connie how structure can generate a comfort of wealth. Therefore, their youngest gained an interest in real estate. Now on the table are talks of him starting his own real estate development company.

Brian retreated to the foyer and placed his jacket inside the closet. Mrs. Grayson couldn't stand it any longer. She decided to quickly phone Avionne. Their daughter will be getting off from work soon. Connie doesn't have all three of her kids there but at least she could get two, she thought.

Overwhelmed with joy she gave Troy a buzz. Even though he couldn't join in on the festivities which are taking place, it is a joy for her just to be able to hear his voice anyway.

"So, Sly Devil, talk to me. How are things going? Some of the fellas told me you look like superman at the press conference just a few weeks ago. I can't believe we missed it. Avionne saw it."

"Yeah, she gave me a call so did Troy. But she and I kept missing each other."

Sly Devil is a term Mr. Grayson adopted for his sons. He uses it most often when addressing Vance. He knows he helped raised good boys, but he always figures Vance has been with more women than he is letting on.

"Are you seeing anybody yet, steadily?"

"Seeing anybody? No, I don't see anybody… else," he said as he looks around the living room."

"I keep telling him to bring that lady here so I can meet her," Mrs. Grayson yelled from the kitchen.

"Come on now, this isn't Troy," Mr. Grayson spoke in a hushed tone. I've seen that look on your face before so talk to your old man. What's going on?"

"Old man? Your bobs and weaves are about as good as mine," Vance then became silent for a few moments.

"There is someone, sort of anyway. I'm very much interested in her, but I don't quite know how she's feeling about me. I gave her the number to the apartment to reach me by. It has been almost two weeks and I have yet to hear from her."

Brian stares at his son for a few seconds.

"Tell me something, Dad, was Mom tough to figure out when the two of you first met?"

"No. She gave me the eye; I gave her an eye and we've been tight ever since," Brian smoothly stated.

"Come on, Dad. I'd like a real answer this time."

"Listen at you Mr. Beat Around The Bush Then Head'em Off At The Pass," Brian couldn't control his laughter.

Vance clapped his hands.

"Good one Dad, that's a really good one."

His father's laughter was catchy. Brian finally stopped laughing as did Vance.

"No truthfully, we did give each other the eye. That Connie, although she gave me the eye as well, she wasn't easy for me. Other than making her smile here and there, I had to leave out my game for that one," he referenced Constance, "and be a mirror for what I was feeling on the inside for her, so there would not be a doubt in her mind as to what she was seeing when her beautiful eyes met mine. And that was love then and we are still in love to this day," Brian pressed his thumb to the stubble of hair on his chin as he spoke to his son.

Just what did Vance's heart reveal to Cadrin? What did it tell her soul? What did it convince of her mind? Whatever she learned had caused her to put the brakes on anything which could further develop between herself and Vance. Vance thought the two of them traded more than just conversation over dinner. If she thought he was so ridiculous, why had she chosen to stay and eat dinner with him, he wondered?

"Are you giving up?"

"No. But maybe I should consider the possibility I've lost and besides, I really don't have the time. Between my client and Troy~"

"Oh, she's a Chicago woman, huh. Where bout in Chicago did the two of you meet?"

"We met at the press conference."

Knowing he raised his sons with more class than to run a woman down in a formalized setting, Vance's father stared into the space straight ahead listening intently for his son to provide a decent explanation.

"No. We formally met at a restaurant, a very nice restaurant as a matter of fact. It's housed under the roof of Stone and Nichols."

"Did you just say Stone and Nichols? That's the corporation you and your client are battling."

"We're not in court yet but so to speak, yes. Yeah, she's a member of the opposing side."

A stunned Brian removed his baseball cap from among the thick ringlets and hurriedly placed it back atop his head in a get out of here, too hot for the contender motion.

"Business and pleasure," Brian stated as he shook his head with uncertainty.

"I know, Dad. I've always done a good job in keeping the two separated. Maybe this time though, this time could possibly be an exception to the rule. The fact of her professional status and my own matters not."

Shocked at his son's admittance Brian raised both eyebrows at his son.

"She must be a heck of a woman, huh?"

"She is," Vance replied, "it makes for a risky move on her part-"

"It's a risky move on her part? You mean it's a risk for the both of you, right?"

"Well, she knows I'm on the Johnson Everdeen team and that's all. That little fact isn't what one would call a plus for me."

"Wait a second. You mean you didn't tell her you're Everdeen's attorney. Your move is a risky one for sure."

"I..."

"Come on into the dining room, dinner is ready," instructed Constance. Avionne will be here in a minute."

Looking towards the dining area, Brian said, “We’ll finish this later before you head back to Chicago.” Both father and son entered the dining area where they took a seat at the cherry oak table. They began to watch Constance busy herself in completing the table for their family meal. Watching Vance intently, Mrs. Grayson cleared her throat.

“Somebody was helping me prepare the dinner table before his Daddy came home.”

“Oh, Mom, I apologize. Let me get that for you,” Vance quickly rose and carefully retrieved the pitcher of iced tea from her grasp, pouring drinks for everyone.

“That’s my boy,” she confirmed while grinning at the thought of the playfulness her husband and their oldest son displays whenever they are apart for too long.

All bowed their heads in prayer led by Brian. As apart of his thanks he mentioned how proud he is to have their eldest son home. Afterwards, they each began preparing their plates when they heard their front door open.

“It sure does smell good in here,” Avionne arrived entering the home’s foyer. “Hello everybody,” she yelled out to Connie and Brian, as she’s unaware Vance is home visiting. Avionne kicked off her shoes. Her feet sank into the living room’s plush carpeting.

“Come on in here, Avionne,” said Constance.

Vance raised himself from the family’s dining table, steadily staring towards the dining room’s entry preparing to witness Avionne’s facial expression.

“Vance!” she ran to him.

“Mom, when you called you didn’t tell me Vance is back.”

“Only until tomorrow,” Vance continues to hug her with a great big smile on his face while watching the light of joy dance about in the eyes of Connie.

“I only wish I could stay longer. Duty calls and look at you. Girl you’re looking sharp,” he spins her around.

"Thank you!" With pivots and flourishes she models around the dining room table for her family. The room became filled with joyful laughter and applause. Afterwards, Avionne bowed then took a seat in front of her place setting. As a reminder, Constance gave Vance the eye, reminding him to remain clueless of Avionne's promotion.

All through dinner, Vance had been willing his personal line to ring and for the voice on the other end of it to be Cadrin's. Before leaving the corporate apartment, he enabled all business calls to be re-routed to his personal line. If Cadrin decided to contact him, it will be the one call he definitely will want to be quickly made aware of.

After dinner, everyone pitched in and cleared the table. The men offered in washing the dishes. Constance told them she'd feel better if they took such time to continue in catching up. She assured them Avionne will assist her in getting things back in order.

Vance followed his father outside along the winding driveway which leads around to the family's back yard. Brian wants to show off his brand-new ride.

"Dang pops! This is some ride," Vance ran his hand along the car's superb red paint job. The car's gold packaging glistens in the afternoon sunlight.

"When did you get this?" Vance continues to admire Brian's new set of wheels.

"Last week. Your mother about had a breakdown. The cruise control is like silk, too."

"I'll be sure to take it for a spin before I head back to the airport tomorrow," Vance resumed his tour around the vehicle while Brian looks on as he fumbles with some loose change he'd found earlier.

"Vance, don't you think you are holding back some vital information from your somewhat lady friend?"

"I know. You get no argument there. I didn't plan to run into her at the restaurant. It just happened, caught me off guard to say the least," Vance said to his father.

Mr. Grayson listened with his undivided attention.

"Our conversation got a little on edge, but I managed to make a quick recovery."

"I believe that. What happened?"

"Naturally, we ended up talking about her client, Jim Grainger. Although I unintentionally struck a nerve, we managed to get through it ending dinner on a peaceful note. However, I'm beginning to think my recovery wasn't good enough due to the fact I haven't had the pleasure of seeing her again or hearing her voice on the other end of my phone."

"Well, my boy," Brian said as he opens a jar of car wax, "if you think she is worth the trouble and it does appear she is, then keep up your pursuit. Give her just enough to think on. Let her be the judge. Be sure to keep this in mind. If the pursuit becomes a battle, leave her alone. For the most part, a union built upon unstable ground will be hell to uphold," Brian handed his son a piece of waxing cloth. "I hear this is the best car wax they got out there on the market," Brian professed, "let's spot test this before we try it out on the car."

To keep product from getting into the silver grooves of his designer watch, Vance removed his own timepiece from his wrist. If he didn't, he knows the band will be hell for him to clean later.

Vance and Brian had just finished polishing the car's windows when Vance excused himself. He needed to check in with Carmichael. Although he hadn't heard from his client, he assumed he should check in anyhow just to inquire on any new activity.

"Hello, Vance," Delia answered the phone in Carmichael's office.

"Hi, Delia."

"I hope you didn't mind I recognized the number as belonging to you."

"It's all right, Delia. Is Carmichael around or can I reach him on his cell?"

"Today, I'm responding to all of Carmichael's phone calls and messages. He'll be in back-to-back meetings for most of the day with the investors. He informed me to make you aware of such in the event you should call him."

"Are the details of the meetings anything I should be aware of?"

"No, just the usual things concerning daily operatives," she responded.

"Delia, thank you for passing along the message."

"Even in the midst of trouble, he can't afford to let other measures fall by his side."

"I couldn't agree more, Delia," Vance suddenly realized he's carrying on a conversation with Delia. The last thing he needs is to send her mixed signals.

"Alright Delia, have a good afternoon."

Before she could reply, Vance ended the call.

Vance rejoined his father who is waiting for him on the passenger side of 'Red Thunder.'

"There's no point in waiting any longer, hop in," Brian urged on.

Vance got behind the wheel and secured his seatbelt before starting the car's smooth engine. Placing the car into reverse, cautiously and skillfully he maneuvered the vehicle around the bend of the second driveway then whipped the car out onto the roadway. Brian gave a sporty laugh as he clicked his seat belt.

Forty-five minutes later, they returned to the Grayson home each entering the family's theatre room where Constance and Avionne are watching television. It wasn't long before the men searched for movies to partake of. The women didn't seem to mind at all.

From wall to wall, the theatre room is surrounded by black and white and color photos. The older of the photos portrays the lives of Vance's Great and Grandparents hailing back to when times were more about appreciation. Sharing family history is of great importance for Brian and Constance. Thankfully, their children are proud recipients. The family's history remarkably curtails the Grayson genealogical traits, including the one responsible for bringing Vance's highly inquisitive nature into existence.

After watching a few of the family favorites, Vance became exhausted and decided to turn in a little early. His mind had been on overload before his flight left out of Chicago. There is the questionable 'case' he's been called to only moderate thus far. At this point, Vance isn't any closer to learning if in fact Carmichael is going after the wrong company. True, Jim does have motive. Could he have somehow gotten himself to the fork in the road then became angry enough to falsely name Carmichael Lewis as a business partner in a joint venture? Vance ponders the possibility. Right now, he'd rather go upstairs and lie down. Vance's other troubles comes down to Cadrin. For the life of him he can't figure out what he might have said to her that was so wrong. Right about now, he will give almost anything to remove any negative thoughts of himself from her mind.

"Mom, Dad, Avionne, although show time has been great, I have to say goodnight," he stretched. "I have that interview at ten o'clock tomorrow morning. Afterwards, I'll be on my flight back to Chicago."

Disapproving sounds drowned out the movie which plays on.

"I know guys. I promise I'll come back and visit, soon."

"We're going to hold you to that," Constance said to her son.

Brian and Constance told their son good night.

"Good night everyone, I'm going to call it a night, too. I have to be up early for work," Avionne headed for her shoes in the foyer.

"Good night Avionne," said Brian and Constance in unison.

"Avionne, wait up. I'll walk you out to your car."

"Okay, just let me get these heels back on. Ma, is my purse still on the coffee table?"

From inside the theatre room, Constance yelled back to her daughter, "Yes, Avionne."

Avionne walked through the dimly lit living room to retrieve her purse, "Okay, Vance I'm ready," Avionne pressed the button on the key fob. Her car's headlights flickered.

Vance walked her to the car and opened its door for her. She was about to get in when he heard her say to him, "Oh! I almost forgot. I made Executive Coordinator the other day! I meant to call you. I got sidetracked."

"Say what, girl. Come here," he hugs her.

"I'm so proud of you, Avionne. Congratulations. You deserve the recognition."

"Thank you so much Vance," she gave him a great big hug, "not that anyone one else hasn't but you," she lovingly points at him, "you have always believed in me. No matter what obstacles I came face-to-face with, you never doubted me not for one second."

Vance felt a drip of water attempting to disturb his focus, but he wouldn't let it win. "Always baby girl," he told her.

"Tell Troy hello for me. Tell him I'll call him."

"I will. You take care," Vance closed her car door for her and watched as his sister backed out of the driveway, watching until she was out of sight. Turning around, Vance walked back into the house and gave another goodnight yawn to his parents as he climbed the flight of stairs. He smiled at their laughter as they continued with movie night. Retirement is sweet.

Vance is in town for only one night. The next night will be offered to re-grouping and thinking about Cadrin.

His mother wouldn't hear of him residing at his own place. Even though Avionne was the only one of their kids who had truly lived there at one point, Connie always keeps and refer to three of the rooms as separately belonging to each one of their kids. She always keeps their rooms neat, cleaned, and ready to receive them if they wanted to come back home for any length of time.

While Vance comfortably slept, the opposite is true when it comes to Claude who is back in Chicago scheming on how to create more diversions. Although Claude never expected things to get out of hand, the situation did do just that. He and his confidant have a solution requiring risky acts to conceal their part in the misfortune of Stone and Nichols, no thanks to the analytical mind of the portfolio manager. What once appeared to be an easy task in the beginning has proven to become quite daunting. Although Claude is without further avail, the pending suit against Stone and Nichols reflecting Johnson Everdeen as enablers of numerous and exuberant lies is still very much a thriving one.

Chapter 9

The Executives

The next morning Mrs. Grayson arose around seven a.m. for her morning meditation and her pilates. Before getting started, she looked in on the Grayson men. She sees Vance is still asleep. Walking down the hall she also peeked in on Brian only to learn he is also sleeping, his forearm across his forehead. *"I cautioned you against that last slice of mid-night apple pie,"* Connie quietly reclosed the door to her and Brian's bedroom suite.

After her meditation, she bathed before retreating to the kitchen to prepare a home cooked breakfast with all the mouth-watering trimmings. She made sure to add salmon croquettes and her homemade hash browns to the morning menu. Once she was done preparing the meal, she removed a pitcher of milk and one of orange juice from the fridge. Crediting the aromas for awakening the men in the house, Constance grins. One after the other, the men rose in a timely fashion. The first to come downstairs for breakfast is Brian.

"Good morning, Connie."

"Good morning, Brian. How was your shower?"

He kissed her.

"Great," he replied reaching for one of the croquettes.

"Stop it, Brian! Don't try and pinch off the patties, their still hot."

"I'm a tough man with tough skin, Connie," he pinched off a section of one of the patties.

"Mmm, Connie these are delicious," he said as he drew air into his smoke induced bite.

"Thank you, but I asked you not to do that. I'm going to brush marinate over them while they're still hot.

Vance is still upstairs sitting on the now made bed. He checked the phone he'd kept beside him all night. There were no messages. He briskly brushes his hand over his face. He finally stood and headed for the kitchen.

For the day he chose a formal crisp white long sleeve buttoned down collar shirt, a pair of tailor-made navy-blue slacks, cuff links to match the gem behind his timepiece and a pair of navy-blue Stacy Adams.

"Good morning Mom, Dad."

"Good morning," they both replied.

"And how was your shower?" asked Connie.

"It was fine. Mmm grits, croquettes…" Vance looks over the spread situated onto the table, "thanks Mom."

"Yep," Brian cosigned.

They took a seat at the kitchen table, gave their thanks and began to eat.

"Are you nervous about the interview with the magazine editor?"

"No. I'm okay. I can't wait to get started. It should be kind of neat."

Brian removed a set of keys from his pant pocket and slid them across the table in Vance's direction.

"What's this for?" Vance inquired.

"They're the keys to my car. You're welcome to drive yourself to the interview. Once you're ready, your mother and I will see you off to the airport."

"Okay, thanks. 'Red Thunder' will be in great hands."

Vance arrived at the Galatians Suites. He's early. The editor has yet to arrive, so Vance went ahead and selected a table suitable enough to entertain such endeavor.

The Suites offers a stunning view. It's picturesque, mainly showcasing an enormously adjacent fountain. The strategically placed jets send spouts of water to tumble high into the atmosphere, mimicking dolphins performing for water park spectators. He wonders if Cadrin would enjoy such a site, especially at night. He figures she probably would. She seemed to enjoy the glory of Vintage very well.

Coming towards him, a tall thin and fairly attractive African American woman who looks to be in her mid- thirties, is heading Vance's way.

"Hello, Mr. Grayson. I'm Virginia Mathis. I hope you haven't been waiting for me too long. Please excuse my inability to arrive on time."

"Hello," Vance said to her. The two briefly shook hands.

"I haven't been waiting long, but you're excused just the same. Please sit down," Vance stood until she was finished getting herself comfortable.

"Alright then, I guess we can go ahead and get things underway," she placed a small pocket-sized recorder onto the middle of their table.

"Did you want to order anything to drink before we begin the interview? It's best we order now to avoid any interruptions," said Virginia.

Each of them placed an order of bottled water. The waiter returned to their table with the two plastic bottles and two glasses filled with crushed ice before leaving them.

"Now that that's taken care of, shall we begin?" asked the editor.

"We shall."

E. Mr. Grayson, from a legal standpoint, your influence in the world of business has been and still is very instrumental regarding the citizens within the city of Maryland. Are you a native?

V. Yes. I am a proud native of Maryland. About thirty-five percent of my family is based here including members of my immediate family. Both of my parents reside here along with one of my siblings. The other resides in the upper Midwest.

E. Being an attorney with such great notoriety within a city in which you can refer to as being your hometown…I'm thinking it must provide you with a certain sentiment of responsibility and nostalgia. In your own words, please share exactly what such descriptions are like, from a personal perspective.

V. As a child, I was often asked and I'm sure you were also asked the same famous question. What would you like to be at the time of adulthood? In most cases as children, we shouted out occupations which we saw and associated with hero and or heroism, including the ones which would take us far, far away from home like becoming an astronaut. However, a little later in life, just as other dreams of ours, that one seemed impossible to ascertain. But let's say for example that particular dream remained to be the most popular answer. No matter what we ultimately chose, our choice always came with some level of duty and accountability. We all should want to demonstrate to the absolute best of our ability in being the voice which efficiently represent and benefit the members of our communities on an individual and group basis. Being an attorney in the state of Maryland makes me feel a great sense of pride. It's great to be able to speak and act otherwise on the behalf of not just local citizens, but those outside of my hometown. A domino effect if you will. My actions do, or in some cases, have the potential to determine the outcome of circumstances in which others periodically are subjected to walk alone.

E. How has your notoriety here in Maryland fared you in other cities?

V. I've been in the legal field for eight years now. I've been blessed and I graciously embrace the gracious acknowledgement of my peers who are based outside of Prince George's County.

E. What would be your advice to others who want to invest their energy into becoming pursuant of the legal field? Maybe one day working along side someone great, say someone like Attorney…Vance Grayson.

He smiles.

V. First, I would want to know what drew them to have an interest in the legal field. It's a wide field, so I would pay close attention to any key words, then associate those terms with the appropriate career. Then I'd tell them to eat, live, and breathe the profession. Never give up. Always keep their eyes on the prize.

E. That brings me to my final question. What led you to become interested in the legal field, ultimately selecting your profession as an attorney?

V. Well, that's also a fair question. I believe the profession chose me. I also learned a long time ago just because a person loves food doesn't mean that person likes to cook or just because one likes to cook doesn't necessarily mean he or she wants a cooking show. Maybe that person can't cook at all but loves trying and we both know nobody says the effort is delicious and mean it.

Both parties laugh aloud.

E. That is quite true, Mr. Grayson.

Vance continues.

V. I said all of that to say the profession had all its makings before I paid it any attention. The profession spoke to me. It told me it knows a lot about me. It was waiting for me to embrace what I morally hold within Vance Grayson. Once I finally did, we've been inseparable ever since.

E. Sounds like you're very sincere and dedicated to your works.

V. Very much so.

"Mr. Grayson, this interview has truly been an enlightening one for me. I really appreciate your participation and open mindedness. I'm sure just from this interview alone, your fan base will increase. I hope I didn't steal away too much of your time from your client back in Chicago. We could have met there you know. Really, it would not have been an issue."

"It's okay. I was due for some catching up with my family anyway. So, believe me when I say everything is just as it should be."

Vance's charm is tugging at Virginia, so off the record they ended up exchanging more conversation until Vance remembered there is a flight due in Chicago with his name on it.

Vance arrived at his parents, climbing out of 'Red Thunder' in a hurry. Before he could enter the home, the door swung open. Brian stands in the doorway.

"How did the interview go, son?"

Vance saw Constance come and peep out from behind Brian.

"It was everything I hoped it would be."

Brian nodded.

"It's getting a little late, son. Are you ready to head out to the airport?"

"Yes, we'd better go ahead and leave now."

Vance's belongings were already packed away inside of his leather baggage and waiting inside the car. The last time he was called out of town on business and had come home for a visit, he left in such a hurry Constance had to mail a few items to him. But this time he made sure to pack ahead of time, giving himself a decent leeway to check and double check for personal things of importance.

Upon their arrival to the airport, Vance's flight is to leave in about thirty minutes. The family chatted amongst themselves until Vance's flight became ready for departure. Brian and Constance walked him to the gate.

"Now, don't you wait almost two months again before we can see or hear from you," Constance said with a motherly point of her index finger.

"I won't. I promise Mom, I love you. Love you too, Dad."

Constance hugs their son.

"Sly Devil, we love you and you be sure to keep me updated."

Vance intuitively knew Brian was giving reference to his love life. Vance nodded his head in agreement. Constance looked suspiciously at her husband and then back at Vance.

"I love you Mom," Vance said again before walking down the tarmac to board his flight to Chicago.

Chapter 10

The Executives

Vance entered his Chicago residence around four in the afternoon. On the ride there, he coaxed Troy out of stopping by Gwyneth's house. It seems everyone has a date for him, or they begged for an introduction as if he's not seeing anyone. The only someone he is interested in repeatedly fails to contact him.

Vance clicked on the television and proceeded to carry his luggage into the bedroom. He began to unpack when he heard the clinking and clanging of cookware coming from the kitchen.

"Hey man, your client really came through. This bachelor pad is tight."

"Thanks. Go ahead Troy, help yourself to the fridge. You should be able to find whatever it is you're looking for in there. Any local updates regarding Everdeen or Stone and Nichols while I was in Maryland?"

"No. Not that I've heard. How is that going anyway? You got any lunchmeat?" Troy yelled from the kitchen back to the bedroom.

"Yeah, it's in there. Keep looking. Things have calmed down. That's for now anyway," Vance yelled back to him.

While Vance separates his clothing and toiletries to their proper perspectives, his thoughts began to drift.

Other than visiting the Stone and Nichols building, while he'd been in Maryland his research involved tracing the company's history. For the life of him, he can't understand how a man of Jim Grainger's character can hold such a grudge, risking everything he and his father worked so hard for. Vance learned Stone and Nichols was founded by Jim Grainger Sr. To broaden the scope of his company, Jim's father envisioned the milestone which would carry the development company through the phases of growth it needed to become a leader in its industry. Jim's father passed the business on with regrets of having been unable to carry his vision to term under his daily leadership.

As far as Vance could tell, so far Jim had been found to carry everything out concerning the building of his corporation by the book, continuing his father's groundwork; growing Stone and Nichols upon integrity as did his father. If Jim wanted to become a tyrant in lieu of achieving his father's dream, he would have attempted to do so way before now, Vance thought. Maybe Vance is wrong. Maybe a bigger fortune and fame wasn't coming as fast as Jim liked.

"Bro, I hope one of those has got my name on it," Vance said of the turkey and salami meat pilled high onto wheat toast with mayo and alfalfa sprouts.

"I got you covered."

Vance bit into the sandwich. The Grayson brothers have a knack for converting ordinary food pairings into something eye opening and mouth watering.

"Dang, Bro. You can leave the other one for me," Vance said after a mouthwatering bite.

"I rather ask you more about your trip," Troy grins. "But seriously. How are Mom and Dad?"

"They're good and Avionne said she'll call you. Pops got a brand-new ride. He said Mom about passed out because of it."

"No kidding?"

"No. It's nice, too."

"I'm sure she'll warm up to it later," Troy said.

Once Troy left, Vance succumbed to doing the very thing he promised himself he would refrain from; thoughts of Cadrin. Vance was never the one to mix business with pleasure. Until now, there had never been a woman capable of dissolving the sacred realm of distinction. There's no doubt in it. Vance had his share of sitting around listening to male comrades as they recited outrageous stories of women who they'd crossed the line with.

He began to recount several stories of embarrassing incidents of how pleasure had rivaled the platform of business. At such moment, there is one episode standing out in his mind. Eugene Whitfield came to terms with a female attorney and ended up inviting her to his hotel suite. She left several hours before Eugene's client stopped by to issue him a badge allowing him access to a conference scheduled to take place later in the evening. To no surprise, they ended up discussing the case as usual. Eugene's client excused himself for the utilities. Once inside, he discovered a pair of heels. He remembered the pair well due to his wife's raving comments regarding the footwear. She was so in awe, she asked where she could purchase the same pair for herself. She ended up exchanging phone numbers with the woman who owned them, plus the bottle of braid conditioner on the sink's countertop confirmed who owned the items left on display.

"*What a disaster.*"

It was three days later before Vance returned to Johnson Everdeen. Building a case against Stone and Nichols is strangely enough a difficult one to gather. If it is anything less than perfection, the judge would be sure to scold them for showing up in his court room. Vance knows better.

Vance and his client distributed so much documentation including the ones from Dun and Bradstreet from one end of the conference room table to the other, until the paperwork ended up resembling patchwork linen, with an in-use coffee pot sitting in the midst.

"Carmichael, have you received any other updates on the legitimacies of existing business relationships involving Stone and Nichols?"

"No. I only have just the partial list of companies which have done business with them prior to the pending suit."

"I hope the answer to this puzzle is somewhere on this table. At least we've gotten a head start in eliminating the obsolete," Vance convinced Carmichael to investigate every aspect of the situation. Some insight is better than none. Vance thought Jim's reaction at the press conference was either an outstanding act or the real deal.

Vance powered up the shredder and placed it on the floor, its cord was left to run along the length of the table.

"How about you go ahead and start with that stack over there using this guide I have here, and I'll start with these."

Carmichael nodded.

"Whatever works. If it clears this table of clutter, I'm all for it."

"Say what? Don't tell me the clutter of paper bothers you," Vance said with laughter evident in his voice.

"No, it doesn't bother me at all," Carmichael lied.

Two days earlier, Carmichael instructed Delia to scan copies of the very documents blanketing the conference room table. Anything he and Vance shreds will be deleted.

Vance is more of a hands-on type of guy when it comes to dealing with documents. He doesn't like sitting in front of a computer for too long unless it is absolutely necessary.

"Vance, we should go ahead and shred any documents you find unnecessary to retain."

"Okay," Vance answered.

The two busied themselves studying and eliminating obsolete information when the shredder jammed.

"What the!-," Carmichael exclaimed. He turned towards the phone, activated the speaker and dialed for Delia. Unsuccessful, Vance had tried hard to free the jumbled paper from the clenching jaws of the machine. Carmichael returned to the disabled shredder, examining it.

"Carmichael, you ranged?" asked Delia.

"Yes, Delia. Would you come in here for a second?"

"Yes, I'll be right there."

"*Great*," Vance disappointingly acknowledged her obedience.

Delia entered the room in a figure flattering two-piece pastel blue ensemble. Her skirt reveals an ample amount of her toned legs. She's wearing matching stilettos, a blue and white scarf around her waist, and a bit of cleavage.

"Whoa. What's all of this?" she questioned the men of the heavily decorated table while she eyed the cord of the coffee pot streamlining across the papers as it drapes over the table's edge, cascading down towards the carpeting. Before either could respond to her question, within an instant Delia noticeably devoted her attention to Vance. Her eyes traveled from his hair right down to the shoes on his feet.

"Humph. *Damn, this man has got it together,"* she confessed.

"Delia, would you take that shredder out of here, please," instructed Carmichael.

"Alright, what should I do with it? Is it broken?"

"We guess. We couldn't free the wad of papers from it. Maybe it's done, we don't know. See what you can do for it. In the meantime, go to the file room and bring us the new one, please."

"Sure will. I'm quite useful in several situations," her eyes remained fixed on Vance as she'd spoke.

"Hello, Vance," she finally said. "I didn't know you were in the building today," she lied.

"Yeah, as you can see it's all about my client," Vance said.

Delia reached out to shake his hand. She held on a little too long for his taste. Vance was ready to release his grip, but Delia refused to let hers go. Speaking with her back turned to Carmichael she picks up where she left off.

"If you gentlemen need anything else, call me," she finally released Vance's hand.

"Yes Delia, we do need something. The shredder. That's all we'll be in the need of," spoke Carmichael.

On that note, Delia unplugged the cord of the disabled shredder and began wrapping the extension around the unit as she studies Vance. Then it happened.

"No!" shouted Vance.

Delia screamed.

Carmichael is speechless. Delia accidentally pulled the cord of the coffee pot, turning it over onto the table which set off a failed attempt of rescuing a few and now destroyed documents.

"Carmichael! I apologize! I can't believe this!"

Vance retrieved the now empty coffee pot from the table, placing it inside the sink. Highly agitated, Delia hurried past him with a bundle of paper towels to soak up the puddle of brew. Vance gently took the soaked paper towels from her trembling hands.

"Don't worry about it, Delia. Everything is fine, we'll take it from here," Vance calmly spoke of himself and the only other useful individual in the room at the moment.

"It's okay Delia, forget about the spillage," Carmichael confirmed.

Delia grabbed the shredder and headed for the boardroom's exit. In despair, she turned and turned again the door's knob. She heard anguish in Carmichael's tone. She froze.

"Delia, on your return please review the documents you've ruined, then I need you to reprint each one of them. Upon your return with the new shredder, you'll find the ruined papers on the table by the door. Please make sure the new copies reach this room, soon."

"Yes, right away Carmichael," without another look at either Vance or her boss, Delia quickly left the room.

"You'll have to excuse Delia. She does have the tendency to be forth coming," Carmichael said. "Oh, I apologize Vance. Did I miss something between the two of you?"

"You didn't miss anything," Vance assured him.

Delia is beginning to really annoy Vance and complaining to Carmichael probably would have gotten her dismissed or on some type of corrective action. If she cranks up the heat, Vance will give that thought more consideration.

"She's a great secretary. Although I don't believe she'll be that out right again, I'll speak to her."

"I appreciate that. And at least not around you she won't," Vance said.

They laughed.

"Carmichael, I have Cadrin Porter on line one. She's PR for Stone and Nichols. Shall I put her through?" asked Delia.

Carmichael is reluctant to exchange ear play. He had been advised by Vance to avoid anything symbolic of bribery. There are still lots of unanswered questions and just in case he is wrong about Jim's character, he doesn't want Carmichael to risk becoming blindsided again, involuntarily providing the opposition with leverage to use against them.

"No, Delia. Please forward Ms. Porter to my voice mail."

Cadrin asked for a fax number to send supporting information backing up the verbal message she'd left for Carmichael. After the call ended, Delia entered Carmichael's office with a hard copy of the information in hand.

"Thank you, Delia," Carmichael began to listen to the message Cadrin left for him. Again, Delia devoted her attention.

"*Mr. Lewis, this is Cadrin Porter. I'm calling regarding my client, Jim Grainger, CEO of Stone and Nichols. I'd like to speak with you in person concerning your recent allegations involving my client. We would like to arrange for a closed-door meeting. Just the involved parties, only. I look forward to hearing from you soon.*"

Before the call ended, Cadrin made it clear to Carmichael that Jim and his lawyer will govern over all the necessary mechanics of the meeting, up to and including the idea of zero press coverage. Jim also instructed her to inform Carmichael she will in fact be in attendance.

Just in case there is something to be verbalized in her area of expertise, Jim wants her to be there to hear it firsthand. And thanks to Pete Monahan's less than professional behavior during the last two point five-million-dollar discussion, Carmichael had no choice but to honor Jim's request.

She also left for him a number to contact her by.

After that call ended, another one began.

"Vance, this is Carmichael. Guess who I just got a phone call from?"

Not up for guessing games this particular morning Vance responded,

"You got a phone call from whom?"

"Cadrin Porter, PR for Stone and Nichols. She said she would like to arrange a closed-door meeting between myself and Jim Grainger."

"What did you tell her?" Vance saw it necessary to quiz Carmichael to learn if he was obedient under his leadership. Sometimes his clients forget they're under his guide and would end up creating bigger messes for themselves and for him to straighten out.

"We didn't speak. I had Delia to forward her to my voicemail," Carmichael proudly admitted.

"Did she go into any specifics?"

"No."

"I see. I'm betting they've worked up some sort of strategy. If she calls back before we have the chance to reach out to them, have Delia to go ahead and arrange a closed-door meeting between the four of us."

"And their side?" Carmichael questioned the number of any likely remaining participants of Stone and Nichols.

"Let them bring whomever they wish," Vance sharply stated.

"It's your call, Vance."

"It's about time we sit Jim Grainger down. I'm surprised it's taken him this long to contact you. Whatever you do, don't contact them right away. Wait for my word," Vance instructed.

The call ended with Vance in an increasingly realm of self deceit.

"Where did that come from?" Without hesitance, Vance agreed to be in the same room again with Cadrin, professionally.

"*It's not supposed to happen this way*," Vance complained." When it comes to Cadrin, he thinks of everything except business. He wants her to call *him*. He wants her to get to know him better. Vance hadn't anticipated on professionally coming face- to- face with her again, and so soon.

He doesn't know how to reach her except by way of her client. That's a solution which he is not in favor of exercising. Now more than ever he needs Cadrin to contact him. Too soon can't be soon enough.

The following week, Cadrin entered the Stone and Nichols building around eleven a.m. It's beautiful. As usual, live ferns are showcased in oversized gold planters. In every direction she turns, no more than three can be seen at a time. As she made her way to the elevator, she discretely informed the lobby attendant of her presence with only a mere nod. No longer did she need to stop and check in; around there her face has become a rather familiar one. Victoria Flanagan only gave her a nod back. Afterwards, the doors of the secured floor opened.

"Good morning, Maureen."

"Good morning, Ms. Porter. Jim said he'll meet with us in the junior conference room. He'll join us in just a bit. By the way, how was your meal the other day at Vintage?"

"It was scrumptious. I'm so glad you told me about it. It offered so many things which left me with a wonderful impression. "*That goes for Vance Grayson, too. I think.*"

"I'm glad you got the chance to drop by there. I told you it would be one you wouldn't soon forget."

"It sure was. They've earned themselves a regular," Cadrin admitted.

"I'll see you again in a few minutes, my cup of mocha waits!"

Minutes later, Cadrin stepped off the elevator on her way to the junior conference room where she began to pace about the floor. Next, she walked over to the window. Staring through the sunlit windowpane, she can't figure out exactly why Carmichael hasn't returned her call. Given the fact he admitted to the media the press conference wasn't orchestrated by him, she believes he would welcome the opportunity to speak with her regarding the matter in a civilized fashion. Evidently, he has preferred to remain faithful in avoiding her. Why? That's the answer she needs, one she craves. After meeting with Jim and Maureen, Cadrin headed home when the most outrageous decision took control. Minutes later, she was parking her Lexus on the premises of Johnson Everdeen. She plans to give Carmichael a piece of her mind.

Being at Everdeen certainly does impress her. Gourmet shops occupy the entire length of a wall. She knows she will definitely check those out before leaving the building. Right now, she has other things to attend to, or better yet, someone.

Cadrin maintained a discreet distance from the lobby's attendant. She's hoping to utilize every direction offered in hopes of being led directly to Carmichael Lewis. So far, he isn't anywhere in sight.

"Excuse me, Ms. I haven't seen your beautiful face around here before. Are you new to Johnson Everdeen?"

"Actually, this is my first visit here. I'm meeting a friend for lunch," she classically responded.

"Too bad your lunch date isn't me. I'm Antonio," he offered her his hand for a shake.

She shook.

"May I show you around the building while you wait for your party's arrival?"

"Oh my God, is he security or what? Everdeen is tight."

He proceeded. "Of course, I can't take you to any of the upper levels. However, you can bet I'll do my best to impress you anyway."

Cadrin wanted to remain on her own. But at least now with an escort, she feels she will not appear to be the snoop she set out to be. Cadrin carefully looks the gentleman over. No credentials of any kind are in sight. His attire is an open brown tweed jacket, his creased slacks are a darker shade of brown, and he sports a long-sleeved white-collar shirt, cuffed.

"Security? It's very nice of you to take the time out of your schedule to be my personal tour guide. What else do you do here at Everdeen?"

"When I'm not on my shift, I like to introduce myself to any new occupants. See that little shop over there," he boldly pointed to a space which neatly occupies a small space at the end of the row of shops, the owners just arrived a few days ago. They're very friendly."

"When you're on your shift?" Cadrin replied.

"Yes. I'm Head of Security."

Cadrin's heart immediately dove to the pit of her stomach. Her suaveness just came to a screeching halt. She tried to hide her embarrassment as the security officer continued in showing off the establishment's first floor. He escorted her or in Cadrin's case, ushered her towards the international gift shop. On her way there, Cadrin admired the twelve feet long forest green marble riser which displays colorful plankton inside the thick glass. Finally, they reached the gift shop.

"I've never seen a gift shop this size before," Cadrin admitted, "it's… wow!"

"I know. It's among everyone's list of favorites. Clients of Everdeen really get a kick out of it, especially the people who come from out of town, of course."

As pleasant as Antonio is, Cadrin desires to be left alone just in case he wants to ask her questions she wouldn't be able to provide any answers to.

"Well Antonio, thank you for the tour. I'll browse about here while I wait for my party."

"Sure thing, enjoy yourself, Ms. Porter," he sported a half smile winking at her before exiting the gift shop.

"He knew my name all along. Thank God he didn't throw me out of the building." He won't, but he's keeping an eye on her anyway. Now with security aware of her presence, that did it for any plans she had of trying to make it to any of the upper levels on her own. After she was done browsing the gift shop, she still wanted to make good on checking up on the where a bouts of her 'lunch date.' Remembering the gourmet shops she admired earlier, Cadrin made her way towards Everdeen's next wow factor. At her arrival, she stands at the shop's

doorway melting in awe of the man she sees standing inside the coffee shop. Vance Grayson.

"Excuse me. Are there anymore stirrers?" Vance politely questioned the individual standing behind the counter.

"They're right over there, Sir," the clerk pointed to a full box of stirrers situated onto the counter across from the right of Vance.

He turned, making eye contact with those stirrers, seeing they are exactly where the clerk said they would be. Walking over to the counter, Vance took one of the straws and placed it in the cup of hot mocha. Before Cadrin could produce bountiful excuses to convince herself in walking away, she found herself to again enjoy the presence of the man she'd been avoiding for weeks. She gave in.

"Someone once told me in order to get a feel for a place, one has to walk where others walk. He showed me I would even have to eat and drink as they do," she said aloud.

Thinking there is no way that beautiful voice can be coming from the woman who has been avoiding him for weeks, Vance curiously turns in the direction of her voice just in time to see her lips round out the last word of her sentence. She stunned him. A pleasant shock. His masculine stance shook only a tinge, which shocked him too. This Everest can be moved and Cadrin would have been aware of his sway, the turbulence she caused, if only she had looked close, closer. Close enough to reach outwards and allow her hand to rest upon his chest. He continues to stare at her. Her background had faded, and he saw her standing inside of a perfect frame. It wasn't long before the dots of her backdrop reconnected from a blur.

She had done better than what he'd hoped for. Instead of calling, she showed up. Seeing her again is causing his world to tilt and glide uncontrollably, his heart to skip several beats. If she were a heart attack, he'd be in a state of emergency right now.

"Cadrin, how are you?" He managed to find his voice to speak to her.

"I'm okay. Busy as always."

"I can't stress to you enough how I've anticipated on hearing from you again after our unplanned 'dinner date.' I have to admit I'm floored of your approach," he said. He's unaware of her true reason for being at the company who is headed towards a legal battle with her client.

"What brings you to Everdeen? Wait. Now don't tell me you were inspired by one Vance Grayson."

"Maybe I was, subconsciously anyway."

"Okay. Now what's the real reason," he said with a smile and the look of concern in his eyes.

"I phoned the CEO a few days ago and he has yet to return my call. I thought today is as good a time as any to try establishing a line of communication with him. We thought by doing so we could keep the situation from getting any nastier. But I suppose he didn't agree with our timing."

Although he's still a bit hesitant, Vance knows it is in his best interest to come clean about his role within the billion-dollar corporation. If he tells her the truth, he knows he will probably be risking any possible chance of getting to know her beyond Stone and Nichols. He knows he'd be a fool if he were not to take advantage of this opportunity to give her the full truth.

"I'd like to buy you a cup of one of the house specialties. What will it be, latte, mocha, sparkling water-?"

"I'll take the latte."

"Then it is one regular latte coming right up," Vance escorted her to a nearby table located at the rear of the shop. "Please sit down. I'll be right back with your latte."

Cadrin sits waiting patiently. She's enjoying the fact of how no matter what any little thing Vance sets out to accomplish, he always does it with sexiness all about him. On his return, Vance seated himself across from her. Over the aroma of brews, she can smell his cologne. It smells like Sebastian. It is Sebastian, and the cologne smells wonderful on him.

"I hope you don't mind my referring to you by your first name to be informal," he said as she took a sip of latte.

Cadrin notices how the contents of her cup are very manageable; Vance must have instructed the clerk to be mindful of the cup's temperature. Cadrin also notices his cup appears to be steaming hot; he placed her own welfare above his own.

"Cadrin, I have to come clean with you. I realize I should have done so before now and letting you out of my sight again without informing you of my role with Everdeen is not an option. I shouldn't have allowed myself an excuse in the first place."

Cadrin's stomach muscles tightened.

"Alright, I'm listening."

"You already are aware of my being a supporter of Johnson Everdeen. It just so happens I'm more than a member. I'm Everdeen's attorney," Vance became silent, patiently waiting for a lecture from her.

As she drew her lips in against her teeth, Cadrin swallowed her sip of latte. Here they are, sitting as two old friends but they aren't friends. That's something Vance knows will require some work on his part for sure. Each time he sees her the more captivated with her he becomes.

Cadrin sternly leaned forward to place the cup she's holding onto the middle of the table. Fearing the worst outcome, Vance tries to calculate her emotions. She's too quiet. He watches her as she stares at their table. After being at a lost of words she began to speak. Instead, she sighed.

"Afterrr..-"

"Before you finish, please let me continue," he gently pleaded.

"My visit to Stone and Nichols the other day was all my doing. I was only there to get a feel for the environment. I wasn't there to bring trouble to anybody."

"You want me to believe that?" her eyes pierces through him.

"Yes. What I've told you is the truth. Please believe me."

"Myself and my client, we are apart of the environment you came to check out," she countered.

"I know. You are correct. Please Cadrin, believe me. If I wanted to judge you or your client, I had every opportunity to be about such a thing during the press conference. I realize I should have told you all of this before now. I had no way of contacting you without...well unless I showed up at Stone and Nichols again, or tried reaching you there by phone. I had no business there in the first place, and to contact you there by phone would have for sure brought others into the matter unnecessarily."

"Can you honestly tell me you weren't there at all seeking verbal affirmatives?"

"No, I wasn't," he truthfully admitted.

"But if you had come across such, would you have turned it down?" her tone of voice now much higher than before.

"No. I wouldn't have turned down any amount of information nor would I have walked out of there ready to share whatever I learned with the world. Cadrin listen. During our dinner, we both gave reference to our clients without experiencing any pressure from the other. If I'd required you to share more, I would have asked you for more but that's not how I conduct business."

"Then just how do you conduct business, Vance? I knew you were hiding something from me. Something told me you are their attorney. You definitely have the look of one. It was just something about the way your pant legs whispered above the shine of your shoes, but I didn't want to believe it," she recalled from the day of the chaos on the premises of Stone & Nichols. She thought he looked darn good then as well as today.

Vance's expression is delightfully questionable. No other woman had ever made such a nice and scrutinized calculation of him and then seen fit to tell him about it.

"What were you trying to do, play up to me for information?"

"Cadrin, I don't conduct business in that way."

There's no mistake in it; she's upset he'd lied to her. She knows what he said makes complete sense to her. She just can't shake how he sat with her for the duration of their dinner, then after the fact continued to hold on to the truth, well the other half of it.

"Why couldn't you have just been totally honest with me from the get-go, Vance?"

"It's plain and simple. I thought the truth might cost me of not being able to see you again, on a personal level. I was hoping-"

"Are you trying to say you're hoping to become romantically involved with me?"

He stared into the brown eyes which makes his body temperature beg for cooling. His silence affirmatively answered her question.

"Vance, although our professional titles differ, they have the tendency to frequently collide. I learned through experiences of my own on why it's so important not to get personally involved with men in similar positions of my own. It just makes for trouble in the long run," she proceeded to explain some of the things which happened while she was working for Lynn Fields, "Vance, can you honestly say to me if we were to go ahead with this, our careers wouldn't be destroyed? Can you protect my career and your own?"

In his heart, he feels like he can.

"Lynn Fields, I swear it! They've done it before!"

He looked at her for a few moments trying to get a take on where she is coming from. She proceeded to give him more insight.

"I did some asking around. Vance, what I'd feared all along is the truth. A client I previously worked for, Lynn Fields," she hesitates, "I found out they had made good on a threat involving a former public assistant of theirs who was caught wining and dining on the job with another professional of her company."

"Sounds like your former client earns a second living at making private matters their business," Vance didn't want to hear anything negative, but at least she's talking to him. She's right. Getting romantically involved can possibly cause complications. Right now, that is what's hurting his heart the most.

"You're not the only one who recognizes the danger, trust me. I have stories of my peers dancing about my good judgment all the time.

This time it's intriguingly different," Vance stares directly into her face, his eyes lock to hers. I take it the prying by your client, Lynn Fields, was due to a close relationship of yours which went public?"

"No, not exactly. My ex ended up punching out a guy at a corporate function. Internally, word quickly spread as to why it happened. A week later, my ex was called into a meeting which quickly led to his resignation."

Vance's heart went out to her.

"Despite my judgment's warning, I have to be honest with you. I'm not going to lie to myself by downgrading my attraction to you. I would like to get to know the Cadrin no other man does. No matter how much or how little you share, I'll accept it or at least I'll do my best in trying not to ask you for more. If I sound overbearing, I don't mean to be," Vance shocked himself. He shared more with Cadrin than he'd set out to offer her. His emotions were lifted; he leans back and relaxes on his chair waiting for her to digest everything he openly offered her.

"Well, with all of that I guess you're unattached, huh?" she wants him.

"You've guessed right," he confirmed.

Cadrin sees something in Vance which makes her want to learn all about him too. But the threat from Lynn Fields made her rethink any thoughts of taking him up on whom he wants.

"Vance, I really appreciate the latte and I would love to share many more with you. But can you honestly tell me you believe it is a good idea for the two of us to try and get something going within such close proximity of our clients? I mean come on. You're working for someone who wants to take my client to court. He could potentially loose his company if this pending suit reaches the courtroom."

"It can possibly be a risk; one we should be able to handle."

"Handle how, Vance? I take it you're the one to blame for the return call I have yet to receive from Carmichael. Ultimately, you're the reason for my being here at Johnson Everdeen getting marched around by the head of security!" She lost it. Cadrin looks around, quickly she gathers her composure. Acknowledging her accusation, Vance inhales deeply.

"I didn't tell you to come to Everdeen."

"That's true but I am here because of you."

Vance offered her no reply.

"Thank you for the latte, Vance. I had better get going. It was really nice to see you again," Cadrin rose from the table as did Vance.

For nothing more than a move of chivalry, Vance rose to see her through the lobby of Everdeen. During their walk he'd come closer to her. In such instant, she swore she felt the ground beneath her move. Their chemistry is loud and direct. She understands his fondness of her to have taken a hold of the anger she has for him. He is winning. It can only take a touch from him, and they will kiss right now, right here inside of Johnson Everdeen. In such instance, both will be relieved of their corporate duties before night can fall.

"Cadrin, no matter your decision I hope to hear from you, soon."

"I don't know, Vance," Cadrin keeps on walking.

Vance continues to escort her from the small coffee shop through the building's lobby.

More frustration energizes the angry sway of her hips, *"Just who in the heck does he think he is?"* Cadrin saucily muttered to herself. No matter how angry she becomes, she can feel the mutual attraction rumbling between herself and Vance. The first realm of chemistry they'd experienced earlier refuses to dissipate.

Vance wants to offer walking her out to her car, but judging from her body's language, he told himself there's no way in hell she will allow him to walk any further with her.

Chapter 11

The Executives

Three mornings and five lattes later, the ball is still in Cadrin's court. She knows Vance could have easily asked how to contact her outside of Stone and Nichols. However, he prefers their next communication be of her own doing.

Surely if she'd informed him of how to reach her, he would have found himself making the first move again. Although her desire to contact him is strong, her warning sign is of greater cause.

Vance not only lied to her, he also posed interference between she and Carmichael.

Cadrin knows she has no right to be angry with Vance over how he chooses to govern over his clients. The thing which weighs on her the most is the fact he has a conscience. She could feel it when he told her he's the attorney who is leading Carmichael in a pending lawsuit against her client.

Cadrin walked over to the card which she'd held in her hand on numerous occasions since she and Vance's dinner at Vintage. She dialed the numbers inscribed on back of it.

At the apartment, Vance walks over to where he left the phone the last time he'd spoken to Troy. Not giving any thought to looking at the caller's information, he answered the call.

"Yeah man, that didn't take long."

She hesitated at his greeting, laughing just a little to herself. She was pleased to have been given the opportunity to have a light moment. It couldn't have come at a better time, for she was apprehensive from the moment she picked up her phone to call him.

"Umm, hello Vance, it's Cadrin Porter. I must say you sound as though you were expecting someone else."

He apologized to her for not looking at his caller id before answering the ring of his phone.

"I just hung up from talking with my brother, I happened to be walking away from the phone when it immediately rung again. I assumed it was him calling right back. He said he would."

Feeling as though she's infringing on his time with his brother, she offered to call him back some other time. He wasn't about to let her get away that easily.

"No. No ah, it's okay. There's no emergency. You don't have to hang up."

"Are you sure Vance? Because I can call you back some other time."

"Please, really its okay," he reassured her.

"You sound kind of surprised to hear from me," she can feel his smile through the phone.

"I am surprised to hear from you," he delightfully confessed, "it has been a while, almost three weeks."

The line grew silent.

"Yes, it has been a while. I hope you don't mind I decided to call."

"No, I don't mind at all. Really, I can't say I'm disappointed you've called. If I did, I would be lying."

He was again apologizing for concealing the full truth of what drove him to pay that visit to Stone and Nichols.

"What finally changed your mind?"

Cadrin paused for a minute or so. She doesn't want to appear as though she's pathetic by unloading her dirty laundry of failed relationships on him. But despite the fact of the matter, she decided to be honest with him from a different standpoint.

"I realized I would like to learn a little more about Vance Grayson. I almost did a little research of my own. However, I would enjoy learning the facts from the man himself."

After a brief laugh, he smiled at her through the phone.

"Well, in that case I'd better not disappoint." On that note, he became more relaxed figuring hurdle number one was defeated, and the more he talks with her, the more he believes he's correct.

"By the way, the number you're calling from, is it yours?" During their light 'getting to know you' session, Vance decided to get her contact information just in case she's to have regrets of having made the call. Without a doubt, he understands her concern.

From the moment he'd seen her at the press conference, he knew he would continue to battle with his own uncertainties of mixing business with pleasure.

After their call ended, Vance's words continued to ring within Cadrin's ears. She could still hear him saying to her, "*You're in great hands and that pretty lady is no lie*." Their conversation ended with their dinner plans in place. When the sun rises again, Cadrin believes her mind will be rested, her thoughts refreshed, and able to let go of the jibber jabber which still pesters what had made plenty of sense to her in the beginning; not to get involved with Vance Grayson. But now she has more on her mind than those things. To never again mix business with pleasure had taken an intriguing turn because on tomorrow evening, Vance Grayson will expect her to have dinner with him at a restaurant of his choice.

Initially, his lead had somehow managed to make her nervous. He certainly has class and plenty of it, so the fact of where she will spend her evening with him are of no worries for her. Yet it is his straight forwardness which has her wondering just what a planned evening with him will in fact entail. She likes honesty and confidence in a man. She even likes surprises. To have it her way, she'd rather talk with him away from the company of others, but at least she's getting a date with him.

The effects Vance has on her, coaxed her ability to forget about Kirk and all the other men who she identifies with the remnants of disaster during the time of their so called 'relationship.'

She never expected to be with the perfect man, but she needs him to be good, honest, and respectable. He could even be her knight in shining armor when she needs for him to be. But is there such a man? A perfect one? She must wonder what he would be like if there is such a man. This Vance Grayson sure hasn't been perfect. Although the answers were all around her, he held back and sat on more than one secret. With ease, he'd kept both pieces of pertinent information hidden from her all through their dinner at Vintage. Vance Grayson isn't perfect, and she's finding it easy to be angry with him for being without error. And he'd made a huge one.

Her career had taken a back seat, passing the buck to their date on next evening. The sincerity she witnessed from within his almond shaped eyes told her he is good, respectable, and a man who has a conscience which he's not able to ignore.

Cadrin blushed at her thought of him sitting across from her while they'd sat together inside Vintage. His untruth isn't going to be forgotten by her. However, her heart is beginning to reposition his secret, defining it only to be a minimal infraction of fabrication.

The blissfulness between the two continues to demand steamy attention.

Chapter 12

The Executives

Vance sees Cadrin as she enters the restaurant. He begins to walk over to where she and the maitre d' are standing. On his walk over to them, he loves the way her gaze of him travels from his head to pass the length of his slacks. Cadrin thinks she isn't being obvious in her scan of him. Instantaneously, he'd noticed her observation. And he's enjoying every bit.

"It's okay, I'll take her from this point he said to the maitre d'. He took Cadrin by her hand. The maitre d' was unsure of just what to do next. Just when she thought chivalry was obscure it proved it is surprisingly getting better with time.

"I hope you didn't mind my sudden invitation to have dinner. My schedule ended up getting very tight. So, to make a long story short, I knew I had some free time coming up, so I seized the opportunity to try and see you, again," he said, smiling, "Oh, I apologize. Please forgive me, I'm sure your schedule is quite demanding as well," he said while helping her with her chair.

"Thank you for the consideration, and the chair. As a matter of fact, you couldn't have chosen a better time. I wanted to see you again too, and I am starving," she said with soft amusement. While waiting for their waiter to arrive so they can place their orders, the two chatted about different restaurants including the entertainment round about town.

"Have you decided what you'll have to drink with your dinner?" He hopes she will mention her taste in great wine selection.

"Yes. I'm having a glass of Zinfandel."

The waiter approached their quiet table in the corner and was directed by Vance to note Cadrin's order first. Before the waiter could ask her what she will be drinking, Vance smoothly intervenes during the order's notation.

"She'll have a glass of Zinfandel. Cadrin, would you like any ice?"

"No ice would be great," she told him. Their waiter continues to make her notations. She's noticeably impressed with Vance's method of chivalry, and so is Cadrin. After the waiter left them Cadrin noticed for someone who is in a strange city, her date certainly knows his way around the menu.

"Do you come here often, Vance?"

"No, but my brother does. I've had take-out from here quite often thanks to him. It's because of him I learned about this place. When I first began coming to Chicago to visit him, I would stay at his place. He would stop by here almost every day to order something to bring home."

"You do the take-out thing a lot?" she thought maybe he is shy of any real work in the kitchen.

"I cook," he smiled at her. "Have you ever eaten here before?"

"No. I can't believe I haven't. I shop in this area quite often.

"Well, the food here is really good. I hope you enjoy yourself."

She observed him for a few moments.

"When you eat out do you always dine alone?"

He looks curiously at her. She didn't realize the stint of her question. She unintentionally informed Vance she's hoping for more out of him than just a friend to discuss hot topics with over dinner.

He cut through the chase.

"If that's your way of trying to ask me if I'm seeing someone, the answer to your question is still a no," he smiles at her.

Pleased and a little embarrassed, Cadrin offered him no reply.

"Are you a native of Chicago?"

"No, I'm from Connecticut."

"Yeah?"

"Yeah," she said before taking a sip from her glass.

"What led you to gain interest in public relations?"

"I enjoy rectifying complicated situations and bringing about adage which will compliment my efforts. It's a nice bonus for my clients and myself," she smiles, "This is so funny."

He smiled back at her.

"Please tell me about it."

Cadrin took another sip from her glass.

"I was only nine-teen when I signed up to be an assistant to an intern who was doing public relations work. I followed the intern and a department supervisor downtown. Surprisingly, we ended up being bombarded by reporters. They came out of nowhere. I still had my pepper spray on me."

They began laughing. Vance shook his head.

She countered.

"You're guessing right. I pulled out the container and let'em had it. I can't believe I did that, but they'd come out of nowhere. They scared the heck out of all of us."

The two of them laughed even more.

"That was back when I was a business major. Studying business was good. But it was also sort of boring. So, I started looking at other areas to study. I figured public relations would give me a nice mix. After obtaining the degree, I continued my studies at the American University of Women and Politics Institute. I was told an addition like that will be most advantageous in allowing me to learn more about corporations and the people operating them."

"Did it help you?"

"In its own way, it sure did."

Vance took a sip of water from his glass.

"Do you get to visit home often?"

"I've only been back twice. Both visits were during the holidays. How about you? How often do you get to visit your family?"

"When I'm away on extended business I try to get back for a visit at least twice. When I'm home just relaxing or whatever, I try to make sure I visit them at least two to three times a week. Speaking of them, I need to get in touch with my Dad, he sent me a text. He has something he's sure I'll be in approval of. I hope he doesn't have another new car," a grin crosses his lips. He shook his head at the thought of his mom's disapproval of Brian's brand-new ride, 'Red Thunder.' "I hate to admit it, but I work so much until when I finally do get to take a vacation, I feel like I'm out there behaving badly, forgetting the purpose of taking time out from work; to relax and for a while, forget about my job as a corporate attorney."

In understanding, Cadrin nodded her head to his confession.

"The two of you are pretty close, you and your Dad? Somehow, I feel he is your hero."

"Yeah, he is. I remember the first time my Dad helped me select my first suit for church. I was fourteen at the time. I told him I wanted to wear a suit like his for Sunday morning church service," he grins, "he said alright, this Saturday I'll take you grooming for one. I looked at him like, what? He told me he would explain on the way to the mall. On the way there, he told me how important it is to be sharp from head to toe. Later that day after we returned home from the mall with the suit in tow, he let me watch him shave. He told me I'd probably have to do the same thing within about six years. After he finished shaving, he took me to the barber shop for a hair cut."

"Was he right about the shaving thing?"

"He sure was."

Cadrin smiled at him. From the moment she'd considered contacting him, she figured he broke a lot of hearts along the way. His attorney status calls for him to travel excessively. She's sure he started up a lot of heated affairs which were finished before he could take the next flight out.

"How do you date or even keep someone in your life traveling from one state to the next as often as you do?"

He gave her a half grin. Her attempt to decently classify him was with class and straightforwardness.

"I was in a three-year relationship which had failed. Over time, it so happened I really didn't have the time to devote in getting to know someone."

He knows she requires more information. He also realizes if he doesn't extend more detail, she will keep up her pondering.

"Although I am around women all the time, I guess I subconsciously pass up opportunities to allow someone into my life. But some of those misses were better off left alone anyway." Cadrin's body language adjusted to his comment. She held her head back only a little. Her shoulders relaxed. And her smile begged for its moment to shine. But her eyes handled that.

"Now that I've told you about my lonely life," he leans forward and began twiddling with her ring finger, "I don't see any commitments here. How is your dating life?"

"My dating life is fine," she lied. "Actually, I haven't had much time either. Work keeps me pretty busy as we both have determined."

That's the truth

Vance agreed, but something told him her hesitancy to contact him had little to do with work and a lot to do with other matters of the heart.

"No unfinished business?" he asked.

"No, Vance. If there was someone else, I promise you I wouldn't be sitting here with you if that were the case. And you?"

"I am without interference, Ms. Porter."

They began to enjoy more of their meal, including each other's company. Once their plates were almost cleaned, Vance hailed the waiter for more ice.

Cadrin is so taken with Vance until she'd forgotten to keep her nerves on edge. However, she didn't know what she would do if Jim or anyone else from her client's company are to see them sitting together. Getting down to the floor and then crawling underneath their table sound rather good.

"You're so relaxed sitting here in public with me. Doesn't doing so bother you?"

"What?"

"Aren't you worried about being seen here with me by anyone from Johnson Everdeen?"

He smiles.

"Trust me. I'm sure we can provide anyone with an explanation decent enough for our public appearance. So, you make sure you continue to enjoy yourself. I know I will."

Cadrin could hardly swallow her Zinfandel fast enough. Vance is genuinely concerned, yet he's bold enough to openly enjoy what is taking place between them. At that moment and those to come, he believes her company is well worth the risk he's taking.

"I apologize. You just seem so laid back without a care in the world."

Before Cadrin could say another word, Vance slowly lifted her hand from the table. She felt the lingering kiss from his lips on the back of her hand. For the duration, he kept his eyes on hers. Who could grab her things now and run for the nearest exit? Cadrin sure can but she won't.

Vance is a catch of a man, and he is a risk taker. She doesn't know which excites her more. Maybe it's the way he would look at her when his smile relaxed on the corner of his lips. She liked that look on him a lot. She noticed he wears a lot of good looks. And right now, he is sitting across from her in a very nice and probably expensive tailor-made suit which shows off his physique very well. When compared to his other jackets this one appears to be lighter in weight, probably one of his dinner jackets. He'd gotten ready for their date hoping he will appear relaxed and down to earth. Everything about him isn't fashioned in boardroom tactics. Well, that particular dress code lingers here and there. He can't help it. Rules and regulations have become a part of him. A reason to break some of those rules is sitting across from him, watching him take another sip from his wine glass.

"Are you beginning to be of more ease now?" he asked her.

Her eyes traveled around the room then landed back on his stare of her.

"Yes, I'm fine," she released a sigh before resettling onto her seat. As dinner progresses, etiquette is having a tough time at this table. Their communication started off with profound annunciations then romantically settled into a bliss of coherent mumbling until the waitress returned to their table to check on them. Once she left them again, it was back to pleasure as usual.

All through dinner their eyes attempted to take their conversation to a deep and passionate kiss. Vance knows this will have to do for now. Reaching across the table he takes her hand in his. This move is more proper, except he is yearning for a spicier encounter.

The way Cadrin samples her food before fully enjoying its goodness is tugging at him something fierce. Right about now, he would love to learn how those lips will lock to his own.

Cadrin took a sip of her drink. She's loving every minute of Vance. However, she hates to admit Vance Grayson is getting to be a private and tempting problem.

"I hope there can be a next time. Hopefully then we'll be minus our Wall Street attire and into something more casual and comfortable like jeans and t-shirts for a stroll around the farmer's market or whatever," his invitation to another date sits well with her.

"Okay, a stroll around the farmer's market sounds good to me, Vance. Speaking of comfort, I wish my feet had more of it."

"Hmm, I have a solution for that," Vance offered.

"You have a solution for what?" Cadrin had already forgotten about the discomfort of her feet.

"Oh no, I'll show you later," he said with a wink.

Vance took care of the bill then in separate vehicles the two of them arrived at his corporate apartment.

"Come on in. I hope you like my home away from home," Vance unlocked the door then they walked into what Vance's brother refers to as being the bachelor pad. Vance smiled a little. The thump of his heart was tripping over its own beat. He likes the way she's checking out his place.

"I'm used to much more space but it's nice."

She gave to him a proud yet questionable stare.

"How much more space?"

"Back in Maryland, I own a six bedroom three-and-a-three-quarter bathroom home."

"You live in that much space by yourself?"

He gave a modest grin.

"Yes, I do. It's generous. It's sort of like resort living. The area is quiet. It really relaxes me especially after airline headaches and client troubles. Being around my family also relaxes me. We especially have a lot of good times together on the deck in my parents back yard."

Cadrin rarely made mention of her family to anyone. All Vance knows about her kin is some of them reside in Connecticut.

"Feel free to make yourself comfortable."

Vance headed for a back room while Cadrin made herself at home. She took a seat on the end of the couch next to a glass end table. She notices how the floor's indoor track lighting gives the room a nice glow. Ever so often, she glances down the hallway towards Vance's bedroom. She misses him already, then suddenly as though he could sense her cognition begging for his return, he strides towards her.

Minus the jacket he wore during dinner, Vance entered the living area. Nothing but his socks are still on his feet. Cadrin looks at him as though she had never seen him before. She admires how he's filling out his shirt. Although she has never seen him without a jacket, there had been no secret toned pecks hides underneath. She's more than pleased at what she sees before her. Once Vance reached Cadrin, he effortlessly knelt directly in front of her.

"Vance, what are you doing?"

"Just a little while ago you were complaining about your feet being uncomfortable. And I see you're already out of your shoes. If you'll let me try, I'll be more than happy to see what I can do for you."

She held her foot outwards. Vance reached and took her heel into his hand. He began to apply a streamline of mild pressure from her heel all the way to underneath her toes then back to her heel again. He began to massage the arch of her foot before working his way back to her heel. He's throwing a lot of heat her way each time he applies pressure to her aching feet. His chest flexing, his jaw line tightening, and when they did, on queue he sucked in his bottom lip.

Although he teases her here and there, his strokes are not mistaken for blunder. She remains quiet as she enjoys his skillful pleasures. Cadrin is too glad she periodically gives her feet special attention, for it would have been very embarrassing to turn such a chivalric offer into a rough experience for Vance.
He repeated his technique for her other foot.

"So how do your feet feel now?"

"They feel warm, relaxed, and rejuvenated. Thank you, Vance. I really appreciate that. Where and when did you learn to give a foot massage like that?"

"I learned a few years ago. It was about seven to be exact. I used to follow, excuse me. I used to accompany Avionne, she's my sister and the baby of the family to some of her pedicure and massage appointments. She had a crush on the guy and just in case he realized it and tried anything, Dad would send myself or Troy to tag along. If the guy had thoughts of trying anything, he would second guess himself and back off. If he had a crush on her as well, he didn't let it show."

"Avionne. That's a beautiful name. I see you're protective of your sister. I love that."

He smiled then nodded.

"I'll tell her you said so the next time I see or talk with her over the phone."

As wonderful as her foot massage was, she couldn't help wondering if Vance had tried to put the moves on her. Gaining her affection so in return he could learn of some if not all the inside activities at Stone and Nichols. He is just so damn suave, and he seems so genuine. In any case, she needs her radar to remain sharp, careful of any hidden agendas he might have. On the other hand, Cadrin is getting a kick out of Vance. She had met other men who held the same disposition. Their association had only been work related; nothing else. They were also the same men who were too busy sizing her up instead of trying to get to know her. Why is Vance so carefree?

"Oh no, think positive thoughts," she wasn't going back to those hindering feelings, not fully.

"Vance, you know I can't share with you any confidentialities pertaining to my client, don't you?"

"Of course. I wouldn't ask nor insist you tell me anything."

On the Everdeen playing field Delia is one thing but without a shadow of doubt, Cadrin is something else altogether.

"Vance it's getting late. I'd better get going."

Vance rises to his feet and looks out over the balcony while she prepares herself for home. He turns around to find her with her purse and her keys already in her hands.

"Thank you for dinner and the foot massage, both were wonderful."

A centimeter from her lips, with a lingering peck, he kisses her goodnight. She peers around his towering form looking for another excuse to part way. After her examination of the timed street lightning, with passion evident in her tone she says, "So the day isn't getting any younger. Is it?"

He looked downwards at her and responded,

"Maybe it is on this side of town."

Her eyes are telling him she will love nothing more than to tell him all about it the next morning, over at his place, sitting at his table, and maybe even in one of his t-shirts. Her lips need to say so with sincerity. Remaining silent, she continues to hold onto her belongings, turning her back to him. All the while she can feel his magnetic gaze pleading for her to stay right there with him for a little while longer. Exhaling deeply, she so heavily headed for his front door feeling as though she's carrying a massive chunk of Mount Everest as she telepathically envisions what their love making would be like. Once Cadrin reached the walk on the other side of his door, she realizes Vance never let go of her hand. At her small attempt to free her hand from his, he held onto her firmer though gentle. Never letting her go, he took the lead.

"I'll walk you to your car." And slowly, he did. She unlocked her car's door of which he held opened before letting go of her hand. She turned to face him, and their fate was sealed. The look of longing and deprivation are in his eyes. He couldn't behave any longer. He leaned in taking gentle hold of her face, and without declination from her, he kisses her lips with so much passion they had almost forgotten they are all but in the streets.

The same muscles she saw go to work during her foot massage she got to caress them, feeling some of his strength as they kissed. He finally eased up. His thorough kiss left her with a dizzying effect. His technique was invading yet respectful, having kissed her mouth and sampled her lips as though edible goodness were about to slowly drip from them. How will she get herself home tonight after a kiss such as the one he had given to her?

"Cadrin," he managed to speak, "will you call me once you're home?"

"Okay," she said.

He let go of her and headed back to his door. He didn't look back. For he knew if he did, he would race back to her and kiss her once more. Seated on the coolness of her car's leather interior, Cadrin held her head back against the headrest. Loudly, she blew a gust of wind out from her mouth. Once she began to cool down, she nervously fumbled with her keys as she attempted to be on her way, for her attention is at his back as he's striding down the short walkway back to the door of his residence.

Chapter 13

The Executives

Two days had past since Vance last spoke to Cadrin. He wondered why she hadn't tried getting in contact with him. He is also curious as to why she wants to meet with his client.

As soon as Vance stepped foot inside of Carmichael's office, he was bombarded with questions of what he believes will probably be Jim's next move and methods on how Everdeen can protect their good name.

"Vance, what's your take on the reason for a face - to - face meeting with Jim Grainger, his attorney and that PR of theirs? I think her name is Cadrin Porter, is that right?" asked one of the Everdeen supporters.

"Yes, Cadrin Porter is her name," Vance strenuously held back a grin of delight, "I think they'll probably try to hit Carmichael with a counter suit in an attempt to get him to drop the charges against Stone and Nichols."

"Well, they got the assets to cover it," Carmichael was being smart mouthed.

"I know there are missing funds out there somewhere. Once your suit is presented before the judge, I'll bet the assets of Stone and Nichols will be nearly frozen in attempts to protect his cash flow. Hopefully, a squeeze like that will move Jim to admitting his incumbency of the funds. Remember, Everdeen is a larger firm than Stone and Nichols. Once they accept the fact we're not backing off, they'll come clean. From the way the bank is telling it, there are two point five million of your company's dollars in the mix," Vance said while waiting for Carmichael to stop pacing the room and throw in his two cents.

"We have to figure this thing out, pronto."

"I know Carmichael, and I'll also tell you this, once your suit does go to court and we're found to be wrong about all of this, Jim Grainger can sue Johnson Everdeen for lost in revenue. I'm sure that due to all of this he is missing out on other deals just as you are. We have got to present the presiding judge with something more solid," Vance's honest opinion stung but Carmichael trust Vance's sound input. He knows it will be just a matter of time before Vance tells him it will be in his best interest to back off with his allegations until they can get their hands on something which will go against the bank's report. There's no doubt Jim will not cease in trying to protect his company's assets. A two point five-million-dollar disturbance will destroy Stone and Nichols.

Vance has a bad feeling about the face- to- face meeting. He also doesn't approve of how Cadrin's client used her to coax Carmichael. PR or no PR he thought, Stone and Nichols' strategy is defined as cowardly. No disrespect to Cadrin though. Vance figured she probably had her reasons for having made the call. He knows she can hold her own, now he's a man who has become protective of his lady.

Carmichael interrupted Vance's daydreaming. He's concerned of the repercussions a counter suit can have on his company.

"Can we stop that from happening?"

"I apologize Carmichael. I hate to tell you right now you're in a no-win situation."

Carmichael didn't like the sound of that.

"Carmichael let's just say if Jim does decide to present you with a countersuit, hopefully we will have generated enough enclosures to overwhelm their board. It'll offer us a nice little extension allowing us to sort through this while Stone and Nichols is left in line with nothing except a case number. Right now, what we can do is give them a little strategy of our own and take them up on the face- to- face meeting their requesting. You know, just to see where it takes us," although Vance doesn't like the idea of another meeting, it's all he and his client now have.

It's Saturday and almost a week has gone by since Vance last saw Cadrin. Now he's on his way to her place for hors d'oeuvres, smoothies, and movie night. Two days after their first date, Vance figured Cadrin is probably upset with him over his last kiss. He knows he's heavily speculating. His fear is really due to the fact Cadrin didn't call him after she got home that night like she promised him she would do. But her broken promise is the least of his concerns for this evening. He's glad he's getting another date, another chance to correct his anxiousness.

"*Date number two. This has to be a positive sign*," he declares as he pulls into her driveway. On his way to Cadrin's, he'd quizzed himself on what he could bring along to help with their plans for the evening. Even though Cadrin informed him any extras will not be necessary, he wanted to pitch in anyway. With Vance being a man of chivalry, he couldn't resist making contributions. Therefore, he'd decided to stop by the market where he ended up leaving with two filled bags of grocery.

Cadrin pretty much keeps her counter tops spotless. She wanted to make double sure there isn't anything in the way which will cause Vance to question her ability to keep a clean house. She had just finished scrubbing down the countertop next to the stove when she grabbed her cordless phone to answer a call.

"Hi Cadrin, is Vance there yet? I hope I haven't interrupted you and your date tonight. Is he there yet?"

"Don't worry, you're not imposing. I'm still getting some last-minute things together. He should be here any minute now. Is everything all right with you?" Cadrin knew Roslyn would call. She'd told her friend about the progression of her and Vance's friendship and now Roslyn has many questions regarding the man she has never met.

"I take it things are as well as to be expected with you and Vance."

"Yes, everything is great. Roslyn, I know what you're getting at and you can believe I have my eye on him."

"Which eye? I hope it's not the one catching the glare from his 'shining armor.' I think you need to watch him. I know he's charming and as equally handsome. He has already lied to you once. Trust me girl, I think he'll do it again."

"Well, that does it for well wishes for quality time."

"Cadrin, I apologize. I didn't mean to come off as unsupportive of you. I just honestly believe you might have placed your career on the line by fooling with him. He could be using you. They don't have any proof Jim is guilty. I hate to see you come out on the loosing end, that's all."

"Now that's better. Now you sound like a friend who cares. And you're right. They don't have any evidence claiming my client is guilty. I don't know. Maybe they figure by bringing in a heartbreaker to play footsy with me will prove Jim to be the liar they think he is."

"I don't mean to infringe on your happiness. I know sometimes it sounds like Vance has taken a genuine interest in you. If you don't mind me saying so, I think you're crazy about him, too."

"Maybe I am. Honestly, I'm trying to be smart about this. Sometimes I feel like I'm behaving like a love-sick fool. Every time I try to find fault with him something about him just makes me want more of him."

"It sounds like you and Vance Grayson have a lot to talk about."

Cadrin peeped through the blinds of her living room, "You're right, and I think we should start right about now, he just pulled into the driveway."

In one swift move, Vance grabbed the grocery bags from the passenger car seat and strode to Cadrin's front door where he rings the doorbell.

With a smile on her face, she opened her door for him.

"Vance what is all this? I expected to see just you not you holding bags of grocery. You really didn't have to do this," she said smiling as she reached for one of the bags," she's impressed at his generosity.

"It's okay, I got them. I'll place them in the kitchen if that's alright with you."

"Yes, the kitchen table will be fine, Vance. Come on in."

Cadrin takes her blender out and is now ready to get started just when Vance began emptying one of the bags.

"Here you go," he said as he passed two clear glass bottles to her, "I brought along two bottles of sparkling water. I didn't know if you really needed any. I'm sure you would like to replace what you may end up using tonight," he said smiling at her.

While Cadrin worked with the ice and blender, she watched him remove paper towels, sugar, cool whip, an assortment of fruit and raw vegetables from the grocery bags.

"I have one more thing," Vance began heading for the front door.

"Vance," she said laughing.

Quickly, he strode back to his car to retrieve a bag of ice. When he'd made it back to her kitchen counter, she stepped aside allowing him to have room to place the heavy bag of ice into the sink. Cadrin admires how good he looks. Silently, she applauds him for knowing how to dress for any occasion. Quite nicely he's wearing a pair of light blue jeans and a navy-blue crewneck short sleeved shirt. He doesn't just work his upper body; the small circumference of his waist and toned rear are filling out those jeans of his very nicely.

It's exceedingly difficult for her to concentrate with him so near. She revels in his fine physique for every inch of him is toned to perfection. Vance notices the finger sandwiches which she prepared minutes before his arrival. The wedge slices were left to sit on a tray next to the refrigerator.

"Mmm, those look delicious, I want a bite right this second."

"Vance, don't you want to wait until the movie start?"

"Oh no," he said wiping dipping sauce from the corner of his mouth, "these are too good to wait for a movie to start," he said as he picked up another and offered her a bite of the other half, "and some for the cook," he said as she chews in delight.

Cadrin left Vance to open a bottle of sparkling water while she added more ice into the blender.

She thought he was so cute when he tried to ask for a colander, having referred to it as the thing water drains from. Despite his error, he's aware of what it is used for, and she likes that. She isn't alone. Like many single women, she admires a man who knows his way around a kitchen. Vance's mother believes one of the plights of manhood is for a man to know how to take care of himself. If the time comes, he will know how to tend to home by himself. Connie believes just because her boys are rugged, have the looks of heartbreakers, and were headed towards successful careers didn't mean they would always have a woman at their side. So, she instilled in them how to prepare decent meals and how to clean up after themselves. Brian supported her.

Cadrin offered him no reply as she fulfilled his request by handing to him the colander. Vance placed it in the kitchen sink then he opened a pack of paper towels. She watched him draw water over the fruits and raw vegetables which he'd purchased from the market. She thinks he looks very sexy in her kitchen.

"What are you thinking about over there?" You've gone and gotten all quiet on me. I want to hear the sweet sound of your voice."

Cadrin looks at him for a few seconds, sizing him up, "I was just thinking about when we dined at Vintage. I don't think you'll be surprised to hear I still find it somewhat strange you showed up at Stone and Nichols."

Vance's eyes darkened in disappointment.

"I have to tell you; I'm saddened to hear that. I thought where we've eventually arrived is an understanding. I told you the truth as to why I was there. And I also informed you I am Everdeen's legal defense," as soon as the words legal defense hit Vance's eardrums, he knew he had spoken the key words hindering Cadrin's ability to further focus on their night together.

"I know that Vance. But if you're lying to me, you can cost my career some really huge points."

"I don't know what else to say to you which will make you trust me. I want this Cadrin. The second I pulled up out there in your driveway I wanted to get out your neighborhood and call you with an excuse, but I didn't want to cheat myself out of an evening I believe will be well spent."

For a moment, she had looked away then their eyes met again. With all her heart, Cadrin wants to trust the man who she is falling in love with. She has big problems with playing the fool. She placed down the strawberries she'd been drying off while she had been listening to Vance. Slowly, she walks behind him. He held up his arms a little, curious as to what she is trying to do. Turning slowly, he watches her out of the corner of his eye. Cadrin slowly looks him up then down. Vance curiously smiles at her once she'd come back around to stand in front of him. He thinks her observance of him is smooth, skillful, sexy, and questionable. He didn't try to stop her. He's curious to see how far she will go.

"I don't know either, but I'll tell you what you can do."

"What?" Vance raises a brow at her. He is clearly enjoying the way she is sizing up his person.

"Hold your arms up and out by your sides, please."

"What?"

"Yes, hold your arms out."

Smiling, he went ahead and did as she requested. She began to walk slowly around him until she made a full circle.

"May I put my arms back down now?"

"No. I need you to keep them right where they are, please," she spoke softly. Her authority is engaging. Vance looks at her with narrowing vision, slowly and sensuously licking the lips which needs to kiss her badly. At her polite order, Vance laughs with so much charisma Cadrin wonders if he can realize just how serious she is about her observation. Clearly, his body's language tells her he is ready for more of this. Not trying to pleasure him she made another full circle around him, then began running her fingers slowly along the seams of the arms of his shirt. Bending down, she followed the inseam of his trousers all the way up, stopping at his zipper. What she discovers is no secret. From his waist down to his ankles, she precariously begins to feel the outer seams. Once she reaches his ankles, she hears him as he asks, "Are we all done, Ms. Porter?"

Vance could almost taste her lips and he can hardly wait until she realizes the error of her ways. Once she does, he knows he will melt his lips to hers. From above his waist, she slowly rubs his abs with the palms of her hands, all the way up to his chest then over the tight muscles of his back. Impressed again, she couldn't help but linger for a moment. She almost grinned at a job well done at the gym. Offended because of her inspection? Almost. He's enjoying this. Her touch to his form is electrifying, inspiring to the lower parts of him. Under her orders there is no room to be discreet. She stands back from him.

"Did you find whatever it was you were looking for?"

Cadrin is relieved she hadn't found anything. She doesn't care if he thinks she's being silly, her career means the world to her and if she is going down it isn't going to be for providing any degree of information for Vance to secretly obtain then use it against her client.

"May I put my arms down now?"

She looks at him like she knows the joke is on her. He isn't going to win that easily.

"Hold your feet up, without your shoes."

"What! Cadrin we've been through this," he thought about it for a second, "okay, I started all of this by showing up to Stone and Nichols. So, I'll play along with you," Vance did as she asked.

She began to look underneath and inside of his shoes and felt underneath his feet.

"I'm not hiding anything from you," Vance knows he should be displeased with her behavior, but he had become excited from the first second her hands began to touch him.

"Are you finished taking inventory of me? If not, you're welcome to continue your search."

Cadrin finished empty handed. Not in his wildest dreams did Vance expect her to check him over, especially like that. She'd kicked that footstool she uses to access the highest shelves in her kitchen to stop in front of him. Vance couldn't believe her gall, and he couldn't honestly say he wasn't turned on by every touch of her hand. Her fingers had glided along side then over his form teasing and exciting him in ways he'd never been offered. He never had any woman to second guess him in the way she'd done. Cadrin's inspection and the way her hands had touched him during such assessment, had him wanting to know in how many more ways she can excite him. He doesn't mind the wait.

However, taking things slow is about to run its course with him. But if it takes more dinners and more nights like tonight that will be simply fine with him. Without a doubt he knows Cadrin Porter is well worth the trouble, and he refuses to run away from any of it.

All Vance heard from her was a huff as she'd washed her hands. Cadrin had found nothing. She thought maybe it is time for her to release all negative speculation of him. She knows if she decides to keep seeing him romantically, she is going to have to trust him or leave him be. If he's capable of hiding something, she knows very well the next time she wants to search him, he will make damn sure she wouldn't be able to find anything. Cadrin took a couple of steps away from him.

"Are you out done, Cadrin?"

"No, I'm not."

Vance closed the gap between them. He lifted her chin to his gaze of her.

"Cadrin, I'm not trying to get any amount of information out of you about your client. While in your presence, I'd much rather talk about anything other than our clients. Even if you were to try, I'd be against it. And by the way, I enjoyed your little pat down, but you are going to have to trust me or leave me. I'm not the villain you think I am but if you want me to leave, I will." Vance hated getting on her case. Being real with her is necessary. The thought of her doing something like that again on the bases of distrust managed to hit a sore spot with him. Whatever it will take, Vance is determined to get her to see she hadn't made a mistake in trusting him this far into her life.

Cadrin is so embarrassed to the point of trying to devote her stare to anywhere else in the room other than on him, but Vance wouldn't let her. He pulls her closer to him. If she had told him to leave, he would have gone out the door knowing he wants and needs her in his life, and he isn't going to allow her reservations of him to govern how he feels for her, especially when he is full aware she's turned on by him. He understands her concern, identifying her fears with those of his own. Her career is more than an investment; it had become a part of her life just like his has become a part of his world.

"I…apologize to you Vance. I overreacted. I hope you can forgive me for the way I behaved just a few minutes ago. Some hostess I am, huh?"

He shook his head at her.

"I want to kiss you now," he said.

She could feel the breath of his whispered words against her lips. When her hands traveled up and had begun to caress his chest, he knew she wanted to kiss him, too. His tongue parted her lips, and he kissed her with so much desire he ended up backing her against the kitchen counter.

The movie is halfway over and Cadrin as well as her date have nearly cleaned the tray of goodness, having sampled a mix of bite sized sandwiches, green olives with pimentos, slices of fruit and smoothies. After a while, Cadrin closed the small gap between them and laid her head on his shoulder. He raised his arm, letting it rest on back of the couch behind the pillows. Cadrin snuggled in closer to him. He figured she must be getting a little tired.

"Hey, I hate to watch a great movie alone. Are you sleepy?"

"No, I just like cozying up to you, that's all." Fearful of how far their relationship would or would not take them, he slowly sucked in his bottom lip. He had unintentionally thrown caution to the wind. Vance had to give it to himself; he had demonstrated a very risqué move. At least now he knows she holds a special place for him within her heart. At the end of the movie, Cadrin rose and headed for the kitchen.

"Vance, there's one more smoothie with your name on it," she called for him.

Never losing focus of her brown eyes, he rose and began walking towards her. Once he reached her kitchen, he sees her standing there holding the glass's crystal stem as though it's holding up a bouquet of roses. She handed the glass to him. He brought it to his lips and sampled. His drink is cool and zesty, causing him to slowly lick his lips. Once he brought the glass away from his mouth, he noticed how Cadrin never took her eyes off him. He wanted his lips to meet hers. He wants to be sure he doesn't overstep any boundaries. He took one step, placing one of his hands on the curve of her hip, then he leaned in slowly allowing her the opportunity to back away before the fireworks began, that is if she feels she needs to. Cadrin thought after what seemed liked forever, their lips finally met. Because of his passion, she melted. His hand smoothly fell onto her other hip, holding her firmly around her waist. He stepped in closer to her frame. Her hands traveled an inch above his waist, soon discovering the toned abs underneath his shirt. Once their kiss ended, Vance caressed her chin with his thumb.

"Thank you for sharing the drink as well as the kiss, it was…," picking up the glass from the countertop he paused, "interesting," he said while softly tracing her lips with the rim of his empty champagne glass.

Carmichael did as Vance instructed and had contacted Cadrin to set a date and time for the face -to- face meeting the two feuding parties are expected to attend. Tomorrow afternoon, Vance is expected to be in the same meeting with Carmichael and Cadrin. How is he going to get through it? It's clear to him Jim is trying to take control over the matter. Vance is already fully prepared in keeping Jim's lawyer in remembrance of which party has control of the pending lawsuit. Vance also did his best to make perfect mental preparations to be in the same room with Cadrin.

It wasn't until right after her first phone call to him, when he'd realized just how risky he and Cadrin's attraction for each other will continue to be. The two of them in the same room together means hot and steamy trouble. There is no way Carmichael will keep Vance as Everdeen's attorney if he should learn Vance is smitten with Cadrin Porter. All Carmichael is aware of is the fact Delia is in no way shy in displaying how she feels about Vance. He sees the way she always eye the hot shot attorney from Maryland. With lustful eyes, her lashes flutters whenever Vance is near her, looking him up and down and riding on a curve when he exits a room.

Once Vance arrived in the parking lot of Stone and Nichols, he did not hesitate in scanning the tremendous parking lot for sight of Cadrin. He wanted to get a word in to her before the other attendants arrived, but he sees no sign of her. He thought if she is on the premises, she must have caught a ride with Jim or his lawyer and is now inside the building. Vance tried to reach her on her cell phone. There was no answer.

After looping the perimeter twice, Vance parked his car on one of the rows designated for visitors. After he exited his car, Carmichael entered the lot and parked next to him.

On their way to the steps of the building, a couple of women began to voice their approval for Vance as they undressed him with their eyes. Carmichael couldn't help noticing the women as they admire his legal defense.

"Well got damn it Vance. What the hell are you, a magnet?"

Vance barely attempted in offering his client a reply, he's too busy looking over his shoulder and beyond the women. He's hoping to see Cadrin but she is nowhere in sight.

As they walked up the spread of steps to enter the lobby, Vance paid strict attention to his and Carmichael's reflection in the glass of the Stone and Nichols large handle doors. He would be better than pleased to see Cadrin's frame fall into step behind them. So far, it appears she has yet to arrive for the second group meeting between the two parties.

Vance and Carmichael entered the lobby. Before they had the opportunity to wonder if someone will acknowledge them, they were speedily welcomed to the million-dollar corporation by Victoria Flanagan. As they were going through their salutations, Jim's secretary joined them. They were on their way to the elevator when Cadrin briskly walked into the building. The clinking of her heels to the tile flooring got everyone's attention. Maureen introduced their publicist.

"Mr. Lewis, Mr. Grayson, I'd like to introduce you both to our publicist, Cadrin Porter. I'm sure the two of you remember Ms. Porter from the press conference held here a few months ago."

"Yes, and please accept our apology for the behavior of our publicist, Mr. Monahan," Carmichael said.

Cadrin extended her hand in a shake to Carmichael and his attorney. She was smooth, very smooth. Vance didn't know if he should have been shocked, concerned or impressed with her ability to be so discrete. He shook Cadrin's hand. Through her slight consideration of him, he was quickly reminded he's not supposed to know her from, Yolanda. His heart beats rapidly for the woman he adores. She shook his hand and hadn't shown any signs of attempting to hold his gaze.

"How long will she be able to keep this up?" He doesn't know the answer but what he does know is it's his best bet to follow suit.

"Are we all ready to proceed to the conference room?" Maureen asked.

The visitors and Cadrin nodded yes. As a group, they began in heading for the secured floor.

Chapter 14

The Executives

Victoria Flanagan buzzed Jim's office to inform him Maureen is in the process of chauffeuring everyone up to the conference room. Jim and his lawyer immediately rose from their chairs before quickly making their way to the meeting room located just down the hall. Jim anticipated the meeting to go well and he's hoping everyone can reach a solution which doesn't involve him going to court.

Finally, the smooth lift of the elevator reached the building's fourteenth floor. During the trip, the ride had sort of been like a game of jeopardy. Everyone carefully chose his and her topic. Vance and Carmichael talked about some of the tourist sites in the area, Maureen and Cadrin discussed Vintage. Maureen couldn't have chosen a shakier topic.

After the doors of the elevator opened, Cadrin was the first to step off. The secured floor is quiet and holds the scent of Egyptian cotton. In pairs of two, Cadrin and Maureen precedes Vance and Carmichael as they all make their way down the corridor.

Eventually, they came to a halt stopping at the door of the conference room where Jim and his lawyer are waiting for everyone's arrival. Maureen stepped aside allowing Cadrin to enter the room first. Out of courtesy for whom she believes is on the winning side, on her way into the room Cadrin shakes Jim's hand. Carmichael almost swore. He was reluctant to shake the hand of the man who seems to have possibly stolen two point five million dollars from someone and wants his company to take the blame. But he figured he would be no better than

Monahan if he succumbed to acting like a fool, even if it were just for a short while.

After Carmichael briefly shook Jim's hand so did Vance, whom of which made very sure he stirred clear of following Cadrin. He ended up being next to the last attending member to enter the conference room.

While coming up in the elevator, Vance had already wanted to brush a strand of Cadrin's hair away from the side of her face as he loves doing so whenever she is alone in his presence. She doesn't realize it, but she is getting to him.

Finally, they all entered the spacious room where they took their seats. Vance sat across from Cadrin, Carmichael adjacent to Jim and his lawyer, then Maureen. It looks as though the tables have been turned. Carmichael cleared his throat.

"Alright everyone, I believe we all know why we've been asked here today," Jim's lawyer opened the floor in hopes for any alternatives in avoiding court room proceedings.

It is difficult for Vance to maintain his focus on the situation at hand. He shouldn't be surprised at all as he observes Cadrin carry herself as a powerful natural and therefore became very intrigued while trying his best not to pay her too much attention.

Ignoring the presence of Jim's lawyer, Vance responded, "Mr. Grainger, I'm seriously speaking here. You're asking my client for a break when you don't have any proof alleviating our suspicions."

Jim's lawyer gave Vance a puzzling look.

Yes, suspicions because over a million dollars are unaccounted for," Vance stressed his point. Jim's lawyer began to intervene on the behalf of his own client, only to be interrupted by him.

"It's all right, I'll respond. Mr. Grayson, is it?" asked Jim.

Vance nodded yes.

"How can you be a part of a lawsuit against my company without any proof? We have checked, double checked, and rechecked Stone and Nichols' financial statements and there aren't any increases in assets to be confirmed."

Vance is beginning to get angry at Jim. He offered him some insight, "Mr. Grainger, let me begin by correcting you. My client is not suing you yet and we have done nothing more than litigate among ourselves without the aide of judicial leadership. And as far as I'm concerned, my client has every right to protect the well being of his corporation. Now, if we're going after the wrong company, give us the right one and myself and my client, we will move on." The room is painfully quiet. Vance gears up to address the room of occupants once more, this time looking only at Jim and his lawyer, "There are documents connecting your company to the funds and until we sort through this mess, my client's pending suit will remain in effect."

Silence again. Every sentence Vance completed, Cadrin had hung onto every syllable. Hot with frustration she dares not look in Vance's direction.

"Okay, everyone, it's obvious Everdeen doesn't have any proof. If they did, there would be a court date in place by now. So, what does that tell us ladies and gentlemen?" said Jim's lawyer.

Vance missed the comment which had come from Jim's lawyer. Cadrin looks downright sexy to him. Vance took off his jacket and laid it across the back of the unoccupied chair next to him. Little does he know, Cadrin almost lost her cognition. The entire time Vance spoke, she didn't look at him fearing if she did, the look in his eyes would have unlocked the yearning she has for him at this moment. In a trade off, she'd devoted her attention to some notes on the table and then over to Jim and his lawyer.

Carmichael began to react to being insulted by Jim's representation. The man offered no decent explanation of his client's proclaimed innocence.

Cadrin intervenes, "Alright everybody. Jim, at this point I think you'll agree that in the meantime, we should otherwise focus on the well being of Stone and Nichols."

Carmichael became astounded at Cadrin's comment.

"Ms. Porter, your client isn't the only one here who stands to lose ground at maintaining the good name of his company," Carmichael spoke furiously as he watches the narrowing of Cadrin's eyes.

A disturbed expression crossed Vance's face. His fingers folded over into the palm of his hand. Before Carmichael could continue, Vance leans over towards him, "Carmichael, may I see you out in the corridor, please," Vance's words numbed the atmosphere, "If everyone will excuse us."

Carmichael rose and proceeded to follow Vance towards the wood and brass doubled doors.

"Where are they going?" Jim had gotten the impression Carmichael and his attorney were walking out on the prearranged meeting.

"Attorney-client privilege," whispered Jim's lawyer.

Once the doors were fully closed, Vance sought more composure before professionally straightening out his client.

"Listen to me Carmichael, okay. Nobody's going to court just yet. The funds are out there somewhere and until we locate its whereabouts, it will be then and only then will we be able to note our next move," Carmichael tried to speak, Vance interrupts him.

"Trust me on this. Even though their own bank documents express otherwise, his guilt hasn't been totally confirmed," said Vance.

"I know it Vance, I'm not lying. I never gave Jim any amount of funding for any venture," Carmichael assured his attorney.

"Relax. I didn't say you did. If we don't find any proof implicating who has incumbency of the funds, at the least Carmichael, if the court awards you with anything and please remember they don't have to, will be some and I emphasize some monetary compensation due to you loosing out on the business deal you had with Gory Trust. Probably a small portion of it and that's it. But don't get your hopes up," Vance concluded.

"I don't like the way things are summing up and I'm ready to get the hell out of here. They've somehow concealed two point five million dollars and I want to know where the hell it is," Carmichael sharply whispered. Clearly, trying to keep his client under control is almost impossible.

"The fact they haven't produced the funds is clearly the only reason responsible for us keeping this case open. Just relax. We can't go back in there ranting and tossing about one accusation over the other, not without something more solid. I absolutely understand what you have at stake here, but you have got to calm down and follow my lead."

Together, Vance and Carmichael reentered the conference room. To their surprise, everyone is standing and are now placing their chairs underneath the table. The meeting had gone very differently as opposed to what they each expected. Thank goodness Monahan wasn't invited.

"Just know my client will continue to protect his good name," stated Jim's lawyer.

"We wouldn't expect anything else," Carmichael responded sharply.

Cadrin and Jim exited the room as well as Jim's legal defense, leaving Vance, Carmichael and Maureen to be the remaining occupants. The meeting should have been over sooner. Vance had caught himself staring at Cadrin. A sly grin crossed his lips. He was betting if he thought about it seriously enough, he could accurately count the number of lines he saw on her sexy brown lips. He hoped no one noticed his spurts of lapsed attention during their meeting as his behavior discretely tipped out of control.

Maureen began to clear the table of the common meeting accessories. Before she could finish, Carmichael's phone ranged. He excused himself and left the room. Vance waited there in the conference room for his client's return.

"Mr. Grayson, I just wish we could come to a final agreement and just end all of this," stated Maureen.

"In due time, we will. In due time," was Vance's repeated reply. Maureen didn't look Vance in the eye again. She hurried as she grabbed up her belongings. She headed for the door so quickly until she hadn't noticed Cadrin had forgotten her purse.

Left to himself to retract over everyone's recent exchange of words, Vance recalled Cadrin didn't appear to have been rattled by Carmichael's behavior. A curve of a smile teases the corners of his mouth. He's proud of her. To his surprise, Cadrin returned to the conference room.

"Oh, Vance, I didn't know you were still here. I forgot something," she instantly feels beads of sweat as they tinkle with the pores of her skin. They both are fully aware they're getting ready to lose control of themselves. No matter how well they had hidden their attraction for each other during the meeting, all it would have taken was slight consideration for the other to ignite the irrevocable likeness each has for the other.

Vance glanced over to where she had been sitting. And she's right, she did forget something. He immediately recognized the purse, knowing it is the reason for her return.

"I just saw Carmichael waiting at the elevator; I assumed you were downstairs already."

Vance wanted to close the door so in private he could ask her what she honestly thought of the way things unfolded. He also wants to tell her how shocked he was at her smooth behavior from earlier.

"You know you surprised me a great deal, right?" Earlier, when we were downstairs you barely acknowledged me."

"Vance, please. We must be careful. If there's any consolation, it was damn near impossible for me to stay away from you just a little while ago," she stated as she began to further open the already half-closed door.

"No, wait a minute. Do you mean just like it is for me right now?"

Cadrin made another mistake and stole a glance of him. She saw passion take him over.

Is he crazy or plain reckless? Jim and Maureen are just down the hall, steps away from the heat generating from one to the other, back down the hall from behind the closed doors of the conference room.

Vance gently grabs her hand bringing her closer to his body. Cadrin barely protested. He brought her hand to his lips, kissing the side of her index finger then her thumb. She slowly backed away from him. Turning her back to him, she cracked the door, then peeked out into the hallway. Carmichael is still out there waiting for an elevator and hadn't noticed her. Cadrin quietly closed the door.

"Cadrin is something wrong?" Vance said to her in a love induced voice.

She could barely speak. All she could do was place her finger over his lips to get him to stop with his seducing mumbles. It is clear he tempts her. She found herself to become halfway pinned to the door. Cadrin quickly peeked out the door again, just in time to see Carmichael's pant leg enter the elevator. No one else is in sight.

"No, there's no problem," she said in a breath of relief. Anxiously, with slow passion Vance brought her face to his and argued no more with the tongue which had wanted to taste the sweet suppleness of her long before she'd arrived at Stone and Nichols. When she let go of the doorknob, Vance blunderingly fumbled for the lock as he devoured her mouth, caressing the side of her face with his hands. Cadrin knows this spell nothing but trouble and plenty of it if they don't quit. The only situation going on there is she has got a hunk of a man standing before her. He is ready and she have no choice other than to get ready to receive him. And when his tongue began to tease hers, it was on. His tall stature now ready to be seduced by her. Her heart continues to beat faster for him. There's no time for re-evaluating the ramifications. He's in her arms. His kisses begging and yearning for them to break all the rules they said they wouldn't break. Their kiss escalated away from the locked door over to the conference room table which they did reach. Vance eases her onto the table. She had fallen and him…he's deep in love. The strength of his body presses against the heartbeat running rampant for him. Vance didn't want to let up. Everything he's giving her; she's giving it back to him. Once she slid across the smoothness of the table, the glide made her get her head out of the clouds, but she's finding it difficult to tell him no. After a minute, she slid again then pushed against his frame. That second slide came with his hands gripping the sides of her thighs, both actions had warned her of how far they couldn't go. He stopped on his own, looking her in the face. She saw yearning all about him and it only took seconds for him to kiss her again, this time like there will be no tomorrow. Finally, he stopped.

"I apologize," he said.

Cadrin tried to secretly shake off the dizzying effect he left her with.

"We shouldn't do this," he said as he gently pulls her blazer back together before helping her ease down from the table. He never stopped looking at her as she untangled her necklace from a button on his shirt.

"Please forgive me, I do have respect, I just…" he said in a continuance of muttered love notes as he strokes the side of her face. They kissed again. The kiss was bound to happen once more, he was so close to her while she worked on freeing the button of his shirt from her jewelry.

"I hope we can talk soon," he muttered.

"Yes, we will," Cadrin patted the button on his shirt back down as best she could.

Vance followed Cadrin from the conference room. He watched her as she sashayed down the hall on the way to her office. As she walked, she secretly fought for control over the heat she has for him.

Chapter 15

The Executives

Cadrin rushed down the corridor to answer the phone in her office, she could hear its constant ring as she hurried faster to answer it.

"This is Cadrin Porter speaking."

"Ah, well hello Ms. Porter. This here is Tim Davenport. I'm with The Weekly Chronicles."

Cadrin didn't recognize the caller's name. However, she is familiar with the company and understands it creates negative publicity for unsuspecting parties.

"For crying out loud, what does he want?"

"Weeks ago, my staff and I became aware of the legal matters of Stone and Nichols. We are almost certain Jim Grainger will be pleased in being offered a real opportunity to express his innocence."

Tim Davenport owns and reports for The Weekly Chronicles, a struggling media outlet located in Lexington. It's a paper which gained its notoriety for its unwavering dedication in publicizing debates, by taking the most crucial information and turning it into smut stretched as wide as the world map. Davenport is out searching for the next best headliner. Two Feuding Millionaires. He began to grin at his own self-proclaimed brilliance as he continues to speak into the phone.

"We hear accusations like these all the time, and I gotta tell you sometimes they're true, and other times…well I'm sure you know how the story can end," Tim smirked.

Cadrin began to reply but Tim sharply took the lead.

"But never mind that, we're prepared to offer him a voice. We want him to be able to tell his side of the situation without any interference. You know, like that circus of a press conference held there only a few months ago. I'd be grateful if you jotted down information on how Jim can contact me. My staff and I would love to hear from Mr. Grainger."

Cadrin's ear was assaulted at the audacity of the reporter. The Weekly Chronicles is associated with anything offering a big payday and the staff has some but not enough regard as to how they obtain their information. Tim is in no position to criticize any unfortunate incidents. Cadrin is relieved he hadn't personally brought any of his foolishness to Stone and Nichols. Tim had taken the liberty to try to secure the story himself. His action is a sure sign he will not stop at anything which doesn't ensure his paper the best headliner it has seen in over a year.

"Mr. Davenport, with all due respect to your industry, I believe Jim will be much better off without any assistance from your paper," Tim tried to intervene, but Cadrin maintained a steady flow, "negatively revising Jim's side of a feuding debate would be hardly helping him."

"Ms. Porter, I have to say I disagree. The Weekly Chronicles has a wealth of readers looking for nothing more than the truth. And my paper offers them such, that's all."

"You may believe that's true, I do not. I'm certain the real supporters of Stone and Nichols are housed right here under the very roof over my head," she paused, "fabricating the truth is a golden rule for you. Am I correct, Mr. Davenport?"

No response was offered from Tim who now has the look of smug apprehension within the contours of his facial expression.

"Jim will be just fine without your kind of assistance, Mr. Davenport."

"We're just trying to do our part in offering him a fair shake."

"Mr. Davenport, you've wasted enough of your time and my own, good-day," Cadrin ended the call.

Davenport is very persistent and starving for recognition. Cadrin doesn't know how he will gain center stage under the spotlight he's so desperately trying to draw. But there is one thing she's sure of - the fact he won't give up easily.

Cadrin finally walked away from the phone and headed over to the on-site files she stores at her office inside of Stone and Nichols. Thanks to Verona of housekeeping, Cadrin's concentration is interrupted by the roar of her vacuum cleaner from down the hall. Looking at the carpet in her office she made her way to the door and motioned for Verona to stop there when she gets the chance to.

To make sure the cleaning lady has full access to the floor which is covered with tiny samples of fabric and other trinkets, Cadrin began removing a few filing boxes from the floor and placed them on top of the round table.

"He has got some nerve," Cadrin spoke aloud as she accidentally let one of the boxes fall onto the table. She heard Verona cut the switch to the vacuum cleaner.

"I apologize Ms. Porter, what did you just say?"

"Oh, I apologize Verona. I was just thinking out loud. I apologize for disturbing you."

Verona smiled her usual warm smile and resumed with her work.

Cadrin was alerted of a personal call. Her buzzing cell phone is lost within the maze of boxes. Her hand nervously searches for the small device. She opened her cell just in time to deter her caller from being subjected to voice mail.

"Hello."

"Hello, beautiful."

In response to the voice on the other end of the line, she begins to smile. It's Vance. Cadrin looks around the room. It was from there she studied the space beyond the opened door looking for anyone within hearing distance. Not seeing anyone in sight she quickly removes herself from Verona and the noise of the vacuum. Leaving the office, she walks a stretch down the corridor.

"How are you, Vance?" she said with soft enthusiasm.

When Vance spoke, she could detect that more than usual he holds an even greater tantalizing expression mixed with mischief upon his face. It's a look he always gets when he is planning something exciting beyond her ordinary to do list. He knows she's a workaholic who doesn't get out much. But when she does, there's no doubt in his mind she can hold her own. He's right on both counts.

"Listen, are you almost done at Stone and Nichols for the day?"

"As a matter of fact, I am."

"Hey, what was that noise I heard a few seconds ago?"

"It was the vacuum. The cleaning lady, Verona, is in my office right now tidying things up."

"If she's in your office, where are you?" Vance is curious if anyone had heard Cadrin mention his name once she answered his call. The two of them can't afford any slip ups. She laughs softly.

"Right now, I'm on the stairwell sitting on a cold step. No one appeared to have noticed I slipped out. Don't worry, I checked the staircase above. It's all clear."

Although Cadrin figures Verona to be harmless, she realized any degree of carefulness can't be overrated.

Chapter 16

The Executives

Vance securely holds Cadrin's hand. His slow steps and smooth discretion protectively guide Cadrin through the after five scenes, pardoning singles and other couples as they make their way through one of Chicago's famous after five venues. There are at least fifty people on the venue's first level drinking martinis, enjoying live jazz and conversation.

Minus any complaints, Cadrin is amazed at Vance's ability to offer the room such a strong presence. Being away from Maryland fails in hindering his level of confidence within a relaxed setting. As a matter of fact, it's Cadrin who is feeling like an out-of-town visitor while she tags closely by his side. Vance is on his usual alert mode giving the venue's first floor a thorough once over. Because of the club's relaxed and let loose atmosphere, Vance doesn't consider this particular hot spot to be a favorite of any notables within the Johnson Everdeen or Stone and Nichols genre. On the other hand, upscale restaurants are a definite yes.

"Where would you like to sit?" he inquired, continuing to keep Cadrin close to him. She's cozying up to the idea of the two of them residing next to the crackling fireplace. All the seats within its proximity are currently occupied; vouched for by couples engaged in the ambiance as they sip imported and house brand wines.

Judging from Cadrin's look of defeat, Vance searches the crowded room hoping to spot an available table just for two.

"You want to sit over there?" she asked.

"No. How about over there?" Vance spotted accommodations just for two near the south wall of the venue. In approval of Vance's choice, they begin to walk in the direction of the neat little table.

Amongst the loquacious crowd, both began to take their seat. Their attention was stolen from each other by the return of the jazz band.

Ready to be entertained, mostly everyone in the room curiously engages the band leader's every word. While the other band members busy themselves staging the platform, the leader of the band took to the microphone. He began quizzing the crowd on how well they have familiarized themselves on their jazz repertoire. Cadrin and Vance tuned in laughing with the participants and other patrons at some of the not so accurate responses.

Seeing the perfect opportunity to check for any notables, Vance politely excuses himself from Cadrin's presence. He'd decided to check out the venue's upper level. Once he did so he quickly realized no one who is recognizable were to be found upstairs. Vance is relieved to say the least. He and Cadrin just hopes no one recognizes the two of them.

To the tune of the band's first note since their last five-minute break, Vance returned to his and Cadrin's table. From the look of calm on his face, Cadrin could tell everything upstairs had checked out alright. Cadrin begins to focus on Vance. Being in the public's eye really isn't a clever idea, but she knows it would have been impossible for Vance to show her the enjoyable time he intends if he'd just given way to what ifs.

As time wore on, the attorney and the woman who won his heart knows while they are in public with or without their clients, no matter what, it will be in his and her best interest to be as slick as they can possibly be. A round of applause fills the room.

"I'm glad you invited me out, this is great. It's nice to finally be able to enjoy some of life's other pleasures again."

He smiled at her before kissing her just past the ring on her finger.

"Every once in a while, I see you over there moving your head to the rhythm of the band," he smiles.

"I love jazz. I'm glad we are getting to hear this particular band perform."

Vance looks around the crowded room. It is filled with laughter and dancing. Judging from the looks of the other patrons, they are surely out to enjoy the festivities the night will bring to them. Vance is determined to make sure he does his part in making sure this will not be a night which Cadrin will soon forget. Vance brought her smooth brown fingers to his face. She begins to caress his chin.

"Look at'em, the lovely couple. Hmmph. The two of them might be my best subject yet. My source didn't lie. The full truth was told and nothing but the truth. So, yawl go right ahead and do yawls thang, because my dividends, pesos and Benjamins are getting ready to look reallll nice." Flash.

Captivated by her touch, he looks deeply into her eyes. Cadrin privately begged to lay her head on his brawn and bare chest.

Interrupted by the incoming crowd of at least thirty, the band changed their current number to something more upbeat. The additional patrons couldn't have arrived at a better time.

After the band returned from another break, the band's leader instructed the men to lead their ladies to the dance floor.

Vance and Cadrin's fingers intertwine as they are on their way to take their place on the dance floor.

Cadrin feels Vance's arms encircle her neat waistline. His embrace pulls her closer to him. Even this evening, here and there she is giving it her best to be angry with him for etching his way into her life, and angry for how he seems to have taken control over her career by leading her to the floor for a dance. He walked that incredibly dignified and sexy stride of his, and once on the dance floor he had lifted the fingers of the hand he holds and led such hand to lay above his shoulder. He dances closer to her. Her only other thought is heaven help her if Vance is as good on the dance floor as he had been in the Stone and Nichols conference room. Flash.

Summing up his confidence, she knows he is a man to be reckoned with. In awe within the depths of his vibe she became mesmerized. Instead of scolding him she found herself wanting to applaud him, make her own sweet music with him. *"Seductive. Confident. Tempting."* Closer to him is exactly where she wants to be. Her reach bumpily travels over the buttons of his shirt. The closer he comes to her the more she can smell every note of his cologne. She marvels in the presence of his manliness. Flash. Credit given to the four-inch heels on Cadrin's leather boots causes Vance's frame to only become slighted. More, he leans in towards her. This time they are inseparable. She lays her hand at the nape of his hair line. Vance wraps an arm around her neat and curvaceous hips. With his free arm, he took her hand holding it just below his chin, gently pressing his cheek to hers, his lips to her ear. Across the overlapping strings of fabric across the skin of her back, Cadrin can feel the impression his fingers are making into her skin. It seems like the closer he joined his body to her own, an ounce of her sweat threatens to weaken her knees. His seductive vibe is so pleasantly intense, she wonders does he even realize what he's doing to her. He's beyond good. Fluent. A natural he is in letting Cadrin know without a doubt, she has most definitely gotten his attention. To be noticed by Vance Grayson is a great thing.

Cadrin knows just about all eyes in the place are on them now. However, she doesn't care. Being this close to him is allowing her to unwind, and invite him into her soul, and when she did rhythm couldn't bounce off time. The connection they're making is positively love. Flash.

Tones of tenor and alto ignites unfamiliar places within her soul. Those sounds from him set off a trail of cold shivers to stream through the clutter of roadblocks she had once built up against him.

The room began to be mesmerized with the tune of a seductive crowd pleaser recognizable by any adult age group. At its induction, the crowd begins to cheer, the dance floor remains packed. The band's leader grabs the microphone from its stand.

Lightly brushing against Cadrin and Vance, a woman passes through closely and yells, "Sing it V!" If Vance didn't know any better, he would have thought she was talking to him. However, he's unmoved. Not even a fine line can be sketched or dotted between himself and Cadrin.

At the song's last lingering note, hand claps and whistles from a satisfied crowd controls the room. Vance joined the other men with hand claps and whistles, but he's the sole recipient of Cadrin's gracious gratitude. Flash.

Once their kiss broke, hand in hand Vance and Cadrin returned to their table. Moments later they ordered bruschetta paired with moscato and a beer for Vance's taste.

After dancing once more they decided to leave the venue. All the way back to the corporate apartment, they laughed and raved about the band's style, and their ability to keep the crowd on their feet.

Vance pulled into his reserved parking space at the corporate apartment. After stepping out of his ride he strode around to the passenger side of the car to help Cadrin exit. Hand in hand again, they came to rest under the glow of the lamp post next to the height of the fixtures of gold numbers on the door of Vance's residence. Vance kisses her lips. After he tore himself away from her for more than five, he unlocked the door of the corporate apartment. Cadrin entered the room first. Before her figure could become a silhouette, it happened again. More than before, flashes danced about the darkness of night. Vance became curiously frozen and stepped off the tile flooring back onto the pavement of bricks just outside of his front door. The very corner of his eye detected only a few flickers of light. A disapproving gesture heightens his awareness. Instinctively, he peers into the night. He sees no one. The only light he now notices is the yellowish glow of the lights from the parking lot including those of the lamp posts belonging to other residents. He said nothing and dismissed the hint of light to be his imagination.

Vance entered the foyer. After closing and locking the door behind himself he calls out to Cadrin. She had already made her way into his kitchen. During Vance's inspection of the discreet light, Cadrin had helped herself to a bottle of water from the fridge. She watches him closely as he makes himself comfortable. Before he took a seat on one of the bar stools, he'd taken his time in removing his jacket before walking into the living area where he begins removing his shoes. He retreated to the bar and sat himself down. For a few minutes, he stared at Cadrin. She looked like there were many miles standing between him and what he'd been quietly begging for since a year after he and Deandra split up.

"Why are you way over there?" he said to her.

"I could ask you the same thing."

"Come closer to me, she heard him say."

Cadrin began to leave the kitchen. Seductively she begins passing through her side of the bar on her way to him. Vance widened the space between his thighs, anxiously pulling her into his warm, hard chest. She just can't denounce the fact she had come so very close to having allowed the most amazing man she has ever met to slip through her voids of loneliness.

Vance is no longer an anticipated wish. Sitting at the island bar, he places a kiss onto the lips which had been driving him crazy the entire time they listened to jazz. And driven he remains to be. His tongue mutually tussles with hers, insisting to dominate then taking over once her head rested against the palms of his hands. From the moment she touched his chest, visions of the pat down she'd given to him resurfaced. Her hands answered every purging aspect of his body from the tongue which caressed her finger, to his abdominal muscles, chest, to the strength of his back's muscles, all the way back to his lower member.

His responses are receptive, speaking loudly and sweating with desire. Due to the way his hands are gliding over her smooth and soft brown skin, his fervor heightens. Cadrin closed her eyes as she felt Vance's hands move from her hips to press then travel above her derriere, straight up the length of her spine. His fingers linger on every curve while his passion licked kisses found their way behind her ears while she continues to carry on with her exploration of his firm body. Vance came face- to-face with her again, their previous kiss reignited, continuing as if it had been frozen by time.

Cadrin begins to work at the belt through the loops of Vance's trousers. Every ounce of him began to intensify in response to her every stroke of him. His chest and tongue lunges for her even more. He pleasures her mouth and face with kisses which are now heading for her ample cleavage. Grabbing her gently by her waistline, his lips met the small space between her breasts. Liking the fullness of them he responded with a slight tremble in one of his knees which without surprise made him grow stronger, gently lifting her from the floor. With her knee resting against his thigh, Cadrin can smell more faint splashes of his Sebastian cologne and aftershave when she kissed him underneath his chin. She took a few moments to enjoy the gripping effect his body's chemistry is doing for the bottled scent. The touch of her tongue underneath his chin nearly levels his senses, the only chance for his recovery is, "God help me," he muttered to himself. He's calling on the right one. She is messing with the fire in him, automatically knowing what it takes to drive him crazy. His desire to take his time with her is boss. She created a rumble within him, a thunder he needs to put into perspective before showing her just how much he is set on making her anything but disappointed in their night together. Vance holds her closer to him; his feet placed a step apart. Leaning into her, his finger settled under her chin lifting it for her lips to receive gentle kisses as he slowly glides a single finger down the center of her back. She thought his touch to be as light as a feather, teasing her with smoldering passion.

Cadrin saw he'd gone for one of the buttons on his shirt, which he quickly grew tired of trying to handle on his own. Unable to keep his hands off Cadrin, through the moans and groans she heard him whisper to her, "Take it off." The buttons might as well have been excluded; she began to ravishingly free him from the confines of his collared shirt. The more she did so, the louder he groaned with his mouth clinging to the side of her neck and face. One of his best shirts was about to succumb to being dethroned from his body. A surprising act, she helped him out of his shirt with slow burning ease. She could feel the perspiring yet cool skin of his chest against hers.

Suddenly, Cadrin associated the smooth wetness of his skin with the rush of spring water. Uncontrollable, she can't resist continuing in the caressing of his skin. Her hand slowly dotes the strength of his back giving him the tender loving massage he deserves. His masculinity keeps begging her for more, moaning and contracting in response to her every touch. Vance's hands travel slowly down to the lowest and smallest part of her back then deep massaging up the length of it. His hands made it to her hair. Vance angled his head on a trail of human electricity to connect his lips with hers. She felt his body flinch in heated excitement when he felt her hands press against his abdominal muscles. He moaned when her hands began to move over his chest. Picking her up with the kiss that's refusing to break, Vance headed for his bedroom suite down the hall. Once they reached his room, he grabbed a packet of protection from the bedside drawer. Like rushing water, her burning desire for him increasingly becomes impossible to regulate. A strand of her hair flowed gently over the back of his hand, tickling the veins beneath. The bass of his voice projects a riveting calmness producing a seductive yearning. "Cadrin, do you love me?" Before they went any further, he needed to know if she had fallen as much as he did. Although the weight of his question originated from deep within his soul, he spoke clearly. Cadrin was totally caught off guard, her emotions and her thoughts became misty, like a soft rain touching the tip of every phase of desire she associates with him. Vance Grayson is so charming and intelligent.

Even through his perseverance of one day totally winning her affection and even through his straightforwardness, he isn't overbearing or cocky. He's equally serious in every action he takes in letting her know he cares for her deeply.

Vance closes his eyes. The way she feels in his arms he's certain he can hold her forever. Her silence had overcome him, his heart began to become immensely filled with possible rejection. She hadn't answered him. He aches to hear the response in which her mouth couldn't say, but he finds solace in what her eyes are saying to him.

"I love you, Vance."

Chapter 17

The Executives

The next morning, Cadrin lay snug in the care of the man who guarded her with his body all night long. She had been pleasantly awakened by gentle strokes, soft kisses on her neck, and behind her ear. Her eyes open, immediately falling upon Vance's shoulder, and the curve of his lips as he hovers over her, continuing to gently stroke her soft brown skin.

In Cadrin's mind sunrise is inevitable. So, she accepted the realization that time does and will move on. Thinking back to their night together, she holds not an ounce of regret.

"Good morning," he said in between kisses, "you sleep alright?" Did he have to ask?

"I did. I didn't plan on staying the night though. Why didn't you wake me?" while she waits for an answer, she notices they are nestled underneath a cushiony navy blue and brown comforter which the light of day seems to make brighter.

"You were sleeping so peacefully I didn't want to disturb you," he's pleasantly taken by her ability to still look beautiful after the eruptions their love making had created.

"Are you hungry?" he questioned.

"Yesss, I am."

"I'll tell you what," he said while caressing her flat belly, "in about thirty-five minutes I will have prepared the most delicious breakfast you've ever eaten."

"Ever, whew," she said aroused at his confidence.

Not bothering to shield himself, Vance rises from the bed for a quick shower. Even from behind, he has her undivided attention, his riveting muscles placed by perfection.

"I'm sure breakfast will be great, but I doubt it will top last night," she said.

Vance's chest involuntarily flexed at her comment. His stride slowed. Once he reached the bathroom's door, he observes her from across the room, inviting her in.

"If I joined you then breakfast wouldn't be breakfast anymore, neither would be brunch. Today I must be at Stone and Nichols no later than eleven," she said from underneath the covers.

He smiled at her with love in his eyes.

"Ms. Porter, I have to give it to you. You pose a strong argument," he wants her in the shower with him. He knows her well enough to know she will not give into him no matter how much she wants him, again. Vance entered the bathroom leaving its door wide open. Cadrin hears the shower. And in a few minutes, she notices steam filling the perimeter of the Jack and Jill bathroom.

After about fifteen minutes later, Vance returned to the bedside wearing a bath towel around his lean waist. He assisted her up from the bed by guiding her hand as though she's stepping from a level higher than ground. Ultimately, he'd helped her to the best seat on Secretariat Lane. He huddles his chin down into the crook of her neck.

"Look at me," Cadrin waved her hand over her entire form, "I hate to put the same clothes back on.

Speaking of clothes, where are mine?"

Thinking about the night before, he smiles.

"My guess would be in the living room. If that's the way you really feel check this out," he grabs her by her curvaceous hips, easing her up from the seat between his legs. Leaving her side, Vance strode to a drawer there in his bedroom. He selected a few items of male clothing from it. He placed them next to her.

"Here you go," he said. He began to put on a pair of blue jeans while she began sorting through the articles of clothing he brought from his drawer.

"What am I going to do with these?" she asked.

"Since you don't want to wear the same clothes back home, maybe you would like to wear one of my sport shirts or t-shirts back to your place," Vance picks up a grey sports shirt, and a pair of black knee length shorts from the bunch, "I think you'll look good in these."

She gave him a naughty look before holding his shirt up against her shoulders.

"I think you might be right. Ooh and this one is sleeveless, and it's cute."

He hugs her.

"Cute? I offer the woman the shirt off my back and she says it's cute," he said with a crisp and playful whisper in her ear.

"It's handsome on you and cute for me," she said as she snuggles into his arms.

"Sorry I can't offer you any pants, but you're welcomed to whatever else works. While you handle that," he kisses her forehead, "I'll be in the kitchen," thirty-five minutes," he confirmed.

"Thirty- five minutes," she concurred.

Before leaving the room, Vance led Cadrin to the door of the bathroom. Slicker.

After Vance had another morning shower, he left stacked on the sink's countertop a couple of folded and fluffed towels, a clean washcloth, toothpaste, new toothbrush, a bottle of lotion, comb and brush all placed for Cadrin's usage. He knows she doesn't quite feel at home. Therefore, he became inspired to do his best at making her as comfortable as possible before she heads back to her own place. While she was showering, he'd brought her purse into the bedroom so whatever she needed from within it, she would have whatever it is at her fingertips.

"Mmm, the food smells so delicious."

After about twenty minutes Cadrin completed her shower. She peeks out into the bedroom to learn if Vance is within reach. She smiled as she heard him in the kitchen working on preparing their breakfast.

"Wow, those biscuits smell wonderful," Cadrin said to herself.

By the time Cadrin finished with her hair and other treatments of pamper, she knows a hot breakfast awaits her. Just a few minutes later, she entered the kitchen. At his table, she sat down in front of grits, scrambled eggs with cheese, slow cooked bacon, and lightly browned biscuits. The last of their breakfast to arrive are glasses of apple juice. Vance took his seat at the table, thinking she's just as beautiful without her makeup. He can't understand why she insist on tussling with it. With or without her makeup he thinks she looks incredibly beautiful.

"Good morning again, you look great," he said while placing a cloth napkin at the side of their plates.

"Thanks. Everything looks so delicious, Vance. You went through all of this trouble for me?"

"You're welcome. It was no trouble at all. I remembered your comment about cooking, so I thought I had better go ahead and throw down," he winks at her with one of his sexy almond shaped eyes. And he is modest, breakfast food isn't the only meal he's great at preparing.

"Yeah, I was curious. But now I don't have to wonder anymore," she said between delicious bites. She continues. "You know, I didn't intend on sounding so doubtful of your ability to cook a decent meal."

"I know you didn't. And right now, you sound like the woman who I made love to last night and this morning."

And he isn't lying. He'd saved the finale for later.

She didn't reply. Quickly she broke eye contact with him the moment his eyes began to speak to her.

"Does he really love me?" she wonders.

Any other time, she would have been thrilled to hear

those words come from a man she's crazy about. Suddenly, she found herself to be deceived by the same heart which previously convinced her with every excuse why she shouldn't get involved with Vance Grayson. Where would the l-word get its nurturing? Her home is in Chicago with no intentions of swapping zip codes.

"Is your breakfast good?"

"It's delicious," she said. She continues eating while Vance sits across from her shirtless in front of his empty plate. He finds himself staring at her every few seconds.

"You look great, too. I really mean it," her eyes went from his handsome face to his bare chest.

"I apologize. Am I distracting you?" Being shirtless at the kitchen table within his own place is no big deal to him. His action is just out of simple appreciation for being in the comforts of his own place, so to speak.

"Not at all, I'm grateful for the view."

Once Vance could take his gaze off her for more than five, he poured himself another glass of juice. Cadrin is doing her best not to catch his gaze. But his stare is so intense, she lost control over her emotions and ended up acknowledging him anyway. Vance took another sip of apple juice and waited for Cadrin to again place her fork back onto her plate.

The night before, Vance had dismissed the flickers of light. The effects of what he saw or only imagined had resurfaced. Taking another sip of juice, his facial expression grimaced at what he now suspects.

"If it's okay with you, I'll see you back to your place whenever you're ready to go. But by all means please take your time."

Once Cadrin finished eating, Vance placed the plates and glasses into the kitchen's sink. Cadrin offered to wash the dishes, he refused her offer. The pair also share the same hospitality. Even though she insisted on taking care of the dishes, she is a guest in his home. He didn't believe in putting her to work, just as she preferred him to park his car in her driveway, and not on the street when he visited her.

Vance placed the dishes into warm sudsy water and began tending to them. Cadrin couldn't resist. Scooping up a handful of suds, she places a poof onto the center of Vance's face. Playfully, he blew the suds from his lips up into the air. Next thing they know they hear a knock at his front door.

"Are you expecting anyone?" Cadrin whispered.

"No. I'm not expecting anyone, especially this time of morning," he whispered while quickly drying his hands before wiping his face. Vance curiously strode towards the front door. The knock came again before he could make any inquiries.

"Vance, its Carmichael."

Standing between the door and Cadrin, in mid-stride Vance stopped.

"Vance its Carmichael! Its Carmichael!" Cadrin said again in a hysterical whisper, "he can't know that I'm here." The doorbell first then Cadrin sang out again. She's losing it.

Quickly Vance knelt, picking up the shirt he'd worn last night. Putting on the fabric Vance walks towards Cadrin.

"Hold it baby, said Vance, "calm down, everything is alright," he said while wiping away remnants of the suds from his nose. Initially, Vance was startled at Carmichael's arrival as well, but he'd managed to keep his composure. Coolly, he assuredly kisses her lips, softly.

"He doesn't have to know you're here and he won't."

This time he kisses her forehead.

"I have to answer the door. Wait in my bedroom and I'll come to you once he leaves," as he spoke to her, he had held her close to him. He'd felt every thump of her racing heartbeat.

He thinks she's so cute in her hysterics. Prior to Carmichael's arrival, the cool and collected woman who had stood before him is now filled with panic.

He almost laughed at the whimsical moment, but his empathy holds the understanding of her concern.

After Cadrin sought cover in Vance's bedroom, he began to work quickly on buttoning his shirt before starting for the front door.

"Hey Carmichael, I wasn't expecting you. Come on in."

Carmichael enters the apartment. By force of habit, he begins to look around the front room. All Cadrin's belongings are behind the closed door of Vance's bedroom.

Although Carmichael is in no position to associate any female items to her, Vance is still glad he'd placed the remainder of her items at her leisure while she had been bathing.

"What's going on? Do we have an emergency? Don't tell me Pete Monahan is stirring things up again."

"Relax Vance, everything's okay. I just wanted to drop by to see how the place is treating you. Forgive me. I should have come by sooner. Actually, Delia is the one who is responsible for making sure everything came together nicely. I left all of the intricate details of the place to her."

"Oh, did you? I didn't know that. Well, yeah Carmichael everything is great. I really like the place. I have no complaints."

"Speaking of Delia, I had her to put together a checklist of some of the items you may need or should have run out of by now," Carmichael handed to Vance the checklist to go over at his convenience.

"Thank you, Carmichael. I'll look this over and get it back to you."

"Or Delia," Carmichael laughs.

Vance cracks a smile, "No that's okay, I'll return it to you."

"Whatever is not on the list and should be just let me know," Carmichael said while heading for the front door. On his way out the door Carmichael began wondering what took Vance so long to open it. To him Vance didn't appear to have been sleeping. He also noticed the pot and pan sitting on the stovetop. Carmichael figured Vance must have been just finishing up with breakfast. The scent of freshly baked bread still fills the air. As the door began closing, Carmichael wonders what would make a man want to bake bread in the morning. Thinking of reasons why, he cracks a smile at one of the explanations as he makes his way back to his car.

Once Vance was certain Carmichael was on his way, he turned and made his way towards the bedroom where Cadrin waits. She'd heard most of his conversation, including the fact a woman is partly responsible for putting together his living arrangements. She also heard Vance mention he prefers to keep the dealings of the apartment between himself and Carmichael.

"Hey, it's me. Carmichael just left."

Cadrin eased out into the hallway. Vance offered her his hand and proceeded to bring her closer to him.

The woman standing in front of him is now at ease and in control of herself. Judging from the look of disappointment in her brown eyes, Vance can tell she's slowly beginning to regret their friendship. It hurt him deeply when she decided to pull against him.

"Cadrin, what's the matter?" he said with concern evident in his voice. "Please don't do this. I promise you Carmichael didn't figure it out. No one knows about us. Everything is okay."

"Okay for whom Vance? getting this far in my career was not easy. Oh no!" she exclaimed. She began to panic again.

Vance countered.

"Cadrin, you're not the only one who stands to lose here,"
he could have kicked himself for appearing to come off
so insensitive.

"Is that what you want Vance, to lose?"

"Cadrin, trust me. I'm taking just as big of a risk in all of this as you are," he took a deep breath. He doesn't want to appear arrogant or even blasé about the entire situation, especially during her weakest moment. And he's not in favor of her walking out of his life. "Listen," he said taking her willing form into his arms again, "I know we've chosen to walk a fine line here and despite the turn of events we're two adults. We are in control of this relationship. Not Carmichael, Jim or anyone else, just us."

Cadrin's eyes searches his own seeking to find any signs of commonality, "What kind of a relationship is this Vance? What are we going to do? I mean come on. We can't run and hide every time we're caught in a compromising situation."

Just to put her at ease again, everything within him wants to tell her no, they can't keep running from and hiding what is going on between them. He wants to share with anyone who will look and listen at the newest joy in his life when he speaks of just how fond of her he has grown to be. He's falling in love with her more and more every day.

Vance gave her what calls for no explanation. He'd gently grabbed her face, leaned in and kissed her lips. Stroking her cheek with the back of his hand he said to her, "You let me worry about us. If you can do that, I promise you nothing will go wrong."

Chapter 18

The Executives

The next morning, the lobby of Johnson Everdeen is definitely abuzz with tender loving care of its own. Blue collar workers work diligently in redecorating and polishing everything from the floor to the wood, and all the windows located within the enormous lower-level lobby.

From the moment the redecorating crew entered the building, Antonio who's the head of Stanford security has been exceptionally busy ensuring the corporation's entire make over process goes smoothly, without even as much as a smudge to be discovered.

He's equipped with his usual gear; an earpiece at his ear, a cell phone at his waist, CB, clipboard, and of course he wouldn't be able to manage without his suave interpersonal skills.

Several levels above are an orchestra of Everdeen shareholders who are on site to meet with Vance and Carmichael. The preliminaries are approaching, and Carmichael needs Vance to assist him in making sure his investors receive the amount of reassurance needed for them to be certain the multi-billion-dollar company is nowhere near folding. Surely if one Everdeen investor decides to fold, his action will result in the other investors to quickly demonstrate a domino effect.

Selecting a date for court appearance was Vance's idea, a strategy he developed in hopes of putting pressure on Stone and Nichols into finally giving up any knowledge of who might be responsible for the unaccounted funds. After the meeting's conclusion, Vance and Carmichael marched into another meeting, the one round table discussion Carmichael needs to devote most of his attention to: a meeting with the CEO of Gory Trust. Gory Trust has the power and the clout to implement a cascade of strong opinions across the board. Because of them, other companies within the industry won't hesitate in pricking Everdeen's ability to remain a staple in such a frugal industry.

Once Gory Trust was informed Carmichael put two point five million dollars on the table, and now those same funds have now turned out to be unaccounted for quickly rose red flags. Gory began to back out of their consideration of a business deal with him.

At the meeting's break Vance headed for one of the elevators. Arriving at the lobby of the first floor, he stepped off the elevator. Greeted with a sign cautioning the strides of everyone's foot movements, Vance took his time moving through the busy lobby.

For a taste of slowly brewed cappuccino, Vance heads for a cup from one of the specialty shops inside the building when he became sidetracked by the appearance of someone much older than himself. A uniformed worker wearing a pair of faded overalls begins to swear at a piece of heavy-duty equipment.

"Awl, come on will ya!" The much older man is a bit stocky and a little under average height. His hair is black and produces streaks of silver hues behind his ears and along his thinning temples. His knuckles looks as though he has been working within the blue-collar field for as long as he can remember.

"Sir, are you able to handle that by yourself?" Vance probed. He didn't want to give the old guy the impression he deems him incapable of managing by himself.

"Good help sure is hard to find," the uniformed worker protested.

"How did your machine get into the lobby?" Vance continues to pry as he looks around for any other guys dressed in similar uniforms.

"The security folks helped me with it. Now they're gone off assisting others I suppose."

"It has been rather busy here today," Vance said of the main lobby. Feeling sorry for the older gentleman, Vance removes his jacket and laid it neatly over the back of one of the empty chairs belonging to the security team. Before he could return from assisting Branford in placing the heavy equipment back onto the van marked Upholstery Cleaning and More, Claude's messenger entered through the revolving doors of Johnson Everdeen. The man proceeded to wait for the return of a lobby attendant.

Branford secured the van's latch and used his faded uniform to dust off his hands.

"I appreciate your help, kind Sir. White shirt and all," he referred to Vance as he doesn't know his name. Usually, guys in executive get ups shunned Branford's blue uniform, constantly avoiding eye contact with him whenever he is on their path.

"It's okay Sir, that's why they make Clorox," Vance said with a smile, "I'm only glad I could help. You take care and have a nice day, Sir." Leaning out of the driver side window, Branford smiled and saluted Vance as he drove the cleaning van away from the side of the curb into the hustle and bustle of traffic.

With his shirt still crisp white, Vance walked back inside the building and headed towards the west exit to retrieve his jacket from the security station where Claude's messenger continues to wait for the return of security. The messenger sees Vance coming towards the lobby. He held the clip board tighter as he backed away from the counter. Not knowing which lie he would repeat first is making him an extremely nervous individual.

Vance believes the fragile man standing in front of the security counter looks a bit pale and scared. He figures the man is obviously worried and heavily agenda driven. Vance said nothing to the man as he proceeded to reach for his jacket when he was erroneously assumed to be a member of security.

"Excuse me, Sir. Will you make sure this reaches Carmichael Lewis?" the messenger asked. He maintains a tight grip on the clipboard he's holding down by his side. The young man quickly placed an envelope onto the counter. Vance was seconds away in politely correcting the young man. Before he could do so, his vision ran across the sender's name on the envelope which had been placed before him.

"Stone and Nichols, what the..." Vance had previously informed Carmichael to refrain from any contact with Jim unless the event is by his instruction. Carmichael is a little hotheaded. Vance thought against his wishes, his client might have contacted Jim anyway.

Vance studies the young man. He notices the visitor appears anxious, in a hurry to leave the building. Considering the nervousness of the young man and the return of any members of security, Vance had only seconds to make a split decision. Sign now and accept the envelope, or waste time and end up allowing security to accept it for him. If he accepted it and came under scrutiny, he figures he can get by with his status, saying the envelope is a personal delivery addressed to his attention.

Liking the way everything sound, Vance coolly grabbed a pen from the security desk. Before he could sign, the young man attempted to present him with the envelope.

"You have important documents for Carmichael Lewis, huh," Vance said while he watches the messenger pay more attention to the envelope than to his question.

"Oh, and you'll need to sign this," the messenger didn't present Vance with a pen, so Vance resumed with his intentions to use one of the pens from the desk of security to sign for the envelope. After completing his signature, he watched the young man make an expeditious exit through the set of revolving doors. Vance began to look around for any signs of security. His eyes fell on the row of surveillance monitors lining the lower deck of the counter. The screens are a clear indicator prompting Vance he should quickly find somewhere else to be. With pen still in hand, he steps out from behind the security desk. He placed the envelope and pen within an inside pocket of his jacket before going for that cup of cappuccino.

On his way out of the shop, he remembered something very odd happening after the young man reached the opposite side of the revolving doors. Vance had seen him toss what appeared to be balled up paper into the garbage. Cautiously, Vance made a dignified stride across the lobby. Calmly, he pushes open the door before stepping onto the platform. Vance reaches into the garbage can which doubles as an ash tray. Grabbing the first balled up piece of white paper sitting on top, he tries to hold only the corners of the once discarded paper as he opens it out. He sees crinkled up letters of the bogus signature which had been no longer needed by the guy who left the building in a hurry. Vance smoothed out the sheet of paper folding it as he steps back into Johnson Everdeen.

Chapter 19

The Executives

Days later, Vance continues to badger himself. "*Good Guy or Bad Guy?*" Or is he plain neutral? He sort of smiled at the fact of how this case manages to cause him to experience more than one first. The fact of his role reversal at the security desk came with its own price. Somehow, falling in love with Cadrin Porter is without regret. Having accepted that envelope is against his ethical standards. He realizes if he were to utilize it as evidence to the court, many questions will come his way. How will he respond to the judge when asked of his whereabouts when he received the package? Even better, how will he explain how the piece of information came to be in his possession?

If he does come under scrutiny, he could always choose not to divulge his source. Depending on the presiding judge and with the help of Jim's lawyer, the information would be declared unsustainable in court. Vance never subjected himself to so much uncertainty. Since the beginning of Everdeen's turmoil, the envelope is possibly the best form of proof when it comes to proving Jim's guilt. Surely, the unopened envelope contains a credible explanation behind this entire matter. Guilt? Up until now, Vance believed Jim to be just as baffled by the allegations against Stone and Nichols as much as he himself.

Bringing his elbows to rest on the conference room table, Vance leans forward. His hands cupped, coming to rest below his chin. What if, just what if Jim Grainger is in fact guilty. This whole contrast of blame and honor is beginning to fashion the behavior of oil when mixed with water.

It's getting late and Vance decided he needs to make his way back to the corporate apartment to shower and change into a fresh pair of clothing. He promised Cadrin another one of his foot massages over at her place.

The next morning Vance rose and gave his tense form an adequate back stretch. He reached for the keys to his car then hastened for the doorway, just then becoming aware he failed to conceal the bantering envelope. He leaned over the table to retrieve it. Immediately, he placed it within the inside pocket of his jacket and headed out the door of the corporate apartment for his commute to Everdeen.

After what had been a hectic day in the office of Carmichael Lewis, Vance was ready to get the heck out of there for the day. Before he could turn around, to his surprise he heard the voice of a female. The sound of her voice is rather familiar.

"If I didn't know any better, I'd say you're unable to tolerate my presence." Yes, her voice is very familiar. He'd done so well in maintaining a low profile until he had just about forgotten about her.

Vance turns around. He notices first her curvaceous legs, a caramel complexion. His eyes travel her figure flattering skirt. Finally, his eyes rest on her face.

"Delia," he spoke with faint recollection. Realizing his stunned expression must have offended her in some way, he tried not to lavish the obvious.

"You look kind of bewildered, almost shocked to see me here. Anyway, what kept you here so late?"

"Carmichael and I had some paperwork to go over followed by a few phone calls we had to make. As a matter of fact, you just missed him."

"I know, I didn't come in here to see him," she admitted.

Without a single word, Vance began to walk towards the doorway where she stands. After two steps forward, he stops and watches her. She continues to stand on the same spot, falsely barricading Vance's access to the corridor. Vance rolls back and forth the keys he's holding in his hand.

"You didn't answer my first question, Vance."

And he wouldn't. He again walked in her direction only to stop less than arm's length of her.

"Delia, trust me, I've known all along of your interest in me. I would have been a fool if I were unable to have noticed your not so candid efforts~"

"But you chose to ignore me anyway. Why?" she demanded.

He wanted to suit her with a reasonable explanation without exuding the nature of a conceded man. But once again Delia's emotions took the lead. She began to paint her initial vision of him.

"I remember your first visit to Johnson Everdeen. You were clean cut, attentive, and attractive. To this day each of those adjectives still defines you to a T. Since then, I've been coming on to you rather strongly. I don't believe my demeanor was earth moving. Yes, it was strong enough, and for that I apologize to you."

Although he's shocked, Vance is acceptive of her apology. He nodded. With their eyes locked she looks deeply into his gaze, hers filled with reasoning. Vance knows her expression is his opportunity to enlighten her on why he chose to dodge ball so well. For a mere second, he broke eye contact with her. When his eyes fell upon her again, he couldn't shun the fact that at this very moment he realizes he doesn't want to hurt her feelings. He knows he must choose his responses carefully. The truth is his best policy.

The fierce Delia he had come to know is changing right before his eyes, her personality now almost demure. Realizing sugar filled words will only act as a cover, Vance admitted to himself he owes her a decent explanation.

"Delia, I'm not going to take you around the world or sidestep, taking you to the four corners of the earth about this," Vance's backward steps brought him to the conference room table where he sat atop. Due to his six feet two-inch frame, his feet continue to rest comfortably on the carpet. Delia doesn't want to know where he is going with such a statement. But she realizes what she needs the most; for him to continue in expressing exactly what is on his mind, and not dance around her, again. He had done enough of that already.

Delia maintains her stance within the doorway and began to nervously fidget with the bangle bracelet which matches the outfit she's wearing. For the first time, in a very long time a man caused her to allow her nerves to get the better of her. To the contrary, an ounce of hope for Vance's romantic fulfillment is still evident in her eyes.

"I'm involved with someone," he studied her for any signs of emotion. When he'd said those words, Delia's nostrils enlarged. In secret, Vance swears her anger is hot enough to toss flames. Although she's hot with anger, his words had come bitterly cold. As a result, her soul began to shake, by the second the room became increasingly quiet.

Trying to conceal her hurt, she attempted to form words, but the terms were so adamantly disobedient, any furthered chastisement to bring them forward would have hailed puddles of water in her eyes. For repair, Delia begins to gather every bit of courage she can discretely salvage. Vance's news is much more than what she was ready to receive.

Vance lowered his gaze to the floor. His focus quickly fell on the set of keys he's holding in his hand.

"*Cadrin,*" he mouthed her name to himself. He doesn't want to keep her waiting much longer.

Breaking the news of his involvement to another woman wasn't the one, two, three explanation he thought it would be. He hated to leave Delia in the state she's presently in. He doesn't want to say anything else, figuring at this point he'd said enough. Anymore words from him are sure to do more harm than good.

Once Delia became anew, she wanted to make good use of the moment and coolly remove herself from his company but being Delia, she didn't allow it. She needed to investigate a little further to find out whatever else she can.

"I see. So," she said with a touch of wind flowing from her lips, "someone from Maryland?" she wanted to believe his lack of interest in her is due to an established union. Surely, not a recent one can be responsible for keeping them from getting together. She certainly believes a man of his magnitude had to be involved prior to leaving for Chicago.

Vance wants to make the moment less offensive, siding with her assumption. She wouldn't have any reason not to believe him but lying to her would most likely invite opportunity.

"No, umm," Vance ran his hand over the hairs of his head, "I met her since being here in Chicago."

Well, that confirmed it. Delia realized he had no interest in her from the start. For a minute, Vance wonders how much more Delia can take before she will throw a fit or something else at him. Vance searches her eyes for any resentment. She appears to have accepted well the shocking news he provided her. But he's still unsure of her ability to refrain from giving anymore advances.

"I see, wow um, I should have known. A catch of a man like yourself; it is easy to understand you would be attached."

Vance knows he needs to get out of there and quick. The last thing he needs for anyone to see is Delia all over him. Surprisingly, to allow for Vance's exit from the conference room, Delia moved aside. Once Vance made it to the door, he turned around to offer her brief consolation. A simple hug. Intuitively, she felt his empathy and with only a wave of her hand she declined his offer to hold her within a comforting embrace. He respected her decision and bid her a good night.

It isn't like Vance to be late for anything he has prior knowledge of. Punctuality is just one of the things he prides himself on. He's late. He hopes Cadrin will forgive him and will still allow him the pleasure of kissing her beautiful smile again. His day had been determined to get the better of him, and right about now he needs such kiss rather badly.

Prior to seeing Cadrin again, every situation he encountered left him with unanswered questions, starting with learning the true identity of the nervous individual who came to Johnson Everdeen with an envelope naming Stone and Nichols as its sender. If Cadrin ever finds out, will she be disappointed in him for the way he gained possession of it? Will Delia make any more advances possibly ruining things between Vance and Cadrin? Although Vance has no intentions of considering Delia beyond work relations, his heart still went out to her. His lack of conceit and compassion is one of the many traits Cadrin admires so much within him.

After coming to a halt, he finally pulls his car into Cadrin's driveway. He climbed out of the vehicle. By force of habit, he enables the car's alarm and began traveling the edged-out walkway. With as much as his presence, her door opens. There she stands in front of him all aglow over his arrival. He takes her into his arms, gently hugging her around her waist. By her touch alone, she can draw every ounce of tension right out of him. Reluctant to release each other, they finally did. Vance stepped inside and locked the door behind himself.

From the foyer, he can see the living room has been turned into a mini spa. She hadn't counted him out. From the looks of the room's layout, she has every intention of making sure he will live up to the promise he made to her, late or not.

"I apologize for not being here sooner, on time to be exact. I returned home to change into jeans and so forth."

She smiles at him.

Vance removed his shoes and sat down on the floor of the living room. She joined him. He thinks she looks absolutely incredible as always. She's dressed in a form fitting pastel blue slip dress with spaghetti straps, and a pair of matching pastel blue leggings. A perfect picture they've created, she up against his dark blue jeans, brown suede and corduroy buttoned down long sleeve shirt. Cadrin moves closer to him, she became nestled into her favorite seat. Vance removed a portion of a strand of her hair overlaying her shoulder, gently he places it where it can begin its cascade down her back. Tenderly, he spoils her with kisses to the side of her neck.

"It looks good on you," he said of the gold chain and pendant he'd purchased for her.

She shifted in his arms, "*Why had he been so late?*" she wonders. Cadrin isn't used to him being late for anything. He didn't offer her a decent explanation and she hadn't bothered to call him. She thought maybe he was just working late at the office or probably watching the game with Troy. If their favorite team is up, the Grayson brothers are sure to be somewhere tuning in. She presses further, *"Could his failure to arrive promptly be due to a woman?"* She didn't want to fathom such thought any further. She didn't want to question him, fearing he would again provide her with half truths. He had lied to her once before.

Cadrin began to feel he very well could have eased her into a relationship with him. Maybe he's using her as leverage, a fool perhaps. She thought maybe he and his client are just waiting for the right opportunity to get the best of her and Jim Grainger.

Seeming to unintentionally shut out the fact Vance is within such close proximity of her, she squirms a little in his arms.

"Are you okay? You seem to be a little restless," he said.

"I'm fine," was her confident reply. She lied. To tell him what she's really thinking is tagged with too much speculation. Their night is supposed to be one of rest and relaxation. Stirring up negative impacts will erase any chance at accomplishing such. Cadrin knows she is probably overreacting, so she snuggles against his chest. He welcomes her.

"Are you okay?" he questioned her again.

She nodded.

"I think it's time for your foot massage," Vance removed his jacket and tossed it over onto the sofa. He began to look over the array of foot oils and massage lotions contained by a wicker caddy lined with tan fabric.

"You have a great selection here," he winked at her, "to start, I'm going to ask you to place your left foot here," Vance holds out his hands for her compliance. He began with her arch. Cadrin didn't want to appear gullible, weakening at the slightest touch from him. So, she avoided eye contact with him by putting her focus on one of the lit candles which showcases one of the far corners of her living room. Closing her eyes, she began to become lost in his smooth strokes. But she couldn't leave alone the fact of his lateness.

"So, how did it go at the office today?" she said with her eyes still closed, afraid if she opens them, she will witness a lie being told.

"Where did that come from?" he wondered of her curiosity. Vance resumed in massaging her feet. Be it Delia or some other woman, Cadrin has nothing to worry about.

"You know, it went…it went okay actually. Despite our incapability to wrap things up early, everything went okay. His thoughts shifted back to his prior moments with Delia. Cadrin has nothing to worry about when it comes to the welfare of she and Vance's relationship, maybe except for the fact his new interest in life has yet to meet his family. To be more specific, his mother and father. From the way he speaks of them she knows they are still with him. Cadrin's hinting about why he had been so late caused him to become somewhat concerned. Had she somehow learned of Delia's obvious attraction to him? For a few seconds, he thought about the possibility.

"Not hardly," he assured himself.

Vance gently reunited Cadrin's foot to the carpet. He's ready to proceed again. Her compliance was followed by sheer delight. He'd outdone the last foot massage as far as she is concerned. She silently prayed duplication will continue to be a small effort for him. During the foot massage Cadrin's posture is a backwards lean, the palms of her hands help in supporting her recline. Purely content, she traded her half recline for a full one.

In a partial push up formation, Vance's form hovers over Cadrin's. Bending his elbows, Vance came in for a kiss then his arms straightened. Again, his elbows bend before giving her lips another kiss. He separated his mouth from hers, but not for long.

At the seams, Cadrin grabs his open shirt; it lightly blows underneath the air of the ceiling vent. Trying to pull his sexy body closer to hers is something else. He began teasing her even more by resisting against her slow, persistent and steady pull of his shirt. Quickly, he gave in and deepened the playful kisses he had given to her just a few seconds ago.

"You know due diligence is key to a more productive outcome," he said.

Her eyes immediately opened at the deliverance of such an unbashful comment. Cadrin couldn't help but raise her head a little before giving him her wide - eyed look, the same one he first saw inside of Vintage.

He then smiled widely at her and gave her the sexiest under breath laugh she'd ever heard come from a man. Then mannishly he said, "I thought we were still talking about work!"

Her eyes playfully squinted at his.

"No, you weren't," she said with a chuckle, "you were talking seduction."

Smiling, Vance gave her foot a gentle squeeze. Before he could speak, Cadrin's phone began to ring. While Cadrin attended to the phone, Vance was reminded of how they were last interrupted by Carmichael when he'd stopped by the apartment unannounced. After being told Delia took care of and finalized the details of his living arrangements, he figures Carmichael and his secretary has a key to the place, leading him to think maybe Delia isn't as forthcoming as he and Carmichael believes her to be. Nonetheless, Vance isn't about to allow either of them to parade with himself and Cadrin. If Vance hadn't answered the door, it would have been interesting to learn if Carmichael would have entered anyway. Vance's facial expression tightened at the thought.

Through the anger, Vance did realize Carmichael has every right to gain entry of the corporate apartment without his permission; his living quarters are through his client's own financial doings.

Upon Cadrin's return, she found Vance in what appears to be a revolutionized state.

"What are you up to now?" she spoke with delight in her eyes.

"I'm thinking about us and our privacy. Do you like my apartment?" he watched as she settled down close to him.

"Uh huh, I love the apartment," she grabbed a bottle of one of the massage lotions from the table. In a waving motion, she hands it to Vance. He politely took it from her grasp.

"Although you love it, what do you have to say to no more compromised moments at my place? Like the one when Carmichael dropped by unannounced." Cadrin looks at him with a big smile on her face as she softly bites down on her lower lip.

"I think I love that idea a lot."

"Well then, on that note I'll start checking out some hotel suites. I'll try to locate a place comparable of the corporate apartment Johnson Everdeen establishes for all of their out-of-town associates."

"Do you think Carmichael will mind your leaving? He may be steered to the impression you didn't take too kindly of him dropping by the other day."

"No, I don't think he will believe that to be the reason. He'll probably feel I have the desire to separate my personal time from business," he gave her a wink, "if not, that's what I'll tell him if he questions me on it."

Vance opens the bottle of massage lotion, "I'm sure personal time is something my client can relate to," he said before he gave a reassuring kiss to Cadrin's forehead and her lips.

Chapter 20

The Executives

"What kind of a relationship is this Vance?"

"What are we going to do?
I mean come on. Vance, we can't run and hide every time we're caught in a compromising situation."

"Excuse me Sir, would you make sure this reaches Carmichael Lewis?"

Two weeks ago, Vance saw Cadrin back to her place where he waited while she made the necessary transformations before she headed to Stone and Nichols. More situations had occurred around him faster than he can provide any answers to or otherwise give resolution. His inquisitive nature is without a doubt overwhelmed. Nothing is adding up.

Out of more than just a demonstration of his chivalry, weeks ago Vance accompanied Cadrin back to her place to secretly learn if anything would further rouse what he suspected to be true. But nothing out of the ordinary had stood out. If what he suspects is in fact true, he and Cadrin had been photographed prior to arriving back at his place.

He'd concluded the churn of events is geared towards himself and not Cadrin. Vance is certain no one at Johnson Everdeen are aware of his relationship with the publicist, he and his lady *had* been very careful. Vance wonders who had taken an interest in him, and why had they?

The day of their face-to- face meeting at Stone and Nichols, Cadrin's stand up was immaculate. She hadn't even blinked twice in his direction. She was scared and understandably so. She needed to do what she felt was wise in order to protect her career. Vance wants very badly to tell her he suspects at some point, he had unknowingly become some source's focal point, and the same is possibly true when it comes to her. Just his concern alone isn't enough. He knows she has every right to know what is possibly developing around them. Vance had found himself exactly where he had once been when he'd sat down for the first meal he'd shared with Cadrin; between uncertainty and deception.

Once Vance came out of his daydreaming, he ran his hand over the slick hairs of his chin. His love for Cadrin told him exactly what he must do. He must tell the love of his life their relationship has possibly been exposed.

After making lunch plans with Cadrin, Vance continued to hold onto the phone after the call ended. No definite time had been set for their lunch date. He just told her the later the better. Pounding the phone's receiver into the palm of his hand, Vance looks over at the unopened envelope. Learning of its contents has the potential of making things much more complicated.

Vance assumed Carmichael isn't expecting the delivery which now poses as a possible explanation to the most recent activities he has experienced.

Deciding he'd waited long enough, Vance picked up the envelope. He turned it slowly about his grasp, eventually clamping it between his index and forefinger. Stalling, he began tapping it on the granite countertop. Wanting to wait no more, he began to open the envelope. What he read caused him to swear aloud. The letter poses a countersuit to Johnson Everdeen if they don't abandon their pending suit against Stone and Nichols. At the letter's conclusion, it displays Jim Grainger as the sender, showing off fancy engravings to a clean background of white paper. Vance took in a deep breath. He exhaled slowly, too slow. He slammed the envelope and the letter onto the countertop. Vance had been certain that by the time Jim unveiled a counter suit, he and Carmichael would have gotten much closer to learning the whereabouts of the two point five million dollars. And from the judge's desk, Vance and his client has been given until the day prior to their scheduled court appearance to cease action if they are still unable to submit substantial proof of Jim's guilt.

Given the situation Jim is presently in, Vance figures a countersuit is characteristic of Jim. But the communication he read is way outside of his earlier projections. Vance thought tiresomely of the message. Personally, he believes Jim Grainger to be innocent. No signs had been given to cause him to think otherwise.

"Why now?" Vance spoke aloud of the sender's timeliness, and of the flashes of light he glimpsed after he and Cadrin's night out on the town. Jim never wanted to go to court in the first place. As they all had sat around the conference room table, Jim and his legal representation had every opportunity to present their threat of a countersuit, but they refrained from doing so. Vance slowly tapped the fingers of his right hand on the countertop's surface. *"What turn of events could have transpired which were not evident at the time of the last meeting?"* Vance wonders. Something isn't right and Vance can't quite put his finger on it. His thoughts shifted back to the young man who delivered the envelope. Judging from the stranger's demeanor, Vance figures he knows way more than just the name on the envelope he delivered.

If Jim Grainger or his lawyer decided to present them with a countersuit, one of the two could have done just as they did before when they'd taken the liberty in suggesting another assimilation of the two parties. But instead, they've resorted to outlandish behavior. Things are beginning to add up for Vance. If the suit ended up going before a judge, there is someone out there who has dire interest in loosing something very important. Something like two point five million. Vance feels strongly the responsible party can no way be Jim Grainger. Personally, Vance still believes Jim to be innocent. Whoever the culprit, he or she is recklessly concerned enough to have sent; as strange as he was, a nervous individual out to Johnson Everdeen to act on their behalf. Vance swore at the peculiar situation.

Cadrin pulled into the driveway of her home. Before she could exit the sedan, Vance pulled his car in next to hers. Vance got out of his car and strode around to the driver side of Cadrin's Lexus. He looks interesting, serious, and sexy as always. Opening the driver side door for her, he quickly became pleasantly mesmerized by the scent of her perfume.

"I hope you're still hungry. I stopped by Kirkland's to buy us lunch."

Vance gently took the twisted straw handles of the oversized brown bag from her grasp.

"I sure am," he continued holding the car door open for her.

Vance walks a few steps behind Cadrin, watching as she fiddles with her keys. Once inside the house, Vance strode to the kitchen and began removing their lunch from the bag while Cadrin looks on from her living room. Again, she found herself admiring him. He's dressed in a pair of semi casual black slacks and a comparable long-sleeved blue-collar shirt that's buttoned at the wrists. A couple of buttons over his chest are left undone. She smiles to herself, *"Is there anything this man can do without looking so damn sexy?"*

Vance exudes a tactful moral standard along with a disciplined disposition about himself, each looks outstanding on him. He wears those attributes about as well as he does his attire with great features to seal the deal.

"You sit down right here my lady and I'll get us more ice for the drinks," Vance began making his way to the fridge as he carries a set of cups. He waited as the ice dispenser filled each one with ice. In doing so, he happened to catch Cadrin's eyes gazing over at him. She'd kicked off her shoes already and had taken a seat at the table before Vance could walk away from the ice dispenser. He returned to the table wearing that sexy smile of his. He placed an ice filled cup at each of their place setting before leaning over and passionately kissing her lips.

"I was surprised you wanted a late lunch today. I thought maybe since you were able to leave Johnson Everdeen early you would have already eaten. Not that I don't enjoy your company. I'm glad you called me," she said.

He smiled at her.

"I'm glad you wanted my company," Vance enjoys her company very well. And in his mind, he knows the true reason of why he needed to see her.

Vance looks over at their dessert. A dampened receipt lay on top of the plastic and foggy container.

"I hope your pastrami stack is okay," Cadrin said as she poured her room temperature drink over the cold cubes of ice.

"It's good, so is everything else," he said before biting into one of the crunchy bread sticks brushed with olive oil.

"Are things pretty quiet at Stone and Nichols?"

"Vance, you know I can't talk with you about anything in relation to the pending suit."

He nodded.

"Yeah, I know you can't. I was only asking in general."

She laughed at herself.

"Ok, well in that case I'm just glad to have left the office before Tim Davenport got another opportunity to annoy me."

"Who is Tim Davenport? Wait a minute," Vance put his elbows on the table then brought his fists to fall underneath the dimple on his chin, "you mean Tim Davenport as in The Weekly Chronicles?"

"Yes, that would be the one," she said exhaustingly.

Vance inquisitively stared at her.

"He contacted you?"

"Yes. He wanted me to pass along his contact information to give to Jim Grainger. He wanted to present him with a chance to offer his side of the story without any major interference. Can you believe the nerve of him?"

"Sorry, can't say that I don't. What did you tell him?"

Cadrin hesitated. It's Vance's humor which provided her the comfort in continuing.

"Basically, I told him we don't have any time for his crap. I don't think he appreciated my honesty."

"How long ago has it been since you last spoke to him?" Vance pried.

"I would say about two weeks ago. The more I think about it I'm certain. Yes, it was two weeks ago. It was the same day we went to hear jazz."

"Oh, really now," Vance became preoccupied with a moment of resolve. *"Tim Davenport. That would explain the flashes of light. Davenport had someone to secure photographs of us while we had been out together,"* Vance is sure of it. There's no way he can be wrong. With no knowledge of what was on Vance's mind when he called her for a lunch date, Cadrin continues to enjoy her food.

The men in her life before Vance came to be probably would have swum in the gumption of leading Cadrin to believe the entire picture taking incident was her fault. Taking a self-centered move, attempting to place themselves in the clear. Not Vance Grayson. He's different; game playing is not his style neither being inconsiderate, not by a long shot. Many of his male colleagues had used one woman after the other for her professional clout. The women were nothing more to them than a melted down pot of gold. Some of the fellas took from it whatever they could get out of them.

As much as it hurts him to know he still stands a chance at losing Cadrin, he'd rather tell her the truth as opposed to playing possum at her doorstep.

"You think he would be partial to obtaining pictures of us, together?" Vance's look of deep concern shakes her.

"I don't know. Vance what are you asking me? Better yet what is it you're trying to tell me?" Cadrin frantically rose from the table. Vance rose a split second afterwards. He reached for her, and she quickly backed out of his reach while she'd thrown him a look he's never seen before on her face. Betrayal is her expression. It's really going to work on Vance's heart.

"The last time you were over to my place, the time when you stayed the night," judging from the worried look in her eyes Vance can feel his forehead heating up with sweat, "I suspected I had possibly been photographed. After you entered the corporate apartment, it was before I had a chance to step inside is when I caught flickers of light." Cadrin eyes closed in disgust over what's she's hearing. "I didn't really see anything or anyone, so I dismissed it as only being my imagination, anything but the media." Cadrin turned her back to him. "We were so careful. Once you told me about Tim Davenport my suspicion was confirmed," he walks towards her. Cadrin turned to face him.

"He got pissed during our conversation. He has photos?" she doesn't want to believe her relationship with Vance will be made public.

"Now wait a minute," Vance said as he lightly touches her arm, "we don't know for sure."

Once more she backed away from him.

"Stop it!" she fussed.

"Have you heard from him again since speaking with him two weeks ago?"

"No! Why would he call? He has no reason to call again, he has pictures now," she sarcastically stated.

She's visibly upset and not thinking clearly. But Vance realizes what she temporarily can't. If there are pictures for the media, most likely he or she would have heard from the local press a long time ago. Vance figures Tim Davenport may be responsible for the picture taking, but he is clueless when it comes down to who is behind the envelope.

If Carmichael finds out about his relationship with Cadrin, his client will ruin any chances of Vance learning the identity of the person who delivered the request for his client to drop the suit against Stone and

Nichols. Instead, everyone will be made aware of the love affair encompassed between two feuding Chief Executive Officers.

Cadrin can feel the lingering stare of Vance's intense gaze at her back. Refusing to be receptive of his presence, she's doing everything in her campaign to override the feelings of the love she has for him. Right now, he has suddenly become a painful reminder of heartbreaks from her past.

"Cadrin, please say something. I need to know what's on your mind."

Hurt, she still refuses to face him. Cadrin holds her head to one side, with her back to him she wipes a tear stream off the side of her cheek.

Vance looks on; he can feel himself slipping away from her heart; it's an agonizing battle for him.

"Vance, this is a mistake. This thing between us should have never happened. How could I have been so naïve? My career is over, and I don't have anyone to blame except myself."

Vance is surely hurt. She hadn't even seen it necessary to refer to their relationship as something meaningful. Having categorized their relationship under simple reference is suitable in her teary eyes.

"Vance, I need for you to go. Leave now. I should have listened to myself."

He isn't walking away that easily.

"Cadrin, you don't mean that. Before you met me, your heart was broken by someone who was a fool.

Before I met you, my life was just that. My life. It never had occurred to me what I was craving until I met you. For more than a year, I worked at making myself content through the demands of my profession, leaning on acknowledgement and bettin on reprise. I did such a great job at it that something within refused to allow me to believe a healthy relationship was possible. You've shown me one can be just that. I'm in love with you. I didn't plan on the underhandedness of the likes of Tim Davenport or Carmichael stopping by the apartment after my being there month after month without any visitors except yourself and my brother."

Holding her head to one side, Cadrin still kept her back to Vance. He wishes he can erase the pain she's feeling.

"Vance, I just want you to leave," she said with tears in her voice. Vance looks so pitiful as he watches the one woman who effortlessly pulled him across the divide of leisure and professionalism as she goes into heavy doubt of him. He knows there isn't much more he can do at this moment to make her want to change her mind about him.

Vance opens his wallet to retrieve the cost of what Cadrin spent towards their lunch; he places the bills on the kitchen table amongst their leftovers.

Cadrin heard car keys being taken from the uncovered tabletop.

"I don't believe you planned on those things either," Vance said.

The next sound Cadrin hears is Vance walking towards her front door. She turns a little more in the opposite direction to ensure she wouldn't meet the one look in his eyes which caused her to fall in love with him.

Vance opens the door. Realizing he had done that of which she told him, it took her only moments to try and steal another glance of him. Racing over to the window overlooking her driveway, it was from there Cadrin stood gazing through the blinds of her sitting room, her knees now weak with regret. She watched as Vance slowly returned to his car. The moment he set foot inside the vehicle; his gaze retraced his way to her arms begging for the comfort of her forgiveness. He had promised her he would look after not only her interest, but his own as well. He failed them both.

"If that pursuit becomes a battle leave her alone,"
the words that had come from his Dad fell coldly upon him. But the struggle he's now in isn't by Cadrin's hands. He had gained her trust and her love the right way. Now the war, oh boy the war. He's in the middle now and have no choice other than to fight his way out.

From behind the steering wheel of his car Vance sits for a while, all the long his heart aches for the love that pushed him away. Finally, he started the car's engine then backed out of the driveway.

Chapter 21

The Executives

"That envelope should have reached Carmichael's desk by now. I tell ya, we have got to stop anymore attention from going forward on this," Claude said while easing his chair out from the desk of his office suite, his stare is very studios of the confidant.

"You did take it there. Didn't you? Claude asked the messenger.

"I don't know if he got it, but I left it there."

"Well, Jim should have heard something by now," Claude spoke adamantly, "two months is all we got," he banged his fist on the oak desk. Claude had heard enough from the messenger who is standing on the other side of the door. He told him to leave. And he did, in a noticeably big hurry, just as he'd done after he'd obtained Vance's 'signature.'

"After you overheard that publicist talking to The Weekly Chronicles, we should have come up with a better plan," Claude finished in a nasty tone.

"Let's just wait it out, I'm sure there will be a press conference soon. Carmichael will back off, you'll see."

"Jim will be a fool to go up against Everdeen. They've got billons of dollars which can destroy Stone and Nichols," Claude continued, "and that is just the reason why your idea of trying to get Carmichael to call this whole thing off is crazy. I don't know why I keep listening to you. Carmichael is not afraid of a meager countersuit."

"Be as little as it may, Stone and Nichols is a rather sizeable entity with its share of clout I remind you. It's your greediness which has gotten us into this mess," the confidant happily reminded Claude.

"Quiet!" Claude shouted, "I don't remember you protesting when all of this got started," Claude rose from the chair. Pacing about the floor he began to seize the congratulatory look of someone who has just been recognized as the next billionaire in the world of development.

"We're so close," Claude made reference of fame, "and we could be even closer if we can get our hands on that money," Claude said while looking out from the window of his office suite enjoying the city's impressive skyline. The warmth of the rays from the sun beats upon his bearded face.

Turning away from the window, Claude folds his arms across his own chest. He's beginning to think sending a Joe Blow to deliver the envelope had been a poor choice on his part. He'd wanted to stay away from using outside assistance, feeling as though a bigger mess will be made of the scandal he helped create.

"None of this would be happening if Gory Trust hadn't been given the heads up. Carmichael wasn't supposed to become aware of the two point five million dollars until after it was in our hands," the confidant said.

Claude appears as though he didn't hear him make mention of the slip-up, "What? Why are you looking at me like that? I knew we shouldn't have sent him over to Johnson Everdeen," Claude continues to complain about, Joe Blow.

"Calm down. I overheard the conversation of Jim's publicist when she was on that phone call with Tim Davenport, and when she was making plans with Everdeen's attorney. We're still ahead of them so stop your complaining."

"And there's another thing! You had no business at Stone and Nichols!" Claude angrily said.

"Okay, true. However, look at what I found out while I was there, so quit with your complaining. After I heard all of what I needed to hear, I high tailed it out of there."

Carefully taking in the details of how all the events unfolded, Claude nodded.

"What should we do in the meantime? Just sit around waiting?" the confidant asked.

"Exactly, that is exactly what we will do. Soon enough, one of them will help us to determine our next move."

"Maureen, the moment Ms. Porter arrive make sure she receives my itinerary for the week, and please make her aware of the changes regarding the dinner meeting we'll be attending on Wednesday evening. If she should finish up before my conference calls are done for the day, please inform her we'll talk when she gets back here on tomorrow."

"Sure thing, Mr. Grainger. I'll let her know," Maureen promised as she watched Jim leave the office carrying his smart phone. Maureen peeked at the itinerary before laying it aside.

Taking a tissue from the decorative box at the corner of her desk, Maureen removed her eyewear. Gently, she dabbed beads of sweat from her forehead as well as from the bridge of her nose. Any mentioning of anything remotely close to the pending lawsuit spins Maureen into an acute frenzy. If it's left up to her, she would seek some institution to donate the amount of the missing funds. And they all would just move on acting as though nothing ever happened. Maureen the peacekeeper; the umbrella over everybody's uh ohs. Just through her words alone brought forth the brighter side of rampant predicaments. But this is much bigger than what Maureen can handle. Interrupting Maureen's thoughts, Cadrin enters the twelfth-floor lobby, her voice carries over the large wait area.

"Good morning, Maureen," Cadrin spoke as she made her way to her office. Before she could get to its entrance, Maureen met her halfway the floor.

"Ms. Porter, I'm glad I got the chance to see you before I headed upstairs. Jim has conference calls of which he'll be presumably attending to all day. He wanted me to make sure you know of his whereabouts, and this is a copy of his schedule. This week's dinner meeting is included."

Cadrin briefly scanned the information, paying most of her attention to the middle of the page where mid-week information regarding when the dinner meeting is scheduled to take place. Ironically, Wednesdays were the days she and Vance would if possible, set aside giving them assuredness in preparing to wind down for the week's end, together.

"All right Maureen, thank you for letting me know."

"There's no problem, Ms. Porter," Maureen began to walk away just when the look on Cadrin's face began to resonate with her.

"Cadrin, are you feeling alright sweetie?"

Stunned by Maureen's question, Cadrin stated a simple yes, but Maureen knows better. She figures her troubled expression is due to some looker of a man. She thought maybe Cadrin was to meet with him, and the changes in Jim's schedule is possibly preventing her from doing so. Whatever the case, Maureen doesn't want to get too nosey due to the fact Cadrin is a newbie to the corridors of Stone and Nichols. Maureen began to walk away again when she remembered the rest of Jim's instructions.

"Oh, Jim said just in case he's not able to meet with you today, he'll speak with you on tomorrow," she said with a smile.

"Okay Maureen, thank you," Cadrin inserted the itinerary into the briefcase she carries daily. She was about to enter her office when she heard the wheels of the mail cart approaching her. She turned around to see the mail clerk coming in her direction. Their eyes meet.

"Good morning, Ms. Porter. This came for you," the mail clerk said. He handed to her a generous sized flat package before walking away.

Cadrin hopes Vance would try to contact her. Getting all thoughts of him out of her mind is one of the most difficult things she ever had to do. Falling for him proved to be one of the easiest. Although her attraction for him came with tempting and provoking technicalities, she had decided to take a chance on their mutual desire. Cadrin wonders if she is being unfair or even self serving. She and Vance had been caught off guard and should have been more careful; using more discretion and creativity when it came to when and where the two of them would spend their time together. She couldn't believe she had been such a fool for love. She has a career to protect and a reputation to uphold.

Cadrin looked at the sender's name. She did the best she could to discretely conceal the large envelope from others who are passing by offering her their good mornings. Privacy is priceless.

Taking count of the wording which informs handlers to be protective of the materials the envelope holds inside, she made sure she holds it with the utmost care. She has no doubts as to what had been sent to her, but she is seriously hoping her thoughts are incorrect. Quickly she tosses her briefcase onto her desk. She usually leaves the door to her office opened, but for the sake of privacy she quickly closed and locked the door to her workspace.

In efforts to maintain control of her racing nerves, Cadrin tries to stop her hands from trembling. She holds onto the mailer tighter than she'd held it once she entered her office. Cadrin opens the envelope gasping as she pulls out photos of herself and Vance, together. They're embraced in a dance. Some of the other takes are of Vance singing in her ear, which on photo paper portrays to be more like a seductive whisper. One is of the two of them holding hands by the fireplace. One shows them chatting over a candle lit table next to glasses filled with moscato and house brand beer. Another is of the two of them standing underneath the subtle lighting outside of Vance's door; he thinks underneath it she looks even more beautiful. And another is of Vance's profile as he had been entering his apartment.

Cadrin quickly placed all the photos back inside the large mailer. If it hadn't been for Vance in the photos, Cadrin would have second guessed herself of her willingness to inform him of what she'd just received. A couple of days after she asked Vance to leave, Tim had called her at the office asking if she had changed her mind about passing along his contact information to Jim. Her answer to him was, "Not a chance."

Cadrin wanted to say more to him about Tim, except she has no real proof Tim is responsible for the picture taking. She doesn't want to end up starting something unnecessarily. She knows quizzing Jim would have equaled staggering inequality to the respected name her client has made for himself. To follow, erased would have been the efforts and pleas aligned by Cadrin's expertise in supplying Jim with the continued support of his colleagues, and the support of others who have their own vested interest in the development company.

Once she takes the time to inform Vance of the pictures, he will surely want to take the lead. Their situation is a public matter; it's also a private one. Shadowing of her troublesome predicament, Jim's ordeal is first and foremost. Now her career is on the line. She can't let Jim find out about her relationship with Vance. No matter how things will play out between herself and the man she's in love with, she knows whatever the result, she needs Vance's help.

In frustration, Cadrin shook and lowered her head at the troublesome situation she's in. She hated to admit she needs Vance's insight which means talking to him. It maybe even means being in his presence again, something she knows she can't handle. They will probably end up in a make out session. She's angry and disappointed in him. She'd allowed him to take the lead in watching over the welfare of her career. She couldn't help herself and look where it got her. She had fallen in love, throwing all caution to the wind. Cadrin hadn't heard from or seen Vance since the day she told him to leave. There had been no phone calls from him or any other means of communication to take place between herself and her man.

Chapter 22

The Executives

Vance can hardly concentrate on the possibility of a countersuit. Each time he attempts to do so, thoughts of Cadrin invades his mind. He doesn't have it in himself to be angry with her for throwing him out. Although he believes he did exercise adequate concern for their welfare, he holds himself fully responsible for having allowed someone of a scandalous nature such a generous gateway in making trouble for himself and Cadrin. Yet, Vance tries to remain optimistic. He and Cadrin haven't officially sought their separate ways, she'd only told him to leave her residence not to vacate her life. Even so, Vance felt as though that was exactly what she'd asked of him. He hadn't seen or heard from her since they'd sat down for lunch together. He knows everything will be all right between them once more if only he can hold her in his arms again. Cadrin Porter is the first woman Vance unintentionally and all but traded his career for. With or without her, he loves her.

Vance removed his shoes from his feet. The palms of his hands cupped together and fell beneath his chin as he sits on the couch. He's in the depths of think mode again, more worried about Cadrin's career than his own. Both he and his lady demonstrate exceptional talent and tenure complimentary of their chosen professions. Vance knows if they decide or is forced to explore other public duties, neither of them would have any difficulty in gaining the attention of prospective clientele. He's keeping his fingers crossed on that one.

Vance had left Johnson Everdeen without having spoken to anyone there about what the envelope holds inside. He doesn't know exactly why he's holding on to it so closely. He thought maybe later down the line it will somehow prove to be beneficial. Something is definitely up with it other than the lie its sender stated within. No one at Johnson Everdeen made any mention of it; their lack of awareness is simply fine with Vance.

Before Vance could change out of his clothes his cell phone ranged. He'd been in the process of loosening up his tie when the sound interrupted him. Forgetting the voice on the caller's end could potentially belong to the one person he's eager to hear from the most, all he can think of now is his latest visit to Everdeen. In disgust, Vance disapprovingly looks at his ringing cell phone. He finally answers it.

"Hello," he spoke dryly into the receiver.

The caller is hesitant to speak, regretful of having reached out to him in the first place. The mood of the quiet moment is spent through their determination to hang on anyway.

"Hello!" Vance said. This time his tone is demanding.

She sighed.

"Hello, Vance."

At the sound of the woman's voice, a rush of enthusiasm quickly brought Vance to his feet.

"It's me," she said to him.

Vance exhaled.

"It's good to finally here from you again," he lovingly whispered in her ear. "I missed the sound of your voice." Their lines grew silent again. Cadrin has a few of her own delights to share with him but she can't. She doesn't want to allow herself to become lost in trading back and forth mind blowing feelings. Her words will bring back more reasons why she should not have gotten involved with him in the first place.

"Vance, I'm at the office," still a nervous wreck, Cadrin is experiencing the most difficult time in trying to inform Vance of what someone had sent to her. Her emotions are all over the place. Vance thought she might be in trouble over there at Stone and Nichols, needing him pronto.

"Cadrin, what is it? What's the matter? Do you need me to come to your office?" Vance asked with a mix of anger and concern in his tone. He doesn't know what's happening there and before he'd realized it, he had sent her a rush of questions faster than she could provide any answers to. Vance knows something is wrong and he isn't about to refrain from going up to Stone and Nichols to check on his lady.

"No, Vance! Please, wait a minute!" his hastiness alarmed her to no end.

"Cadrin what is it?" Vance said. He began to listen tentatively for her explanation.

"I have pictures of us together."

Vance lowered his vision to the floor, his free hand rest firmly on the top of his head as he prepares himself to listen to more of what Cadrin has to say.

"I don't know who sent them or where they came from."

Vance sighed deeply.

"I thought maybe they came from The Weekly Chronicles, so I checked Tim's latest publication which had not one photo of us in it. I found nothing about us at all," Cadrin knows what's coming next.

"Stay where you are."

"Is he serious? What does he think he's going to do here at Stone and Nichols?" Cadrin wonders.

"Vance please, you can't show up here," she warned him.

"I know I can't," calming down, he paused. "You're right. How long before you leave the building?"

"I have to meet with Jim. He's handling conference calls right now. I'm expecting to leave within the next hour or two."

"Once you do, meet me at my place."

"Vance, I -"

"Please, Cadrin. I need you to come to my place and bring the photos with you."

"Vance, I don't think that's a very good idea."

"I'm quite sure the photos say it all. You might as well come to me or I'll come to you. I don't like being away from you," he honestly said.

"How am I going to get these photos to you?"

"We need to talk about our clients. I'm not going to let them stand between us anymore. I won't allow it."

"We can meet anywhere except our place. It's the only way I see you getting a hold of these pictures," she said.

"Pictures or not, we need to talk about our clients Cadrin, and us."

"I know what I'll do. I'll send them to you by mail. That's right, doing it that way no one will see us together," before Cadrin could come close to pulling her plan into full motion, she could feel Vance's objection coming through the phone lines.

"Cadrin, don't do me that way."

"What way?" Cadrin said acting as though she is just flat out clueless of what Vance is getting at.

"Cadrin, you're treating me like a stranger."

"I don't just call up strangers to share my problems with."

"Well then who do you share your problems with?" he frankly asked her. Vance thought she would give him a brief rundown of the fanfare their relationship had once brought to them when the terms were much better, only she didn't fall for it. It will take much more cleverness from him to break that code.

"Cadrin, I need you to bring the photos to me. If you're unable to do that, then I'll stop by your place and pick them up from you."

For lack of a better excuse to keep him away, Cadrin accepted the fact no matter which decision the two of them reach regarding the photos, she is going to see Vance again. She doesn't believe she can be in the same room with him without touching and running her hands along the masculine and toned ripples upon his stomach. If not that luxury, she will be grateful to have the privilege to sit across from him and again become lost in his engaging brown eyes.

The pair realizes the complications of their relationship will become heightened if they meet in public. Also, in objection to the appointment is the seriousness of the matter which is an unforgiving one. It's one without compassion as it pummels down onto her and Vance.

"Vance, I'll see you at my place around six-thirty," she said while trying to sound every bit of business without leisure. If a daunting reporter were to show up at her place, she believes at least she will be in the position to immediately throw him or her off her premises. Declaring it to be indeed private property will be the classification giving her a welcomed chance at regaining the control she so carelessly lost.

"Vance, I just hope we're not getting ready to make a bigger mistake by meeting up again. But who am I kidding? What have we got to lose now?"

In response to her doomed comment, Vance looks towards the vaulted ceiling of his living room seeming to pray desperately her comment was not meant to be descriptive of him and everything good he's brought to their relationship.

"Okay, Cadrin. Once you leave work, call me and I'll meet you at your place."

"Alright," she said.

They were about to hang up when out of anguish, Cadrin remembered something about the photos. She remembered in almost every take there's one individual, a man of a youthful appeal who is presumably early to mid-thirty something.

"Wait a minute." Who is this?" she spoke aloud.

"Cadrin, who are you talking about? Who's there with you?" Vance believes her attention may have been diverted by a visitor to her office.

"There's a man. No no, this is unmistakably the same man who is in almost every one of these photos of us."

Shocked at her response, Vance sat down on the bar stool.

"Who is he? What man?"

"I don't know who he is, Vance. He's in the shot with us at the fireplace, the bar, he's occupying a seat just a few tables behind the one we had. And he's pictured behind us as we were headed for your car," she rambled on as she informed him of her attention to detail.

"Hmm. It's unlikely just a simple explanation is within reason," Vance said.

"Vance, what are you thinking?"

"I can't say for sure. We'll talk more about it once I get over to your place."

The call ended. Without having had the opportunity to sit down with Jim, a couple of hours later Cadrin left the office for home. She's thankful her client has other things to attend to. She has other things on her mind as well and they all sum up to equal one Vance Grayson.

Cadrin arrived at her home expecting to see Vance there first. *"Maybe it's not too late to call and stop him from coming over here,"* she tried to convince herself. Even though she had been caught off guard herself, she's certain she could have handled this misfortune alone. She thinks maybe the only person who has something to do with the photos is Tim Davenport or her former client, Lynn Fields. Cadrin knows Tim is hungry to get Jim's story for a headliner. She never thought Tim would stoop to sneaking around her private life waiting for the right time to use her moments of intrigue against her. Tim had always been known to obtain images of sources during press conferences and preludes to private meetings, only. Never has his snooping occurred after his subjects had ended their day and had gone on about their private lives. She can't understand why he would suddenly take keen interest in her and Vance. Figuring their careers are probably now more at stake, she wonders if Vance will eventually receive his own set of snapshots. Cadrin believes either Tim or one of his reporters had done some snooping around, eventually learning of her relationship with the high-powered attorney. The findings of their relationship will award Tim with the right amount of leverage he needs to obtain then rearrange Jim's side of the conflict between himself and Carmichael.

Cadrin's punctuality gave her the opportunity to freshen up and get a bite to eat before Vance's arrival. Food had been the farthest necessity from her thoughts. Throughout the workday, Cadrin pondered over the very pictures which threatens to tear at not only her and Vance's relationship but also their career, taking a huge step into her and Vance's private matters.

Before she began to freshen up, she decided to place the photos onto the coffee table before warming up the slice of meat lovers pan pizza of which she'd been too full to finish off the night before. Also, into the oven went a dish of broccoli and cheese.

"Mmm delicious," she took another bite. After Cadrin was finished getting ready, she stood in front of her full-length mirror. She halfway anticipates Vance's arrival while she nervously checks over her form fitting jeans, and the way her lightweight grey sweater shows off a front and back v-shape design which accentuates the curve of her hips. Now that all of that was done, she gave her attire a quick second approval before she made her way back to the kitchen. She removed the dish from the oven rack and placed it onto a wooden chef's board. Right on her last fork full of broccoli intertwined with strings of cheese, she hears a knock at her door. With a little tension, Cadrin raises herself from her chair at the kitchen table. Before heading for the front door, she grabs the photos from the coffee table.

Cadrin has the exchange of events all laid out. Vance would ring the doorbell. She would open the door for him, say hello, hand him the photos, then give him what she hopes to be a believable excuse as to why she has little time to cajole. The two of them would say their good-byes and he would…leave.

Peering through the peephole Cadrin was about to open the door when her heart sunk. Thinking she might be a little afraid, he calmly identifies himself.

"Cadrin, it's me."

It wasn't just her sight of Vance; it was the sound of his voice. His husky tone had set off flutters of lulled emotions throughout her body. Cadrin slowly turned and pressed her back up against the still closed door. To her surprise, she is pitifully and emotionally unprepared for his arrival. She can hear her subconscious ridiculing her for making the phone call which brought him over there.

Cadrin takes in a deep breath, gripping the doorknob she holds it tightly. Finally, she turns around and opens the door for Vance. She studies him with a slightly nervous gaze causing him to want to take her into his arms to kiss away the doubt he knows she now holds of him.

From the moment she'd opened the door, he'd picked up on her edge. She'd stepped backwards signifying to him it's alright for him to enter, again. The sparkle from the diamond pendant and flat gold chain are also well. Glad to see she still thought it necessary to wear it, he smiles a little as he slowly runs his finger along the jewelry. Vance is set on going against her every attempt to derail his gestures of how fond he has become of her over the past months. His focus is one of consideration. He comes closer to her. She looks up at his eyes, apologetic they are. Even with his clean-cut appeal, he's managing to look every bit of a desperado. His presence is overwhelming, denouncing every excuse of hers, even the ones she might want to try and use to get him out of there.

His entire body still aches for her, moaning for her touch against his skin. Somewhere between the communications their eyes are having, Cadrin settles the pictures of the two of them above a small tabletop next to where she's standing with Vance. She can feel the weight of his frame cascading over her. With a gentle lift of her chin, he reads desire in her eyes, he sees passion on her lips, and he feels love from her heart.

His kiss explores her mouth, never wanting to let go of the seemingly never ending and passionate journey. Their kiss deepened when she gave more into him. He's so thorough. Direct. At that moment, she honestly believes she will slip into another world if he keeps this kiss of his going. For a moment, their lips separated. Vance turned his head for another angle on the kiss just when she began reaching for his chin. Vance barely noticed her fingers had come from the condensation of his back, and now closer to his face. Succulently, he tasted those fingers before his mouth glided back to her lips, another rhythm unmissed.

He misses her. She'd become such an important part of his life. Having been without her, he'd felt a definite strangeness to his life, an empty feeling. He watches her as she diligently undoes the buttons on his shirt. He feels soft caresses over the strength of his chest. Suddenly, the pictures don't seem to be all that important anymore. But they do realize the snap shots are vital for they are the reason for their separation. A prelude to one more kiss, Vance takes hold of her hips once more, pulling her willing frame into his own. Their kiss goes back and forth. Vance placed his arm over her shoulder and relaxed his stance on the wall behind her.

He gazes into her face. Through the passion, he vividly sees the same amount of concern she'd shown to him when she'd opened the door. Still burning with passion, Vance turns around and slowly walks towards the middle of the room. Turning around he notices the large mailer envelope she'd picked up from the table.

"Are those the pictures of us?" he managed to find the voice he needs to speak to her.

"Yes. These are it. All of them," she responded a little out of sort.

Never breaking eye contact with her, Vance slowly took the pictures from her. He thought she would have been all tears when he'd arrived. She was thankful he missed that episode earlier in the day. Not eager to lay eyes on the gearing evidence of their relationship, he slowly begins to open the envelope. Cadrin watches him closely. For what he is about to see she inhales deeply for him, on her exhale his heart went out to her.

Taking her by the hand, Vance led Cadrin over to the sofa. They both sit next to each other with little space between the two of them.

Vance began to shuffle through the photos again. After taking count of each one he said nothing, calmly placing them back into the envelope. Vance's thumb and index finger ran over the smooth hairs of his chin area. It's true. The pictures of them together definitely announces sizzle between him and his lady.

"I hope you know who that person is Vance because I sure don't. There isn't any explanation which will make me believe whoever made these photos doesn't know where and whom we work for."

"I agree. Without a doubt in my mind, I believe you're right," he paused, "Cadrin, I hate to tell you this sweetheart, but I believe somewhere along the line you became the focal point. Otherwise, I would have gotten my own set of photos."

"I know but whoever made these photos of us followed us to your place."

"That's because you were with me," Vance repeated his shuffle through the photos again.

"Whoever is behind this is in no hurry to expose our relationship," he said as he situated all the photos together which pictures the blonde and slender young man wearing a wrinkled short sleeved t-shirt and a pair of blue jeans.

Protectively holding her hand, Vance hesitated. Vance doesn't take too kindly to being in a situation in which he can't provide any solid answers to. And until he can sort things out to where they make sense to him, he decided right then and there he wants Cadrin in his care.

"I need you to do something for me. I need you to get some of your things together and come stay with me for a while, until this thing blows over." If he must, Vance is prepared to extend his stay in Chicago. Cadrin can tell from the look in his eyes, he's taking their situation to be profoundly serious. His straight forwardness has placed her in an uneasy state of mind. The concerned look in his eyes took her cup of fear from its rim to spill about the career she so cherishes.

There will be no winning for her, so she didn't argue with his suggestion. He wants to protect her. Eventually, his idea came as a form of comfort for her. With so much uncertainty around them, she realizes she needs Vance near her, demonstrating nothing less than the true hospitality he's gearing up to give her. Just being in the mix of watching him get ready for work every morning, then to become wrapped in his arms once the stars come out at night is nothing to argue about.

"You're still residing at the apartment compliments of Johnson Everdeen, right?"

"No. We can't have Carmichael dropping by at any hour," every ounce of Vance wants to passionately kiss her lips right about now.

Cadrin is quiet. Vance failed to make any mentioning of Delia. The way Cadrin heard it, his thanks to Delia are in order for ensuring a wonderful job be done in making sure his temporary living arrangements came together nicely. Delia's efforts didn't fall by the wayside. Cadrin had to give it to her. She thinks whoever this Delia woman is, she sure does have a knack for putting together an impressive bachelor pad.

After Vance loaded down Cadrin's Lexus with half of her closet, he helped her with the dishes. Since it had been his idea for her to move in with him, he felt he should do whatever is within reason to assist her with the transition. Vance isn't surprised she expects to be at his place with him for only a few days. But looking at everything she loaded up, he sure can't tell.

"I'm so embarrassed Vance, look at all this stuff. I hope I won't be putting you out of your place."

"You don't have enough stuff to make me feel displaced," he winks at her.

Soon after they arrived at the apartment, Vance retrieved Cadrin's belongings from her car and his. He then showed his house guest where she can put away her belongings. While he left her to those things, he returned to the living room to finally return Troy's phone call from earlier in the day.

Once Cadrin finished getting settled in, she slowly and cautiously walked around the large bedroom. The sun is in its second stage of setting. Here and there a hint of light glistens the very room she's slowly walking round and about in. With her arms folded, Cadrin rubs her forearm. For her, it is kind of strange being at the new place Vance calls home. Standing here in his bedroom brings back reflections of the last time she visited his former residence, the time they made love. Memories owns the moment. Having been in his arms was better than anything else she can think of.

From across the room, Vance stands leaning against the frame of the doorway. Cadrin is unaware of his presence as he admires the way her lightweight sweater drapes just above her waist and how her jeans gorgeously compliment the curves of her hips and derrière. Right now, he will be grateful to have knowledge of what has her so preoccupied that she didn't hear her own name being called. In his sexy tone, again he said, "Cadrin."

This time she turns around. From the look of curiosity on his face, she can tell he has been observing her for a while.

"You all settled in?"

"Yes, I was just thinking about all of this craziness."

"Well, if you'll remember, I told you I can be very interesting," he studies her underneath a raised brow.

"Finding out who made those photos of us and why the person figures us to be so interesting in the first place is not going to be easy," she said.

She got him again. Ignoring Vance's attempts to find the laughter in their trials made her feel she's back in control of her career. Being solemn is her new precaution of which she's beginning to use more of. Doing so ensures her she won't get herself recklessly caught up in his charm again. Vance nodded and gently brushes her cheek with his hand.

"You're right. I hope by inviting you to come stay with me will take away some of the stress you're feeling."

"I know I can go into hysterics, but I am stronger than you think, Vance."

"I've taken note. During the closed-door meeting at Stone and Nichols, I thought I was going to have to stand between you and Carmichael."

She laughs.

"If you don't mind me saying so, your strength looks good on you."

She gave him a naughty smile.

"Ah, there it is," Vance thought to himself.

"Speaking of the pictures, what did you do with them?"

"They're in the living room. While you were unpacking, I placed them next to the shelf."

"I thought you would have thrown them away or something," her arms fell by her side.

He smiled at her.

"I wish things could be that simple. If they were, for you I would do just that if I knew it would free you of your problem, our problem and anything else in your life destined to cause you grief," he said.

She wanted to put her total faith in him, but he had made such a big mistake. So did she.

"I'm not here to disappoint you and I don't want you to believe for one second your dilemma is an objective of mine. I'm not that kind of a person. I'm a good man, Cadrin. I've been the good luck charm of several women looking for opportunity. So, I am used but I'm still just as good," he sees the water beginning to fill her tear ducts. Honesty is the best policy, so he keeps on going. "When you threw me out of your place three weeks ago, you basically brought my world to a halt. If it hadn't been for all the craziness coming from the crew at Everdeen, by now I probably would be on somebody's island skipping rocks over the ocean or out relaxing on my yacht, the mountains, or a desert island."

She shakes her head at him. Watching the smile which is about to appear on his face and before she knew it, she burst out laughing. He got her again.

"There it is. I've been waiting on that beautiful smile of yours since you opened your door for me."

Vance looks into Cadrin's eyes. It is there where he'd seen the first peek of her forgiveness.

Chapter 23

The Executives

Cadrin was still standing almost mid-room when Vance had gently squeezed her around her waist. Leaning down he kisses her softly on her cheek bone. The gentle mannerism of his finger once he touched her upon her back, "*swuuu*," felt like a cool autumn breeze known for teasing the fine hairs of her skin, further arousing her need for that man.

Keeping her face forward from his any longer would be an injustice to the rhythm he will be left to strum alone, begging for the indulgency of her affection.

"All I have to offer is unmistakably yours," he said to her in a seductive whisper, "if you want it, all you have to do is tell me. I don't care where in this world I may be, call me. I know I've said it before, but baby please trust in me. I promise you won't be disappointed."

"Thank goodness. This welcomed man is finally in my life."

Cadrin was still sleeping peacefully when Vance opened his eyes. Worried their situation will eventually go haywire, he stares at her for a few moments as she sleeps. He's aware he needs to make things better for her. But how will he do that? How can he diminish the threat of Lynn Fields from her life while revealing not an inkling of what he and

Cadrin mean to each other? Groaning softly, he looks at her again to make sure his anxiety hadn't awakened her.

After Vance showered, he pondered around a bit.
He didn't want to worry Cadrin. The testosterone in him refuses to let her know he's unable to get the photos off his mind.

Once Vance opened the blinds in the living room, he opened the envelope containing the pictures. This time he concentrates on the unidentified male. Minutes later, sounds of shuffling hails from his bedroom. Cadrin is up and probably going through her bags, he thought. Vance quickly placed the mailer and the photos inside his briefcase to join the envelope and the crinkled paper abandoned by the messenger. After breakfast, Vance kissed her a see you later before leaving for Everdeen. Before leaving, he poorly attempted to engage in small talk over orange juice. Cadrin can tell something is bothering him. She can't help feeling partly responsible for his worries, but the playing pieces of the blame game has worn thin. She'd rather be in this with him than without him.

Cadrin placed the glass picture of orange juice back into the fridge and cleared her plate from the table. On her way back to the bedroom, she noticed the mailer containing the photos aren't next to the shelf as they had been the night before. Right then and there she suspects the photos and the person behind them are constantly on Vance's mind. She's glad she didn't mention them to him during breakfast. It had been clear to her something else about their situation is bothering him, and he doesn't want to talk about whatever it is.

Later, more than two glasses of juice failed to measure up to Cadrin's special blend. She and Vance had gathered and loaded up some of her belongings so fast until she unintentionally left behind her packets of coffee beans. She couldn't wait to get her hands on the famous brew the beans aroma will bring to Vance's kitchen. The fact she hadn't finished unpacking slowed her down a little. Placing her belongings on her side of the walk-in closet was certainly a welcomed experience. Although Vance sometimes throws some of his belongings around, he's very neat and has expensive taste which raises a ruckus to the eye and to the sense of touch. She notices all his suits are expensive and tailored made, navy blue, grey, light brown as well as black in color. The rhythm of repeat didn't fool her.

When it comes to the length and color of his jackets each piece holds its own. The design of his lapels; some of the jackets are without them. His row of formal shirts, all long-sleeved ranging in shades of blue, crisp whites, tan, deep burgundy and grey. Of complimentary shades in respect to the remainder of his formal attire there are vests galore. Cadrin notices a few of his vests shows off clasps on their back sides. Situated next to two rows of expensive cologne and a bottle of after shave, she then notices shined cuff links, a row of expensive formal footwear, and five designer watches neatly laying above a piece of felt material.

Cadrin can't resist. She picks up the bottle of her favorite scent he wears most often. After removing its cap, she brought the bottle to her nose, closing her eyes, she slowly inhaled. Tricked by her senses, for a split second she looked for him. Smiling, she presses the cap back down over the nozzle before sitting the bottle amongst the other masculine scents. Everything she'd seen inside the sizeable walk-in space speaks stud, power, rugged and influential black man. Her man. Next to his luggage are two pairs of almost beaten-up sneakers he wears when playing sports with Troy and the fellas whenever the latter can tear themselves away from their wives. Another applauded glance over Vance's belongings within the custom-made room makes her want to jump and shout back at the hummin masculinity within it. And she did!

Hoping to get back to the corporate apartment before Vance, Cadrin grabbed her purse then headed for the front door. She closed and locked it with the key which had slid from underneath the grasp of her fingers and had dramatically fallen onto the coolness of the sheet as she awakened that morning.

She needed to hurry over to her place to collect her packet of coffee beans. She knows Vance will definitely be critical of her for returning there without him. Upon entering the front room her eyes roam around the room for a few seconds. Everything is in its place just as she and Vance had left them. Cadrin planned to be there long enough to grab a few extra things as well as the beans from the cupboard. She had been at Vance's not even a full day yet and already she missed lounging on the chaise in her sitting room. Cadrin grabbed her bag and headed for her front door. She swings it open.

"Well dang girl! Hello. Where are you rushing off to? I came by here yesterday evening to only find you weren't at home. I left several messages on your cell," Roslyn said as she took count of Cadrin's overnight bag and the packets of coffee beans she's holding in her other hand.

"What's all of this?" Roslyn inquired.

"I know how this must look to you. It'll only be for a little while," Cadrin answered.

"Now girl please, this is Roslyn. You do remember me, don't you? I came back by here last night and you still were not here. You stayed the night with that hot shot attorney Vance, didn't you? And it looks like you're going back over there. I take it on yesterday you forgot the overnight bag you're holding."

"You guessed right and for real, I was going to call you," Cadrin said reassuringly, "You won't believe all that has been going on with me lately."

Roslyn looks completely puzzled.

"Somebody found out about my relationship with Vance."

"Uh oh!" Roslyn throws her hands up into the air, "here we go. Who found out? Girl, I told you that man is a repeat of Kirk!"

"No, he isn't," Cadrin quickly stated in Vance's defense. However, she managed to remain calm.

"Well, I don't mean like that. Vance is quite the contrary. Cadrin you crossed the line again. Now you're saying somebody has found out about you and him. You told me about him," she said frankly, "but you didn't tell me you were thinking of moving in with him."

"I didn't tell you because it's only going to be for a little while. I wanted to make the decision of moving in with him by myself. I hope you can understand and forgive me for not letting you in on this one," Cadrin sighed.

"Because of our 'secret,' I'll be staying over at his place until we can get to the bottom of this."

"Judging from the look on your face I don't know about that."

"I wouldn't be surprised," she said of Roslyn's observation, "we thought we were being so discreet. We really were. Neither one of our clients are aware of our relationship."

"So…who did find the two of you out?"

"That's a question Vance neither I have an answer for. Whoever the person is cleverly took pictures of us while we were out late together a few weeks ago."

Suddenly attempting to shield her face from anybody, Roslyn held a manila folder over her head ducking as she peeped from both sides of the shade the folder provided her.

Playfully and jokingly Cadrin said, "Girl, stop it! Look at you, you are so crazy! Nobody is trying to take any pictures of you."

"Yeah, that's what you think. Neither you nor Vance for that matter knew what was going on when the two of you got yawls pictures made."

"Please girl," Cadrin said still laughing and shaking her head at Roslyn, "come on in. Obviously, the reason you've dropped by has something to do with what's inside of that folder."

Cadrin unlocks the door again, "I'm just trying to stay positive about all of this, girl."

"Yeah, I hear you girl," Roslyn said.

"What brought you over here last night? I'm guessing the reason is inside the folder," Cadrin said as she closed then lock the door.

"We'll get to this after I find out how you're doing. I know it has got to be rough for you to go through this again."

"It is, to be more honest with you if this happened when I was with Kirk, we'd be on every news channel by now thanks to his temper. Vance can get angry as well, except he is more cool-natured. It took a lot for me to get my career to where it is today and I'm not giving up on it."

"You sound incredibly determined to not let this compromised time in your life have the pleasure of defeating you. I'm cheering for you all the way."

"Thanks, Roslyn."

"Oh, by the way how is Vance dealing with it?"

"Vance is…dealing. I really don't know how this has affected him; he hasn't said much about it. However, this morning I noticed the photos were not where he'd placed them last night. I looked over the place searching for them with no luck."

"Why would he move them?"

"I don't know, Roslyn," a look of worry crossed Cadrin's expression, "what I do know for sure is since the delivery of the photos he doesn't want me to be far away from him."

"If he really didn't care for you, he would have looked the other way. This whole issue of spying would have put an end to your relationship. To protect you, he wanted you at his place not just anywhere." The possibility of exposure isn't stronger than the love he has for her. Any other man of influence probably would have gotten as far away from Cadrin as he possibly could have. Maybe keeping Vance in her life isn't such a bad idea after all. There is only one thing which remains constant within Cadrin's emotions and that is where Vance really stands when it comes to her and her client.

"He's a good man."

"Yeah, that's what I keep telling myself, anyway," Cadrin pointed to the manila folder, "what's that?"

"These are some of the sketches created by the new guy at work, Samuel. He's the twenty-seven-year-old guy I told you about. He's extraordinarily talented and passionate about his desire to make some noise in the field of architectural design. I get a kick out of his creativity," Roslyn carefully opens the folder. With care she handed it to Cadrin, "he has such great precision I asked him if it would be okay if I were to show off his sketches around to a couple of people who has an equally abstract way of thinking. The encouragement will be nice for him. He said he will be thrilled if I share with him any thoughts I get from others about his latest work."

Giving more attention to the artwork, Cadrin nods.

"This is a sketch of the walk-way in front of that famed skyscraper, right?"

"Yes, it is," Roslyn responded.

"He has great attention to detail. He has documented things in this sketch which some sketch artist usually deems insignificant. These are great."

"I'll tell him you said so."

"It sounds like you and Samuel have been getting more acquainted."

Roslyn smiles.

"We get along."

"We get along? Is that all you have to say?"

"I mean, well. Yeah, we get along. I mean for real now, he's new to the company. I only work there part-time. And it's not like we get to see each other every day."

"What about the time you do get? Is it enough for you?"

"Ha, listen at you!" Roslyn laughs.

"What I mean is, okay it's obvious the two of you get along quite well regardless of how little or how much you get to see each other. And he's letting you walk around with his sketches. He's showing you he has trust in you. It seems like you are growing fonder of him as well."

"Maybe I am."

"Believe me when I tell you, he's taken an interest in you."

"I'll have to let you know, Cadrin," Roslyn said as she smiles with hope in her heart to one day receive romantic attention from Samuel.

Chapter 24

The Executives

"I can't believe this!" Avionne abruptly placed her car's gear in park before jerking the car keys from the ignition. Quickly exiting her vehicle, she hurries along the curve of the second driveway way in front of her home. She unlocks the door of her residence. Pushing open the door she breathes a sigh of relief as she sees the fancy grey ribbon neatly situated above a square gift box. The box holds a birthday gift for Lelani, a co-worker of hers.

Previously, she'd made it to her car not once but twice holding an arm load of decorative trimmings for the surprise party. Gently, she lifts the box and its content from the sofa table. Before she could get herself and the box out to the car, her phone rings. Turning around to answer it, she felt the toe part of her right shoe hit the foyer's baseboard.

"Oww! Ouch! Please don't let this be who I think it is. I promise I'm on the way ya'll," she promised while grabbing the ringing phone in a hurry.

"Hello!"

"Baby girl, I was hoping I reached you before you headed to work."

"Vance! Is that you?"

"I had better be the one and only."

She laughs.

"No. I'm only kidding. How's my baby sister?"

"I'm fine. Just behind schedule."

"I dare to ask the reason behind your near tardiness?"

"It's nothing serious. I just can't seem to get myself away from the house this morning. I've been running back and forth from the driveway to the foyer. I keep forgetting one thing after the other."

"Hmm, well I'm grateful for your forgetfulness, otherwise you would have missed my call. I called you up on your cell several times with no answer from you."

"I don't doubt you. Sometimes I get so many morning distractions until I end up with a mind overload before arriving to work. For that reason, I decided to power off my cell in the mornings if I'm on my way to work."

"Staying busy is a good thing so is rest. And you really should keep your cell phone powered on a little more often so you can be aware of who's trying to reach you. Especially when you are away from the house. Besides, you never know when you'll get that million-dollar call."

"Yeah, a million would be fantastic. But it wouldn't mount up to getting a call from my big brother."

"Thanks. After we hung up last week, I forgot to ask about your overnight trip to the Massachusetts office. Did things go alright there, Ms. Coordinator?"

She nodded.

"Everything went extremely well. My trip to Springfield was the first time I had to stand in for our corporate trainer. Everyone was pleased with my contributions. I don't think they had a clue as to how nervous I was."

"You're Avionne Grayson. They'd better be pleased with my little sister."

She laughs.

"Vance, quit it."

"No, I'm serious. You are very serious about your duties. I hope your out-of-town colleagues are truly able to realize your professionalism and generosity."

"We both hope so," Avionne can feel Vance's smile through the phone.

"So lady, I know you're trying to get to the job so I'll let you do that, but before I do I need a favor from you."

"Sure, anything for you, Vance."

"I need you to go over to my place, go into my study room. You'll be looking for my rolodex which will be on the desktop. Flip through it. There is a bed and breakfast card in the mix."

"Did you say bed and breakfast?"

"Yes, and don't ask. You'll see a phone number on the back of it. No name attached just a number. If you wouldn't mind, please send the number to my phone. The sooner I receive it the better. It's really important to me," Vance said.

Still trying to figure out her big brother, she gently bites the corner of her lower lip.

"Ok. Alright…sure. Vance, umm….is everything okay?"

"Everything is fine….but you will do that for me, right?"

"Yes, Vance," Avionne understood anxiety to be in Vance's tone. He seriously needs the number of whomever rather quickly. She's curious as to why any other information doesn't accompany the numbers on back of the card.

A few hours later and during her lunch break, Avionne sent to Vance the information he needs. Next thing Vance knew, he gained possession of the numbers he had in question. Avionne had tried to probe for details after learning the cute little card promotes a bed and breakfast located in Wyoming. Vance did nothing but grin his way out of the pressure. Finally, he told her she's cute and a tad bit nosy. Before the information came to him, Vance made a second trip to the jazz club where he showed a couple of the photos to various employees, especially to the ones who were on duty the night he and Cadrin were photographed. He needed to learn if the man in the pictures happens to be recognizable by anyone who works there. Having learned nothing more than what he already knew prior to arriving, the next place he wants to check out is Stone and Nichols. If it weren't for Vance's own low profile, he would have invited himself back to the very corporation his client wants to sue. Snooping around there will now be left up to Creighton's discretion. Vance thought maybe by now it is likely Creighton had grown tired of his line of work. Not hardly.

Vance searches for the detective's private contact number he'd saved to his cell's list of contacts after he'd received Creighton's number from his sister. In the past, Creighton had done some work for a prior client of Vance's back in Baltimore. After being hired, Creighton always remained slick and suave during his findings which were always accomplished through his unique investigative measures. Vance grins at the detective's initial greeting. It's so Creighton.

"This is Ms. Hadensworth. To whom do I have the pleasure of speaking with?"

"This is Vance Grayson, corporate attorney for Johnson Everdeen."

"Hello, Mr. Grayson. I've heard a lot of good mentioning about you through some of the media channels. I must say it's a pleasure to be able to speak with you. I wish you were in person."

"Thank you, Ms. Hadensworth. If possible, would I be able to speak with Creighton Jamison, please?"

"Mr. Jamison is out to lunch as we speak. I'll be glad to jot down your message for him. Of course, we have your contact number. Is this a good number for Mr. Jamison to reach you by?" for Vance's ear the receptionist repeated Vance's contact information.

"Yes, that's right. Please let him know I need to speak with him as soon as possible. It is rather urgent I do."

Vance was surprised to have spoken with hired help. Creighton had always been a solitaire act. The last time Vance saw him, the detective was minus an entourage, understandably so. His lone dedication to the field is just as effective.

Over time, Creighton's increased popularity awarded him with the right amount of attention he needed to expand his business into the two offices he nicknamed, The Thin Line. All his employees are housed behind the same office door. Nothing except their airtight knowledge for their respective skills, and a blue runner down the center of the aisle is placed to distinguish one operational aspect from the other.

The sound of Cadrin's cell phone startled her. This time around only a couple of hours had past since the last time Vance called to check on her.

"Hey, I'm bringing dinner home. I got one of your favorites. It's barbeque."

"That's g-great. I-I will get the table set," Cadrin had ordered dinner after looking through Vance's nearly empty cupboards and refrigerator. One of them will have to go to the grocers, soon. Her man showed her he can cook. However, shopping for groceries is on a whim. For the most part the items he shops for regularly are heavy, bulky and sports handles to be supported by. Vance sound so happy when he told her he's bringing dinner home. So once Cadrin got a hold of their ordered meal, she transferred the contents from their cardboard containers into various sized plastic ones with lids, then placed each into the fridge.

"Wow, my kitchen table hadn't look this good since I've been here in Chicago. I take it everything went okay today. I hope you really like this place. I think it adds up to a hotel suite. Troy won't show it to any buyers, not until two months or so down the line.

"Everything couldn't be better," she answered.

He probably would have hit the roof if she'd told him she'd gone back over to her own place without him.

"You know you can always move in here with me, permanently."

"Vance, you know that's not going to happen, your home is in Maryland. Remember?"

"Yes, I do remember something about that," he gave her the grin which made her want to pack up the rest of her belongings, then have her mail forwarded to her new address. His.

Mr. Prince Charming is unaware of just how close he has become in getting his desire to fruition. But he still hadn't told her exactly where she stands when it comes to their secret union.

"Wings, fries and one lemon lime drink on the rocks coming right up, my lady," he said as he sat his cell phone down next to a glass of sparkling water. Cadrin began to assist in emptying one of the bags until she felt Vance's hand close over hers.

"How did your day go? I hope some of it was dedicated to thoughts of me," he said as he leaned in towards her.

"Thank you for being so concerned of me. And some of it was dedicated to you," she kissed him on his lips.

"I want to thank you for everything you're doing for me. I-I don't know…I don't know what I would have done without you. You've invited me into your home~"

Vance rose from the table. Taking her into his arms he whispers, "My heart."

"You've made me feel welcomed into your life," she holds onto him tighter.

Vance feels her emotion. He strengthened his embrace.

"You could have turned your back on me, but you didn't," Cadrin feels tears of joy arising.

"Shhhhh," is the steady constant from Vance stilling her emotions.

A few moments passed by before Vance let go of her and helped her to her seat at the table. After half the wings had been eaten, Cadrin poured herself another glass of water.

"Vance, is everything alright? Since we sat down to eat you've looked at your cell phone like twenty times."

"I apologize. It isn't my intention to be rude. I'm expecting a call from Carmichael on my cell concerning the corporate apartment," he lied. He's really waiting on the detective's call.

"I thought Delia would have been the one to take care of that for you."

Vance could hardly contain his obviously stunned expression. Unfortunately, that moment was the first time he'd ever heard Delia's name come from Cadrin.

"She probably should be my contact in regard to the place, but it was his company's money which covered my stay there."

Vance moved his chair away from the table. No matter which way he turns, Delia's name always pops out of nowhere. Occasionally, he noticed her paying close attention to him. Through the hurt and embarrassment, there is still no denying it. Vance Grayson manages to hold her undivided attention. Delia still wants more from him than just the simplicities of everyday common courtesy.

Cadrin studies Vance. Figuring him out is a process. At all costs, Cadrin must know exactly who she's dealing with.

"Vance, isn't there something you need to tell me?"

He hopes she's inquiring on why the photos next to the shelf had suddenly become obscure. He'd rather discuss that for it will be easier and less intense.

"I apologize. I didn't know there's something you're expecting me to share with you. May I ask what it is?"

"It's concerning the day Carmichael stopped by when I hid in your bedroom."

With only a nod, Vance acknowledged his remembrance of the surprise visit from his client.

"From down the hallway I heard Carmichael make mention of Delia. He said she is responsible for putting together that apartment for you. Who is she? You've never mentioned her to me."

Vance didn't want to have this conversation with her. He had just defeated what appeared to be the last bit of trust issues between the two of them. He must banish any remaining doubt she fears.

"I didn't think it was necessary for you to learn who she is, howbeit she is not a secret. She happens to be Carmichael's secretary, and it is true she is the person who took care of all my living arrangements, which I was unaware of up until Carmichael informed me. She is his colleague not mine."

"Is it true she makes you uncomfortable for some reason or another? I could hear your tense reaction in your voice. Is there some sort of tension between the two of you?"

For someone under accusation, Vance remains very calm.

"I have to admit she can be a handful at times, but her flirting is nothing I can't get around," Vance can see where this is trying to go. Immediately, he left his chair and led Cadrin away from the kitchen table and over to the couch where she sat between her favorite seat. Vance's arms reached around her waist and overlapped at his wrists. She snuggled in closer.

"*Ahh, relaxation,*" Cadrin felt a whisper at her ear as he began to provide her with an answer.

"Please don't get upset," he said to her.

Cadrin began to shift in his arms, he held tighter.

"No, listen. It's not what you're thinking."

"No, Vance you listen to me. I know women check you out all the time. You are a very attractive man. Heck all you have going for yourself; you are a package deal. You can't tell me you don't have a lot to hide then expect me to believe you're not lying to me."

"Ms. Porter, if it's possible to be right and wrong at the same time you've nailed it. I don't share my private life with a lot of people. If I share it with anyone it's my Dad, only if he presses. A lot of times when folks think there is something to tell, I know there isn't and that's the case when it comes to Delia. Yeah, she has flirted at me not with me, there's a difference."

Cadrin knows the difference. However, she needs to hear him say it.

"What is the difference, Vance?"

"I'm happy to tell you I have no interest in Delia and that's the truth. From day one she's been aware of my lack of interest for her." There was no way he was going to tell his lady Delia is the reason he'd been late for their date a few weeks ago.

Cadrin and Vance had ended their night, a truce they called. They vowed to end accusations and put their focus on finding out the person who threatens to expose their relationship. Over breakfast, Cadrin got caught up in the lingering of overnight pillow talk and playing footsies underneath the table with Vance. Because of their playful activity, she forgot to ask him why he changed the location of the photos. Once he realized Creighton's call could come at any minute, Vance had 'hit the door' almost simultaneously.

The entire day was almost gone and still Vance has yet to hear from the detective. Ready to be about other things than work, Vance exited the Everdeen building heading for his car parked on the front row along with other luxury vehicles. Before he could get inside, his cell phone began to ring. Not recognizing the caller's number, Vance answered anyway.

"Who's calling please?"

Creighton immediately recognized Vance's voice.

"Vance, this is Creighton. How are you man?"

"Man, you're busier now than ever and that's a good thing."

"You know it. And I hear you're still a hot shot attorney."

"That's what people tell me, so I guess I had better maintain, right?"

"You better know it man, being the best is what we know. So, what's going on? I take it something or someone has got you on high alert."

"Yeah, that's for sure. I've been out here for a while in Chicago on business, playing catch up with my brother, and I've had the pleasure of getting to know this beautiful and intellectually compatible lady," Vance bought himself some time with small but good talk while he separated himself from public ears. Once inside his car, he locked the door. Now secured inside the vehicle, it is from the tip of the iceberg where Vance began informing Creighton of his and Cadrin's situation.

Vance returned to a quiet home. The only thing buzzing is the lingering scent of Cadrin's body wash, and after bath lotion she uses to smooth onto her damp skin. Curiosity first sent him to their bedroom. He didn't see her. He peeks inside the Jack and Jill bathroom, but it too is vacant. Vance strode back into the living room just in time to see the wind's graceful ruffling of Cadrin's skirt. It's about five- thirty in the afternoon. The sunlight glistens over her face and legs as she relaxes comfortably on the balcony. Turning towards the door her eyes opens and a smile tickles her cheeks the moment she sees Vance. He steps out onto the balcony.

"Hey pretty lady, you got enough room on that lounger for a big guy like me?" He knew she most likely missed her lounger back at her own place, so the other day he stopped by a hardware store on the way home from Everdeen and purchased one for her. "I mean I don't want to crowd you or anything," he said jokingly. Cadrin smiled then she eased down to the weakest part of the lounger, Vance sat behind her. Once he was comfortable, she slid back to lay her head on his chest. He groans, kissing strands of her hair then snuggling his mouth under the lobe of her right ear.

"Did you have a tough day at Everdeen?" she waited for his answer while watching the wind lightly blow the pulled shade back and forth.

"Everyday is a tough day at Everdeen. If it's not Carmichael who I'm dealing with, it's the people from the board and that damn Pete Monahan. Carmichael has been avoiding them. Until he is ready to face them, yours truly is it."

"Well, Carmichael knows he has the right man on the job, so don't expect him to be willing to sit down to talk with them anytime soon."

"Thanks for the compliment."

"It was my pleasure."

Through the glass door of the balcony, Vance can see his briefcase resting against the lower half of the bar stool. The photos, crinkled paper and the envelope are still inside of it. During his appointments at Everdeen, he keeps the hard copies of unanswered questions inside a safe deposit box. Balancing the scales of work, pleasures and trying to stay one step ahead of whoever made those pictures of them are persistent in battling for the upper hand, Vance has bet his hand on winning.

That night Vance had gone to bed thinking of his early morning appointment with Creighton. It will be then when Creighton will see firsthand the kind of situation Vance and Cadrin are in.

Vance didn't want to tell Cadrin about the envelope. His discretion is mainly due to her reaction when he implied her client to be guilty. Although she'd kept her cool, it's quite obvious to Vance that clearly, she doesn't appreciate his earlier diagnosis of the man who signs his name to her paychecks. Before the unfortunate picture taking, Vance knows if he were to tell Cadrin about what he has in his possession, she will assume he's again up to premature accusations against her client. It seems Cadrin's and Vance's moments of bliss always graduated to measures of uncertainty and other issues of trust. Through it all, sincerity and love always has the final say, but telling her about his possession of the letter is forbidden.

Chapter 25

The Executives

Creighton always advises his clients to meet with him on location rather than showing up to his office. With or without an appointment, seclusion is everything. And his net worth is nicely endorsed by his chosen order of operation. From behind a pair of GQ shades, Creighton watches as Vance enters the restaurant situated on the outskirts of Chicago. One of the many reasons Creighton's business experiences the unprecedented growth and success it does are credited to his vague persona. On every occasion, he fluently demonstrates a unit depictive of how he and his dedicated group of associates come through for his clients. Without question, they always get the job done the right way.

Vance spotted Creighton sitting in a quiet corner of the restaurant which is steadily approaching its busiest time of the day. Vance doesn't require much time to convince Creighton of what he holds inside the briefcase and how such goes hand in hand with his need for paid assistance. Vance calmly approaches Creighton.

The detective sees him walking over and removed the semi-dark shades which had temporarily altered his appearance.

"Creighton, man it's good to see you again. Too bad our meeting couldn't have been under better circumstances."

"Those are my thoughts exactly, Vance."

The two briefly shook hands.

Vance placed the black briefcase upon their table.

"This is my problem," Vance opened the briefcase, from it he handed to Creighton the pictures of himself and Cadrin. Creighton busied himself reviewing the eight by ten sized photos while Vance removed the envelope and the crinkled piece of paper from the briefcase. Then, he slid the items across the table to the detective. Vance watched him as he read to himself the words on the piece of paper discarded by the messenger. The header holds a bogus name of a messaging company. After he was done observing the photos, he said nothing. Therefore, he proceeded to read the letter which calls for cease of the pending lawsuit against Stone and Nichols. Creighton did just as Vance had done and separated all the photos from the ones which doesn't have the unidentified male pictured in them.

"So, you think there is some kind of connection between them?" Vance spoke of the envelope and photos.

"Which one came to you first?"

"I received only the envelope. The crinkled paper was retrieved by me after it was discarded. My lady received the photos."

Creighton gave a stunned expression. Usually, his clients produced pitiful answers. Creighton soon realized this client is no comparison to any of his former or current clients.

"I think this is a good time to inform you she is the publicist for-"

"Don't tell me you're getting ready to say what I think you are getting ready to tell me. She's PR for Stone and Nichols, isn't she?"

"Yes, she is."

For a minute or so Creighton offered no response to Vance.

"You said you received the envelope. Who gave it to you?"

This is no time to hold back information. Vance knows any bits and pieces of it are not to be overshadowed by the photos, neither the fact of where he was when he accepted the envelope. He didn't hold back in his explanation.

"My lady received the photos after I gained possession of the letter from a so called 'messenger.' He took me to be a member of security.

There was no one attending to the station at the time, I happened to be there to assist one of the blue-collar workers. I ended up leaving my jacket behind at the security desk. Upon my return, the 'messenger' who was nervous as heck was there waiting for...security. I glimpsed the sender's name on the envelope and became sort of furious at my client. He can be kind of hot tempered and disobedient. To make a long story short, I thought he went behind my back and developed a line of written communication between himself and Jim Grainger. So, I accepted the envelope on what I assumed to be on the behalf of my client. I've had it in my possession ever since, and my client has yet to make any mention of it."

"I see," Creighton said. He continued to remain impressed over Vance's answers.

"Wait, there's more. My lady received the photos two weeks after speaking with Tim Davenport of the Weekly Chronicles. We also think a former client of hers -Lynn Fields- may have something to do with the photos, but we're not for sure. She threatened Cadrin's career if she were to ever learn of compromised practices."

Creighton nods his head.

"Do you believe Jim Grainger is guilty?" Creighton had learned about the pending lawsuit along with everyone else.

"Truthfully, somewhere near the beginning I had my doubts Jim Grainger could be capable of stealing anything from anyone. My client believes differently of course. So far there hasn't been any substantial evidence to be acquired. So as of right now I'm still Everdeen's attorney, ready to go to court to defend them if need be."

"Sounds like you're telling me this letter could not have come from Stone and Nichols."

"That's exactly right. When the messenger left the building, I saw him ball and toss the sheet of paper of which he thought I foolishly applied my signature to into the garbage."

Creighton began trying to press more of the wrinkles out of the once balled up sheet of paper.

"Man, I need your expertise. I did some searching around on my own and it got me nowhere. I need to keep a low profile, so I need you to find out for me who had that letter delivered and who made then sent these photos to my lady. I also need to learn who is the man who keeps appearing in photo after photo."

"I sure will, Vance," Creighton has several sources and methods to obtain information regarding any possible contributions which can lead back to Tim Davenport, Lynn Fields or even elsewhere. He figures the newspaper to be a great starting point. He hopes his sources will be able to provide him with enough information to report back to Vance before next evening.

"My Burgundy enthusiast, Pinot Noir is a delicate wine of its category. I'm happy to say it is amongst our most favorite of reds. Just a swirl or two, or maybe even three," he laughs, "will spruce up the flavor of this light to medium bodied wine. Notice first the aroma." Everyone brought their glass near their nose to enjoy the scent of finely matured grapes.

"Never gulp, the grapes from the vine are meant to be cherished, savored before attempting to swallow. And ladies and gentlemen, if you'll notice the smoothness of the wine as it trickles down, be aware of the warmth it brings. I'm sure it will not be soon forgotten. Everyone taste," the connoisseur instructed the crowd of evening wine participants as they whet their palates.

Vance noticed first the aroma of the wine. On his palate, he discreetly and gently swished. Then slowly he swallowed. Impressed, he nodded to Cadrin after she did the same. She winked at him.

"Everyone I hope your glasses are at least halfway empty, my fellow tasters and swallowers. Please follow me on a journey over to the Empire room. It has been especially and beautifully prepared for this experience," the Connoisseur led the group through a set of doubled doors as he begins to present the final stage of the evening. Vance and Cadrin entered the elegantly designed Empire ballroom. Its ambiance is a mix of rustic flair.

There aren't any tables to own the room. The presence and chatter of the wine tasters are left to make up the difference, as well as the entourage of twenty servers waiting to oblige the participants beck and call. As the group enters the large room, it is at the door where some of them accept white paddles resembling the appearance of the ones used when playing racquet ball. The participants are to quietly exercise them when requesting crackers, cheese, or fruit from one of the servers constantly moving about the room.

"A night out for wine tasting sure does beat staying cooped up at home in front of the television," Cadrin thought to herself. Well, half the night anyway. Staying home with Vance never offers her a dull moment, he always keeps her entertained. Often, he would burst out in tune singing some of his and her favorite songs. For the most part, he would sing some of them word for word, then relic in her naughty smile. Then *mmmm,* he would kiss her as though he doesn't know how to be well in this world without her. Vance refused the opportunity to walk around the ballroom with a paddle. He left the gesturing to Cadrin. The opportunity he craves the most is much nearer than arms reach of him.

"Having a good time?" Vance asked Cadrin as he gently embraces her around her waist, pulling her closer to him. They walked the room some and Vance couldn't resist in stroking her back. He isn't discreet but chooses to be open with his affection.

"So, this is the real reason you didn't want to carry the paddle around the room, huh. You wanted to be free to do whatever you want to," she said with her index finger underneath his chin. Vance's spontaneity sent tingling shivers causing her skin to want to break out in a sweat every time he touches her. He's doing it again, showing her how to throw caution to the wind. And if the force of the trials tries to separate them, he will be ready and more than willing to weather the storm with her.

The breeze above their heads is cool, quickly becoming frost like. The four doors of the ballroom are wide open. Within the frame, each of those from inside the ballroom can see evening has been found by the brink of night, and it's calling for Vance's attention. Vance is certain the other men who are here with their ladies picked up on the hint just like he had done. Before the candle lit walk became crowded, Vance asked Cadrin to give her paddle to one of the servers. She inquisitively stared at him with the beautiful smile he is so crazy about. Once the server left them, Vance grabbed Cadrin by the hand leading her through the center side door.

The night's air is refreshing, its comfort seems to free Cadrin and Vance from their troubles as they walk pass the motif candles lighting up their path. Vance doesn't know if he should have her stop mid-way or continue down to the end of the walk. The farthest point will ensure they have the amplest of privacy if not on one side of them, at least they would have the other side all to themselves. For him, walking to the end is symbolic of "*we've come to the end of this wonderful time together.*" Just what are the two of them to each other? When it comes down to defining the time they are experiencing together, the good and the bad, it's no secret they are an item. The bond they have created has been compromised. And eventually, Vance will be leaving Chicago, headed back to his home and his life in Maryland. More and more, walking to the end doesn't seem like such a good idea to him.

Reaching the most comfortable point, they stopped middle ways the walk. Vance figured at least there he wouldn't have to give way to a finale of un-mercifulness.

"You know coming to this event with you was a really good idea. I think the two of us have given up enough of our freedom," she said.

He smiled at her.

"I couldn't help in feeling I owed you some sense of normalcy. I thought a change of pace would supply us nicely. So far so good," Vance said as he looks around. The risk of them being seen by a credible associate of Johnson Everdeen, Stone and Nichols or the one who threatened Cadrin's career from early on are still very possible. Mouths can speak the truth and lies, as well as images on photo paper. Vance and Cadrin have a solution for such if need be. But in their case photos and comments from other people will be and are true. He and Cadrin are definitely an item.

"We need to be in control of our own lives again, our own fate," he said with strong determination in his tone. Through his seriousness, Cadrin can feel the still ever so present uncertainty their ordeal presents. Are they in fact back in control of their lives? In some respect, they are. Cadrin wraps her arms around Vance, she looks up at him.

"I know baby, I know," Vance said to her, "we still have to be careful, as much as we can be. But I couldn't allow us to keep going the way we've been going for the past few weeks. Hiding the newest joy in my life is inexcusable," Vance gently brings her gaze to look him in his eyes.

"If you will accept my invitation, I'd like for you to come home to Maryland with me. I think you will like my family. I believe they'll most definitely like meeting you."

Cadrin took a step backwards and slowly ran her finger along her lip,

"I'm shocked, Vance. Are you serious? You want me to come with you back to Maryland? Without a doubt, this is a night filled with surprises that's for sure."

Vance grabs a hold of her hands. His heart rate begins to increase.

"You haven't said yes yet."

She laughs aloud.

"Yes, I will!" Because of the noise Cadrin made, she and Vance got several stares from other couples who are as nearby as they should be. They kept observing the pair, waiting for Vance to place a ring on her finger which will glisten in the night. But all their vision is receptive of is Vance and Cadrin's hugs, followed by one long passionate kiss.

Chapter 26

The Executives

In complete awe, Cadrin steps into Vance's home office. Vance watches as she walks around the room with a grade of confidence he thinks is just absolutely sexy. She can't believe the size of this space. There are other ample rooms which are to her liking as well, just as the roominess of his huge bedroom. His office gives off a degree of coziness mixed with professionalism galore. The hue of the walls within his office is a combination of taupe and beige. Up above, Cadrin sees the ceiling within such room has track lighting. She notices his office is also decked in dark brown oak, and cushioned chairs which looks like they are suited for a theatre room. He has one of those as well. The huge oak wall mounting is placed against a wall to the right. Inside of it is its own track lighting within each section of the unit. Next, Cadrin's eyes went directly to the antique golden and hand painted stems and leaves showcased inside of a crystal vase sitting on the middle section of the wooden shelving.

"Your office is very inviting. It looks like your very own private library."

Standing off the room's center, Vance said nothing. He grins a little, continuing to watch Cadrin's every expression while she continues to marvel over his home.

"My clients like it too, only a select few of them get an appointment here," he finally spoke aloud.

Cadrin raised her brow at him. Did he mean only a few female clients got the invite? Or were they not really clients of his?

"I'm only kidding. Actually, I use this room for conference calls and compilations. You know, strategies, proposals, drafts, you name it just so it involves adequately assisting my clients. The chairs add a nice touch. They're mostly used by members of my immediate family who have just got to get a word in to me while I'm working."

"Then I'll bet your awareness of their presence is a closed mouth or one-word answers."

Vance's eyes lit up at the obvious caption in her ability to refer to the things his family members had lovingly brought to his attention. Obviously impressed and ready to see more of his home, Cadrin gives Vance a curious smile.

"So, what else is there to do here?"

He began to answer her but not before a smile spread slightly to his dimples. She shows him a look of flatter; he can almost taste the naughtiness which will occupy the remainder of their evening and most of their night.

She had seen his kitchen. A couple of instructional cookbooks were left on the granite countertop. One of the full baths is big enough to engulf another bath and a half. More, Vance's study exemplifies enough concentration to evenly divide up between the two of them. To go on, his living room is very hospitable, it's the room where she'd placed her purse and kicked off her shoes. Before leaving the room, her attention had been drawn to a large window overlooking the sprawling green lawn between his home and the neighbor's back yard. The neighbor's home appears to be a lifetime away from each of them.

"Before we settle down, I'd like to show you the bar downstairs."

"A bar? Downstairs?" She stared upwards at him. He'd been cool in his statement. He doesn't have a conceited bone in his body, and she likes that about him, too.

She can't believe there is a home bar added to his space. A bachelor. With more thoughts regarding his personality, Cadrin is no longer surprised. The house's vibe appropriately exudes the man which others respect and admire once they finally got over his other attributes. They praised him for his toughness, fairness and honesty.

They reached the downstairs, having walked down a short hall from his kitchen then down an inviting short flight of steps. On the other side of a solid oak door, they took four steps down into a room showcasing the most captivating home bar she'd ever seen. The bar's counter is of beige and tan granite with a mix of dark-brown oak here and there. There are eight bar stools, eight place settings made up of brown paper napkins, the elegant ones along with eight wine goblets sitting atop the elegant fabric. A huge case holding a variety of wine glasses seems to sparkle as much as the glasses themselves. And the boss of the room if that's possible is a mounted plasma television. The floor of the room is ceramic, its tile shined to perfection. The entire time she showed how impressed she is over his Maryland home, Vance stood near the doorway watching as she slowly and carefully strolled around his space of entertainment.

The stars are getting ready to find their place within the cool night sky. All night, Cadrin had slept silently in Vance's arms. It's nice for them to be free of the chaos going on back in Chicago.

A few hours later, Vance had awakened first. He didn't want to disturb her rest, so he continued to let her lay there in his arms. After about a good hour she'd also awakened.

"I'm glad I bought some extra hair care products with me. Otherwise, I would probably look a mess during breakfast with your parents this morning."

"If you hadn't, I'm sure you would still look every bit as beautiful as you do right now."

"You keep those compliments up and you'll make us late for breakfast at your parents' home."

"What? Listen to who's willing to be late in the name of some extra activities. Let me see now, PR for whom…Stone and Nichols is it?…Ha Haaa."

Cadrin smiled widely at Vance. She knows full well she had it coming, always conveniently working her way around one more session with him. Her choreography was for the sake of keeping her client happy with how seriously she believes in the importance of arriving on time.

"Well, we're not in Chicago right now. Are we baby?"

Vance licks the lips she's about to kiss. He could almost taste those kisses on his shower wet skin. She had willingly made his first dream of her a reality as they made love in their morning shower. Cadrin felt like they had been there before, it's so very real to her just as Vance's dream had been for him. Cadrin's strokes to his muscle toned back felt amazing to Vance. He was all but asleep as she'd strummed through the trickles of water which rolled down his back. Cadrin's question struck Vance to raise a brow at her. She's serious and he likes her game.

"No, we're not," he answered her, contemplating her next move.

"Well then where are we, baby?"

"She's going to take this thing to the point of no return," Vance said to himself., loving every minute.

The PR and Attorney are behaving as if they're determined to get Mrs. Connie Grayson over there. By the time the two could finish their game, Connie would probably be at Vance's doorstep. Brian almost wished Vance hadn't told Connie she's finally going to get her wish; to meet the new lady in her oldest son's life. It was yesterday when Vance made the announcement of his visit and his surprise guest. Brian was all but forced to induct the state of Maryland to stand between their home and Vance's. Their oldest son had finally brought home that special lady and Connie is too eager to meet her.

"I'll tell you where we are. Maryland is the place. Remember when I told you no matter where in this world I may be, if you need me, don't keep your desires to yourself. It doesn't matter what your call is concerning, call me. Although there will eventually come a time when our careers will intervene, I will not disappoint you. Do you remember my promise to you?" he said in is romantic and husky tone.

Getting back to normal and running to the aide of their clients will one day do its part in establishing many miles between the analytical public relations expert and the high-powered attorney. Hearing how Vance feels about her gave her valued assurance when it came to thoughts of other women and how they constantly try to become the love of his life. She's the love of his life and he doesn't hesitate in letting her know she is.

"That's a very generous offer. Soon after your business with Everdeen is done, some other mogul is going to need your leadership. Sharing you will not be easy for me."

Having confidence in the continuance of their professional duties, they keep their conversation going.

"Just the same, I'll maintain. By the way Cadrin, I feel the same about you. You're giving all the credit to my career, but your roster looks pretty damn impressive. You may begin to be called abroad more often. Sometimes companies can tend to need a public relations expert more than they need attorneys."

"That may be true," Cadrin answered, "but when you're called upon you tend to be away for weeks at a time."

"Come here lady. Do I need to again state my claim with you?" he said with laughter in his smooth tone.

"You better be willing to say it often," she told him.

"Cadrin, being without you even for a day is more than I can handle. From the moment I saw you standing there behind that podium, you excited me in ways I couldn't ignore. But every time I tried to convince myself I could overlook my feelings for you, my heart began to protest," Vance truthfully admitted.

Sitting down above the covers of the king-sized bed Vance reaches his hand out for hers. Cadrin came to stand between the gap of his knees.

"You know it's going to take some creativity on our part to make this work out," Cadrin said.

"We'll be fine," he assured her. "Somebody sounds like she might love me. Could I be right or am I the wrong man for you, bright eyes?"

Cadrin began to run her fingers over his, now they're holding hands.

"Vance, I have been crazy about you ever since…our second dinner, maybe it was after our first. So much had been going on with Stone and Nichols then you came along. Out of nowhere you came, abruptly causing me to do everything I said I would never do again. Oh, and I don't mean that in a bad way. Really, I don't. It was like I was placing bets with myself, while trying to come up with every reason as to why I should devote all of my attention elsewhere."

"I didn't pressure you. Did I?" Vance asked her.

"Honestly, no you didn't. However, you had a hold on me from early on. It just took me a little while to realize it. Then it became clear to me I was falling in love with you."

Before the invite to meet Vance's family, weeks had past and Vance still hadn't heard the sound of l-o-v-e to come from Cadrin's lips. The day when she'd told him to leave and before he did, he told her he was in love with her. She didn't offer any returned feelings to him; it was understandable why she hadn't. The mood had taken on a different course; Vance knew even through the building pressures of emotions; she'd heard him well. In Cadrin's mind, prior to arriving in Maryland, the L-word didn't have enough footing. Now standing underneath the roof Vance owns shows her some security in allowing the word to manifest, to sail and careen with strength, purpose and yes, true love.

"Wait just a second," he told her.

"What? What's the matter?"

Cadrin watched him dial a set of numbers. Judging from the look on his face she knows what he's up to. This is one spontaneous moment which will be no secret. Over the phone, Vance apologized to his parents. Breakfast will have to begin two hours later as opposed to the eight-thirty a.m. start time Connie is hoping for.

Chapter 27

The Executives

It was difficult for Brian to talk Connie out of seeing Vance and Cadrin off to the airport. Adoringly so, during their visit Connie didn't have any trouble speaking of her oldest son as if he's seven years old again. During her visit, Cadrin had never seen so many baby and other childhood photos of one person all at once. Every stage of their children's lives has a place inside the family's photo albums.

After Vance's last relationship, Connie waited for so long to be introduced to the next lady in her oldest son's life. For that reason, Vance didn't try to pose interception between his mother's hospitality and Cadrin's undivided attention. Connie was so ecstatic until Brian had to tell her to allow Vance and Cadrin some time alone; his thoughtfulness didn't do them any good though. Once Connie had gotten the word of the two of them heading out to Maryland for a visit, she went into the kitchen and began to take inventory of the goods currently on hand. She then drew up a list of items to purchase from the market. Vance told her there was no need to prepare any overnight accommodations for them, he and Cadrin would be residing at his place.

After dinner Cadrin offered to help Connie and Avionne clear the family's dining table. Connie wouldn't hear of Cadrin pitching in. She'd reserved additional time for Cadrin to be treated like royalty.

Cadrin could do nothing except let Connie know if she ended up needing extra hands, she was still more than ready to help.

After Avionne received the word it is okay to skip her usual duty of helping Connie after a meal, she and Cadrin quickly left the kitchen. Therefore, Vance thought he would catch up to Brian and Troy. Little did he know, Connie wasn't about to allow him to leave the dining room so quickly. She had slyly grabbed a hold of the back of Vance's shirt. She'd wanted to talk with her son about his surprise and why it had taken him so long to bring her there. After Vance ended things with Deandra, it had been three years since her son mentioned a love interest. He wasn't pining over his ex like most people believed him to have been doing. Even though work became a huge part of his life, Cadrin happened to spark a special place within him which most definitely got his attention. Connie's biggest question was, does her son love the woman he'd brought home to meet his family; the answer to his mom's question had been, "Very much so." His mother figured he does. However, she'd wanted to ask him anyway. Sometimes dinner and meeting the family is what it is. That's all.

During dinner, Vance's eyes often stared at Cadrin. He lovingly listened intently to her every word as she spoke to his family. Vance told his mother he has deep feelings for the beautiful, fun-loving intelligent woman he'd met in Chicago. He had to admit, he is a little skeptical of how she will feel about him if her career becomes damaged due to her decision to see him based on romance. So, he must live in the moment, a moment which shows him she is as crazy about him as he is for her.

"Hey what are you thinking about?" Vance said over the smooth glide of their Southwest flight.

"I was thinking about your family and what a wonderful time we had. Thank you for inviting me. It was a pleasure getting to familiarize myself with your siblings and the man and woman responsible for raising such a wonderful man."

When he thinks of her, and he does think of her often, a smile teases a corner of his lips. As always, a soothing kiss from her lips burns with passion. The thought of the sensation holds him ever so comfortably, and he can't wait until the moment when they're to privately come face-to-face with each other again so he can receive more of what he is missing. His hours at work are extensive, each hour seem to be frozen into eternity. Cadrin means a lot to him. Often Vance finds himself wondering if she really knows just how much he does depend on her loving him. Every time they make love; he sure does show her he is in love with her. And he enjoys doing so. Taking his time kissing her, getting reacquainted with the way her skin feels through his touch. Their lips tangoing as they live life through each other's ability to define what those kisses mean to them. He's so thorough. She is always so thankful. He never leaves her feeling as though there is something or someone of greater significance in his life which requires his attention the most. Her former lovers, humph. The men flaunted great pride in believing unionization with her was defining of what she'd meant to them. Regretfully so, initially she'd believed them. So much more of her begged for greater attention. Thoughtfulness and consideration go a long way. Superb affection.

"*Wonderful…hmm, I like that,* "Thank you very much."

Cadrin leaned over and gave Vance a short but sexy kiss on his lips after the flight attendant passed their seats.

"That was a great getaway for the weekend, Vance. And in less than four hours we'll be back in Chicago," Cadrin relaxed back in her seat, "your family didn't mention anything about those photographs of us. Did you tell them what's going on?"

Inhaling, Vance realigned himself in his seat by the aisle. He grabbed a hold of Cadrin's hand.

"In strict confidence, I mentioned our situation to Avionne. I would have told my Dad, but I didn't want to put him in the position of keeping that kind of information hidden from my mother. I know she wouldn't be able to handle it. Now Troy, he's a different story. I would like to let him know what's going on, but he can only hold family water for so long. I needed to tell someone, so I told Avionne. She panicked a little but she's okay now. I trust her. She'll keep it between the three of us."

Cadrin squeezed Vance's hand.

"I trust your judgment, Vance."

Having visited Maryland with the man she loves allowed her to not just physically but also to emotionally separate herself from the ordeal which continuously test the authenticity of their love, and their ability to walk with courage.

"When all of this is over and our careers are off the line, I think we should take another trip. Just the two of us," Vance said.

Cadrin loves his optimism.

"Where will we go?"

"I was thinking The Keys, Turks and Caicos, maybe."

Cadrin is aware of what he's trying to accomplish. He wants to make sure even if things don't work out in their favor career wise, he doesn't want her out of his life.

"Vance, you don't talk much at all about what is going on. I'm a big girl, Vance. You can talk to me. It would be great if you would begin telling me why you moved those pictures."

Vance's thumb slowly caressed the back of her hand.

"I don't talk about it because I don't want you to worry any more than you are right now."

"If only you would talk to me, you wouldn't worry as much as you do."

If they had been on a private flight with just a pilot to tend to the controls, Vance would have shown her just how much her comment touched him. Holding back his urge, Vance kisses her on her cheek.

"Are you sure you're not an attorney? You are rather convincing," they laughed, "you said you dibbled and dabbled with a few law classes along the way."

"That's right. And I enjoyed every bit."

"Between that and your PR skills, you'd be a heck of a counsel to reckon with."

From the moment Vance complimented her, Cadrin never allowed her expression to fade away. She's serious about Vance's silence.

"So, talk to me, let me be your attorney, confide in me. Whether I feel you're right or wrong, I will listen to whatever it is you must say. Because somewhere along the line, I believe we will be better than alright." Her persistence is stirring up a yearning in him.

"Listen. I knew early on you would probably realize the photos have been absent for weeks," he told her.

Cadrin nodded.

"I was sure you became concerned, but I didn't want to say anything. However, not talking about them won't make the trouble they hold to go away. Unfortunately, neither will the time we'd spent in Maryland this past weekend. Watching you sometimes mope about the place…all I wanted to do was put a smile on your face."

She shyly looked away and laughed softly to herself. Vance only smiled but he wouldn't allow himself to look away, he stroked her arm, "I couldn't think of anything better than to finally introduce you to my family."

She smiled at him. Because of his disposition, Cadrin can tell he is holding something back from her besides the information concerning the photos. She thought by mentioning those to him would serve as an ice breaker. Finally, he let out a deep sigh.

"What else is going on, Vance? You've been really quiet?"

"Trust me. I'm not relaxed in what has come up against us. Knowing the situation is constantly on your mind….I figured talking about it with you would only make you feel worse about it. We've come over one hurdle and I didn't want to be responsible for putting up another. By placing up roadblocks, how would that make you stronger?" Silence.

"I wouldn't have to be. I can lean on you."

Nodding his head in agreement, Vance smiled.

"Trying to handle this on my own will surely bring more unwanted attention to us, so I hired a private investigator."

Cadrin's eyes grew with shock at what she just learned. However, she knows their predicament is a serious matter. And now learning there is professional and discrete assistance on board nearly caused her to faint.

"You hired…a private detective? Oh…is he a good one?" she asked, trying to keep a hold of her nerves.

"I know. It's okay. Yes, he is. He can ask questions we can't, and he can also go certain places in which we don't need to be seen in. I know of his practices, trust me. We'll be all right. I also told him about Lynn Fields. If she has any involvement in this situation we're in, the detective will inform me."

It was around ten on Sunday night when they arrived back at the new apartment, walking hand in hand all the way to Vance's door.

As soon as they began to unpack, Vance received a text message from Creighton. There has been a small break in the case.

Chapter 28

The Executives

"Good morning," Vance removed a shy amount of covers from Cadrin's grip. She was holding a small section of it as she continued to hold onto her dream of him, and the reality of the night before. Letting go, Cadrin opened her eyes to see Vance smiling over her glowing skin. He was partially ready for another morning meeting with investors at Johnson Everdeen. Wearing a long sleeved crisp white collard shirt, he snuggles close to her with every button on his shirt left undone, and he has yet to turn down his collar.

"Good morning to you," Cadrin said as she softly rubs his chin taking in the scent of his after shave and Sebastian cologne, "mmm Sebastian."

"I'm glad you like it," he said of her compliment.

"Carmichael is something else with these early morning meetings," she pouted. Her hand glided from a loop of his black and starched slacks. From there she ran her hand up to his chest. She began to rub his chin again.

"Are we still in Chicago?" she asked.

Vance laughs aloud.

"Yes, we are. It has been two days back in the rough," he spoke of their predicament. The day after Vance and Cadrin arrived back in Chicago, Vance had gone to meet with Creighton. During their trip to

Maryland, Creighton had heard back from the business next door to the jazz club. On their surveillance camera is footage of the man who boldly appears in several frames during that bold yet careless night by all. The man had loitered around inside their establishment and left shortly after Vance and Cadrin arrived at the jazz club.

With the news the envelope had brought to him and the photos own secret, who knows what impact Creighton's news would have been able to have on her.

"So," Vance kisses the space behind her earlobe, he took in the scent of the cocoa soufflé she'd smoothed on the night before. With her body's chemistry, the scent mesmerizes him, "have you figured out which outfit you're going to wear to Jim Grainger's charity function?"

Cadrin sat up and looks Vance in his face, "Yes, but I wish you could be my date for the evening," little drops of perspiration on his nose and those on his forehead are calling her name. If she answers, she will have to give Jim a pathetic explanation for her tardiness. Looking at the covers and the way her brown skin lushes over them, neither is Vance doing well in running from temptation.

"I wish I could be there with you, so does someone else."

"Someone else? Who are you talking about?"

Vance laughs. He can't wait to see the look on her face.

"Carmichael."

"What? Vance, you're kidding me, right?"

"No, I'm not," his voice took on a serious nature, "my client wants to attend the event your client has been giving for the last ten years. Carmichael says he's been showing up for it since it first began. He understands no reason as to why he shouldn't remain faithful to his record of perfect attendance. Personally, I think it's a bad idea...then again, this event is for the sake of charity. Just as long as he stays away from Jim everything should be alright."

"Yeah, and the guest list is minus of any reporters," Cadrin informed him.

"So, you know what that means right?"

"Sure do. They'll be practically huddled up around the front entrance. Dodging them will be impossible," Cadrin told him.

"Don't worry about it. You'll be okay, make me proud," Vance laughs.

She laughs back.

"Vance quit it!"

"I have to get going," he said while buttoning down his sleeves, still grinning.

After Vance left for the office, Cadrin rose and got herself together for the morning. Once she entered the kitchen, she found the table to be already set. While she was sleeping, Vance prepared her favorite breakfast. On the breakfast table are French toast drizzled with peach glaze and butter maple syrup, two slices of slow cooked bacon and a cup of mocha never looked so good. She couldn't do anything except pull out her chair and enjoy her breakfast. Afterwards, Cadrin sent Vance the sweetest text message.

"Cadrin, I'm so glad you were able to make it this evening. You're looking quite fabulous," Maureen commented amidst the glitz of the evening glam.

"I finally made it. I must have stood in front of the mirror at least ten times before getting here. You know how we ladies can be sometimes."

"Oh yes, too often sweetie," Maureen noticed Cadrin appears to be without a date. She expected the young and beautiful woman to come showing off a handsome hunk of a man. Her solitaire act has left Maureen to feel rather confused.

Cadrin found it very odd everyone thought it to be a crime to be seen at any event without a date. Sometimes even she was one of those people. Even though Vance couldn't make it, Cadrin decided she may as well make the best of things.

Although Cadrin never spoke much about any aspect of her private life; just like many others Maureen always automatically figured her to be involved with some lucky fellow.

"Where might your date be this evening?" Cadrin questioned Maureen. Maureen almost crumbled from her embarrassment.

"Oh, um he's right over there. My husband just loves those tiny little blocks of cheese with olive and pimentos. He's simply crazy over them. I'd better get back over there to him. I'm sure we'll talk again before the evening is over, and you can tell me all about the beautiful ensemble you're wearing."

"I will be sure to do just that Maureen, have fun."

"You too darling, talk with you later," Maureen swallowed before making her way over to her husband who is just about to flag another waiter for more hors d'oeuvres.

Judging from the head count, the event sure had been anticipated. The numbers fell just under a count of four hundred which is great for Creighton. The detective is in attendance as well as Carmichael. Walking around the room, Creighton is fitting right in wearing the same tenure and class of other attendees who are honored to be a part of a great cause during this evening.

This year is different. Jim is really excited about the additions to Stone and Nichols' annual charity affair for multiple sclerosis. Once legal matters fell into place, those in the city who are experiencing their own personal battles with the disease are now in attendance to personally share with others their stories of strength, hope and courage.

Creighton is positive whoever defined the activities of Vance and Cadrin to be of great importance will show him or herself to be present for the evening affair. To ensure the culprit will be in attendance, Creighton told Vance he should plan on attending as well. Vance and the detective arrived at different times with Creighton's name near the top of the guest list.

Paying no specific attention to other guests except for Cadrin, Vance took his time walking around the large ballroom. He spotted Creighton. Each of them maintained their distance from each other. Creighton is in usual character of himself, mostly conversing off and on with other guests and a few of the servers. From afar, Vance studies Cadrin with those come here sexy eyes of his. She seems to be enjoying herself, laughing and talking with others. Each time she shook hands with someone, Vance saw her hand gracefully flow from underneath the wrap of silk fabric which partially covers her almost form fitting dress. She's stunning and amongst the crowd of people, she looks as if she is happily reuniting with old acquaintances as she makes new ones.

Creighton passed by her often, he sometimes hated the grade of distinction he commonly demonstrates while on the job. However, he's thankful his client didn't try to introduce Cadrin to him. It's better she considers him to be just another guest.

Cadrin is beginning to feel a little out of place. She didn't realize just how comfortable she has really become with being at Vance's side. The charity event seemed to have drawn couples from every side of Chicago. Just when she took in a deep breath to hold her subconscious high, she turned around to see Vance from across the room. He had come closer. She's shocked to see him. She thought he had been seriously speaking when he'd told her he wouldn't be able to attend. She smiled and shook her head at him. Vance placed a finger over his own lips to remind her whose event they are attending.

"How can a still best kept secret manage to be so funny," she mused. And Vance is right. He is a very interesting man. When Creighton informed Vance he should attend the event anyway despite the fact of his client and Cadrin being on the guest list, Vance had known since then she would have a date after all.

From across the room, Cadrin notices the look of seduction in the eyes of her man. His longing is very enticing. The way he flirted with her when no one was watching was risqué, but he didn't care. He thought he could control himself around her. Bold and brazing love is sneaking back and forth between them. Next, Vance wrote a note asking one of the servers to deliver to Cadrin a single long stem red rose he'd brought there along with others which are placed safe and secure within the inside pocket of his jacket.

When the server returned to her tray, she noticed the rose first then the note. Studying the crowded room, she's trying to get a take on the spontaneous gentleman. The only thing he left behind was the scent of his cologne. Sebastian. It took all of ten minutes for the server to locate Cadrin. Vance truly knows how to get a woman's attention in a way which makes her bubble over with anticipation. Cadrin looks around a few minutes longer. The men she sees appear to be fully engaged in conversation. With a slight turn of her head, she finally sees Vance again. He's standing on the other side of the room. He sent her a toast of champagne.

Cadrin doesn't know exactly why Vance is here. She thought he must have seen it necessary to attend in order to keep Carmichael under control. She'd seen Carmichael earlier and he acknowledged her with just a nod. She did the same.

Not wanting to set off any reminders there is a lawsuit in the making, Vance and Carmichael are making sure to keep their distance from each other. Preparations are still being made for the charity dinner and Cadrin still has time to contribute. After she presented her check, another waiter holding a long-stemmed red rose approached her. She's playing Vance's game well. Standing a considerable distance from her, he gives her a wink before he toasts her again. Their flirting is interrupted.

"Cadrin, did I just see you submit a check?" Jim questioned.

"Y-es, yes you did. Donating to charity is really a big deal for me. I'm glad to have been able to do something," Cadrin feels a little awkward yet liberated in defense of Jim's stare.

"Please accept my apology Ms. Porter, how I must have sound. I wasn't looking for anything from you. You've done so much already."

"I wouldn't hear of sitting this one out and the way I understand it, you've been supporting this cause for ten years."

"Yes, I have. Ten long and rewarding years and only two of them have included my son. It's very daunting to gain his attention when it comes to giving," Jim told her.

"I'm sure with all the attention you're getting," she waved her hand, "I'm sure he'll soon realize the importance of supporting charities. He'll come around, you'll see."

"As a matter of fact, he is here this evening."

"Really, he's here tonight?"

"Yes, I can't believe it."

"Well, you'll have to introduce us. I'd love to meet your son."

"I will do that, Cadrin. Oddly enough, he'll be sitting on the panel with us and if I didn't mention it before, thank you Ms. Porter for accepting a seat there."

"No problem at all, anytime."

Before Jim left her, he kissed her cheek barely getting a reaction out of Vance who is watching them closely. Vance knows the kiss from the old man is innocent. As for the other men there, Vance doesn't know what he might do or say if he catches one more guy staring at her. She's stunning. Her knock out dress is also making a few of the women turn their heads. Vance knows he must remember to stop behaving like Cadrin's date and pay more attention to the detective who keeps repeating no more than one word at a time. It's probably some slick communication to one of his guys on patrol.

Creighton moves through the crowded room. From the moment the detective saw the peculiar man in the photos, he'd made a mental note of him. If the man is in attendance, he will be apprehended. Creighton could feel it. Yep, trouble is here, and it won't be long before it speaks out. Prior to the event, Creighton assured Vance if something were to come up, he will do his best to be as discreet as he can possibly be. Jim doesn't need another embarrassing scene, especially during this particular evening.

And Cadrin? Vance couldn't help it. Before he realized what he's doing, he'd began watching her again. She looks so innocent, and he feels like he's betraying her. She's aware of the pictures and the fact a detective had been hired, nothing else. Whatever is to happen, he's praying she will not be in harm's way.

So far everything is running smoothly, the event looks like any other. There are the usual conversations, mingling and the carrying around of champagne flutes inside of a crowded ballroom.

"Vance these are so beautiful," Cadrin brought the petals of the roses closer, "they smell even more beautiful than they look," her eyes scan the crowded ballroom looking for Vance. She spots him. Immediately, she picked up on his gesture.

"Here's to you, beautiful," he mouthed the words to her. From across the room, he lifted his glass to her. She smiled and lifted her glass to his. Cadrin's eyes roams the room. She hoped no one picked up on the eye she and Vance hold for each other. Her man is so charming and so very smooth.

Cadrin had no time to lend to discomfort. But maybe it's his discretion which is responsible for her being so at ease. He has skills which she is more than grateful for. And she's more than glad he knows how to be creative with his discretion. She came out of her daydreaming soon enough to see Vance walk away.

"*Why is he here? He said he couldn't make it....Vance what are you up to?"* she wonders, though still intrigued. There she is, holding three long stem red roses searching for her man. He isn't the only tower here. The only difference is his build and mmmm, he is extremely handsome and the way he walks is a sure give away. If only she can see him again. He had started up heated anticipation and Cadrin is not going to let him forget where he'd left off. Vance Grayson will finish what he started. Tonight. The fact he surpassed her earlier expectations of him means nothing, tonight will be about new accomplishments.

"Hello, beautiful lady. Would you be looking for me?" Vance had come closer to Cadrin. Her back was turned to him. To him, she looked as though she was on a discreet treasure hunt. Vance spent several minutes watching her smoothly navigate her way through the crowded room as she tried not to be so obvious in her search for him.

Cadrin turned to face him. She's shocked and as equally pleased. She didn't expect him to come so close to her, but he did without a single scold from her.

"Vance, what are you doing here? You said you couldn't make it," she whispered sweetly to him. His presence is making her sort of nervous but in a good way. Right then and there Vance wanted to take her into his arms. But people who answers to the names of Jim, Maureen and Carmichael forbid him from being so obvious. It made no sense to him to press his luck. He's supposed to be on the job, now his duty is all about Cadrin.

"A while ago I saw Carmichael go through one of the exits, to smoke probably. My client will be back, soon."

"And the rest of the crew?"

Vance notices the slight cute little swivel of her hips as her eyes roam the room looking for her client and Maureen.

"I don't know about Maureen and Jim that's why I'll be brief. Would you like to take a break from the hoop-la in here once Carmichael returns?"

She smiles at him. Cadrin knows very well where he's coming from.

"Uh huh," she replied.

"Meet me outside on the other side of the fountain," Vance whispered as he holds her hand rubbing the back of it. As a shield, Cadrin used her silk fabric to conceal his caress of her fingers. When he asked her to sneak away, his lips barely moved. Cadrin took his spontaneity to be the perfect opportunity - as Jim seems to be well occupied - talking with another guest. They are examining the work of artists whose paintings adorns the walls of the ballroom's foyer. She gave her attention back to Vance.

"There's a fountain here? You really know your way around, don't you?" she whispered back to him.

He looked at her and tasted his lip. *Quick Vance, you'd better get out of there before you kiss her. He sure is dying to.* He said nothing else and walked away from her. She watched his stride as he went through one of the side doors and out into the night's air. Only a few seconds later, Carmichael came back inside the ballroom.

Cadrin looks around the crowded room. From the looks of it, the coast is clear. On her way to the side exit, Cadrin became sidetracked when she noticed Maureen heading her way.

"Hi again, sweetie. It's getting pretty crowded in here, isn't it?" asked Maureen.

"Yes, it is. Right now, Jim is probably feeling a smite bit overwhelmed."

"Probably so. I'm sure he'll get through the evening simply fine though. Oh my, what do we have here?"

Maureen said while she admires the roses Cadrin had been given.

"Thank you," Cadrin said as she accepted a flute of champagne offered by one of the male servers.

"They're just a little something~"

"Well, a little something sure is lovely," Maureen said as she looks within close proximity of Cadrin in search of a man who looks like he may in fact be her date for the evening, "So where is this man? I know he didn't leave you here, alone. Did he?" Empathy is present in Maureen's eyes. Cadrin reached out and gently taps Maureen's wrist.

"No, I assure you nothing like that happened. The roses were delivered to me."

"You're a lucky woman. I hope to meet Mr. Romance, soon," before Maureen walked away, she gave Cadrin a look of you'd better not mess this up.

Cadrin finally made it outside the venue. With her every thought of Vance, she got a tingling rush of excitement all over herself. To follow him up in his request she knows her act is foolish as well as irresponsible. She wants to see him in private and no one is going to stop her.

Just as Vance had told her, there is a fountain. Cadrin watches as spouts of water falls within the large pool. With her roses in tow, she walks down a few steps before strolling across the courtyard. Before she had gotten around to the other side of the fountain, it was through the shots of water Cadrin began to see the shine from Vance's cuff link, and then she saw a part of his jacket. When the darting of the water changed direction, she saw his masculine chest. At the half circle of the fountain, Cadrin sees Vance standing directly in front of the railing which encircles the pool of water. Once she made her way around to the other side of the fountain, she saw the seductive look in Vance's eyes. Preparing to wait for however long it will take for her to reach where he is standing, Vance reaches out his hand to her. Cadrin keeps walking while she began to look for nosey folks.

"It's okay, there is no one out here except us," he said in a love spent husk. Without a doubt, the two of them know they are taking a big chance at being seen together.

Their hands touch. His grasp folds over onto her fingers. Now they are standing behind the protective eyes of the falls of water. Vance lifts her chin. The closer he comes to her, the more Cadrin thinks it is impossible to wait before feeling the slight wetness of his lips earnestly seduce her mouth with the true love he hasn't been able to display around anyone else other than his family. Cadrin feels as though her knees are uncontrollably shaking. Next to their feet, her roses began falling onto the moistened pavement. Cadrin managed to keep a hold of the one rose which ended up over his shoulder then behind his head. She held onto it and their kiss for dear life. Vance holds her closer. They kissed like they had everything good in their lives riding on their passion. His kisses trailed downwards to the cleavage her outfit models. Modestly, it offers her man just enough opportunity to explore just some of what he knows is to come later in the evening. The mystery of his actions is enough to drive her absolutely into a swank of private curiosity.

"Vance, are we crazy?"

Close and as far away as he could see, his eyes wander the pristine perimeter. He stares at her.

"I don't know. Maybe we are crazy or just in love," he smiles.

"You've been walking around this place, haven't you? Not even I knew about this fountain."

Cadrin peeks around his frame at the gorgeous cascade of water.

"I happened to look out the door earlier. I was checking for any uninvited guests, if you know what I mean," Vance gently strokes his thumb over Cadrin's lips, "I'm quite sure Jim wouldn't object to my observation."

"You can't fool me," she took his hands into hers.

"You're worried, aren't you?"

Vance held his head back; she had gotten to know him well.

"Concerned is more like it. But what's getting to me even more is the sexy way you hold your lips after we've kissed. I wouldn't trade it for anything. I feel bad for taking you away from Jim's shindig. I'm sure you understand I had to see you in private."

It had been getting incredibly difficult for Vance to go another second without getting Cadrin outside and into his arms. Under the night's moonlit glow, they sat down on the cement steps the water's splashes over shot. For a short while they had been quiet, enjoying the breeze and the sounds made by the water as it continues to splash into the pool behind them. Finally, Cadrin brought her head from Vance's chest. Looking up at him, she rubs his chin with the one rose she's still holding.

"Thank you for being my date this evening, your being here is….very nice."

He smiles at her. She shyly licks her lips at him before turning back around. Knowing they have overspent their time of privacy; he reaches over her shoulder and led her chin around to meet his face before he covered her mouth with his. Leaning against his thigh, under hypnosis she went. She swore heat reached her toes. Vance had her in a backwards bow as she celebrated his bold yet classical skills.

"Wait Vance, you're spinning me out of control. I'm not complaining but…" he knows what she's getting ready to say to him and she will be right. The last thing they need is for Jim, Maureen neither anyone for that matter other than Creighton, to come out there and see what's going on between them. In his own mind, Vance praised himself for not having introduced Cadrin to the detective. If she knew of his presence, her panic would probably ward off the one person who they are waiting for.

"Sweetheart, we had better get back in there. I'll miss you right here with me. We'll have our privacy again, in a few hours."

"Yeah, I guess you're right. We'd better get back in there before we tear down our secret."

Vance licked his lips. Nodding, he smiled at her. They both stood and kissed again.

Cadrin began to walk away when she turned and knelt to reclaim the roses Vance sent to her. Before she could stand, she dropped one of them again. Slowly, Vance knelt as well. Picking up the rose, he then placed it back in her grasp. Their eyes reached an agreement to stay outside a little while longer. Only because of an opened door of a corridor, the noise coming from inside the ballroom brought them back to the realization of why they made the decision to head back into the event. In disapproval of their short separation, Vance drew in both of his lips. Releasing the words, he said to her, "I would see you to the door, but I think you better go without me. I'll see you soon."

"Alright, Vance," she stepped back from him, "then I'll see you inside."

He finally let go of her hand.

Cadrin turned to walk away then quickly she turns back to him, "oh, someone wants to meet you."

He looks puzzled.

"It's Maureen," cutely, Cadrin fanned the night's cool air with the roses he'd given to her.

Smiling, Vance winks at her.

Chapter 29

The Executives

Vance waited at least five minutes before he deemed Cadrin to have safely made it back inside to rejoin the festivities. Once Vance did the same, he casually strode around the crowded room. He's growing tired of waiting on nothing. The event is heavily attended, its capacity all but makes it impossible to recognize a face from photos which holds many answers. Vance still finds it difficult to abide by Creighton's instruction; to be the look of little concern and to remain casual is growing old. Vance, the detective as well as the guys on patrol has been attentive for just over two hours without any signs of reporters outside of the event. And Cadrin hadn't heard anything from Tim Davenport, not since his second call to her when she'd told him there was no chance she'd changed her mind about passing along his idea of a headliner to Jim.

Knowing the man trying to sue him would most likely remain faithful to the event for charity, Jim has a few more hours to go in containing his differences with the CEO of Johnson Everdeen…and Vance Grayson.

"Everyone, may I have your attention, please. The dining room is now ready to receive everyone. Go ahead and take your seats, and again I would like to thank each of you for sharing this evening with us." Well, some of them. Surrounded by chit chat, Jim turned off the microphone and began heading to the dining room as well.

Maureen stood off to the side entrance holding the door for the guests to make a smooth transition into the dining area where they will settle down to dine. Next to enter the room is Vance.

"Hello, Mr. Grayson. We never know what to expect from you and your client," Maureen said with a questionable smile.

"Are you labeling me as a troublemaker?" Vance said smiling back at her. The person in line behind him waits patiently as he and Maureen continue to speak. Vance knows full well even for the sake of charity, it's quite odd for he and Carmichael to have shown up. He even got a few disapproving stares because of his attendance. He doesn't care at all. Right now, he has other matters which require his attention.

"It's good to have seen you again, Maureen."

"Jim's a good man, Mr. Grayson."

Vance almost nodded in agreement then he caught himself. Later down the line, he'd stopped believing Jim could be responsible for the things Carmichael is accusing him of. Cadrin's date for the evening entered the venue's dining room.

Although the room is much larger than the lobby, it's filling up rather quickly. Just from a few tables away, Vance sees Carmichael. His client is just about to be seated when he'd recognized another familiar face amongst the loquacious crowd. That face belongs to Creighton. He hadn't seen the detective since the moments before leaving for his secret rendezvous with Cadrin.

Sitting at the head table are sponsors and other big-time contributors in support of the annual event. Also invited on the panel is, Cadrin.

"This is a wonderful surprise. I hoped no one got the boot because of me," Cadrin said to Jim.

"Non-sense, you belong up here with us. We're honored to have someone of your stature here. It's just another way for us to thank you for all you've done for Stone and Nichols. You made a lot of heads turn for the better and changed a lot of minds on how my company is perceived by others. Our gratitude for all of your support will never be enough," Jim praised her.

Cadrin shook hands with Jim, Maureen and others seated there at the table. Moments later, Jim's son entered the room from the kitchen. He took his seat on the other side of his father.

In formation, the servers walked down the aisles then spread out about the room to serve the guests iced water and tea. By the time a picture of tea could be brought to Vance's table, he'd consumed both water and tea from two pre-filled glasses.

Vance's attitude had taken on a turn of hopelessness when Creighton discreetly informed him nothing qualifying as suspicious had taken place. If Creighton can't find anything, everyone on the good side of the spectrum will remain at square one.

"Would you like more tea, Sir?"

"Yes, more tea will be great. Thank you," Vance said.

Stragglers from the lobby entered the dining area searching for a table where they can be seated.

"Excuse me Sir, are you holding this seat for anyone?", a stranger asked of Vance.

Vance stood halfway while the woman began to take a seat at his table.

Seeming to grow a bit impatient as well is Creighton. The detective looks across the room where he sees Vance. Vance's stare is steadily producing the most serious concern, a look which is quite different from the one he'd displayed since his arrival. He's staring at one particular individual. Creighton attentively followed Vance's line of vision. The young man seated on the panel notices Vance staring at him like he knows exactly who he is. With a wisp, Vance's eyes trailed back to Creighton then back to the panel. The young man fought to compress himself from doing the next best thing; to high tail it out of there. Cadrin watches Vance as he begins to walk around the table, appearing as if he's headed for the panel. His vision never lost sight of it. Puzzled, Cadrin looks to the left of her seat then right into the eyes of Jim's son, Quinton Grainger. The piercing of her eyes nearly sent Quinton on a race from the raised panel.

"It's him!" Cadrin shouted.

Quinton jumped from the platform running for the nearest exit which will get him out to the streets. Cadrin's frame jolted from her seat, the force rocked back and forth the water glasses sitting before each guest of the panel. In her heels, she trotted to then down the very steps of which Quinton fled. Vance and Creighton abruptly rattled clueless bystanders as they ran across the ballroom floor in pursuit of the man who is pictured in the photos with Cadrin and Vance.

"My God! I can't believe this fiasco! Someone please call for security! That's my son their running after!"

"Jim! For crying out loud, what's going on?" exclaims Maureen.

"I don't know Maureen, but I'm going to put a stop to it!" Jim proceeded out of the venue's ballroom. Finally reaching the sidewalk, he had been too many steps behind to know for sure which way they all went. Frantically, Jim reaches into his pocket for his cell. He quickly needs the help of the authorities. "It's past time I put a stop to Carmichael and his games. First this ridiculous threat of a lawsuit and now his attorney and who knows who are chasing my son!" Jim shouted.

Vance hustles down the sidewalk after Quinton, Creighton trailing a sprint after them.

"He ran into that sandwich shop!" Creighton yelled to the others.

Once Vance reached the shop, he burst through the doors. Halting, he stares into the faces of the people sitting quietly at their tables.

"Which way did he go?" Vance barely huffed. The owner of the shop points towards the back. The shop's patrons again reared back in their seats when Creighton burst through the door of the shop along with two other detectives from his office. One of the detectives watched a plate of burgers and fries hit the floor.

"Where is he!" Creighton shouted.

"He went out back!" Vance shouted.

Creighton looked to the back of the small restaurant and sees Vance sprinting towards the back door. Vance and the detective almost tore the back door off as they went through it and out onto the driveway used for deliveries made to the shop. Before entering the restaurant, Vance could hear Cadrin picking up speed behind Creighton. Her ranting had become louder. Vance thought she must have taken off her heels because Creighton did have a substantial lead on her. Vance prefers her to be back at the event with Jim. He doesn't want to see the woman he loves to perhaps end up in some kind of a stand off with the man they are blaming for having increased the logistics of their secret.

With every pound of his feet to the walkway, Vance is running for the chance to restore every tap of normalcy to his and Cadrin's life. He had done a lot of crazy things in the name of love before. Only sprinting down a public sidewalk hadn't been one of them. Nonetheless, he will catch Quinton. The answer regarding the whereabouts of the two point five million dollars are in front of him at about five feet six inches, scared and weighing about one hundred and twenty pounds.

"Wait! Taxi!" Quinton shouted through his own huffs of wind, waving his arms and hands back and forth hoping for a chance to put more distance between himself and Vance. Quinton pulls on the door of the cab. Poor luck. The force from Vance's grip to his upper arm caused the door's handle to snap away from Quinton. Rustled up against the cab, Quinton struggles to break away from the fist filled grasp Vance has on his shirt. Vance man handled Quinton away from the cab as he kicks the door for closing.

"Let me go!"

"Not until I get some answers! Who are you?"

Quinton said nothing, continuing to try and break free of the angry grasp Vance has on him.

"Who are you, damn it?"

The cab driver had no longer wanted any parts of whatever it is that's behind this match. The cab's tires screeches as the driver speeds away from the unfolding scene. His vast departure caused Quinton's foot to score gravel away from the curb's side. He almost fell onto the street, but Vance took care of that. He angrily ushered Quinton across the sidewalk throwing him up against the windowpane of a jewelry store.

"Vance, hold it!"

"No, Creighton. I need answers from this evading scoundrel."

While Creighton tries to talk Vance into letting him handle things, from down the sidewalk comes Cadrin carrying a pair of after five heels in her hands. She knows Vance will hurt Quinton if the detective doesn't step up.

Vance shook Quinton once more. Creighton watches the fear in Quinton's eyes begin to show everyone he absolutely understands he is not going to get out of this.

"Who made those photos of us? I just dare you to say you don't know! Who are you?" Vance is losing it. He isn't geared up for halfcocked responses, he needs information like yesterday.

"Quinton Grainger! My name is Jim Quinton Grainger," Quinton's truth grumbled down into the bitterness way back from his years as a teenager. He blamed the success of Stone and Nichols for wedging a gap between himself and his father. Just before Quinton entered college, Jim tried to sell him on the temperament he will need to have before going into the family business. Learning the rules, regulations and other managerial aspects of what it takes daily to successfully operate the development company passed down to Jim from his father, is fundamental. But Quinton still showed no interest in learning the family business, not until he'd graduated from college.

Often, he'd worked from a side office within Stone and Nichols where he ran budget reports; a duty borrowed from an employee of the administrative floor. Quinton seriously thought Jim was being a heel for not taking his haphazard advice to cut cost by opening a new position to be ran by himself, and it had been ever since then he resented his father for the declination. All it had taken was for the likes of Claude to have led Quinton astray.

Everyone gasped and their eyes grew with shock.

Vance's angry eyes narrowed at the slight resemblance Quinton has of the CEO of Stone and Nichols.

"Well, he shocked the hell out of me. Quinton, you have a lot of explaining to do. And before you begin, allow me to provide you with some encouragement to use any last remnants of integrity you might have," in a nutshell, Creighton informed Jim's son he is in fact a detective, and the scheming is over for him and whomever else he's under handedly associated with.

"Start from the beginning," Vance chastised. The four of them kept Quinton blocked off while he made himself 'comfortable' sitting down on the store's windowsill. Vance's arms remain folded. The look on his face shows just only a fraction of accomplishment. Maybe now he will get some insight on the things which transpired before he arrived in Chicago.

"Starting a company that was better than Stone and Nichols was what I was after. When my Dad failed to gain Johnson Everdeen for that joint venture, I took that failure to be the opportunity we needed to get our plans off the ground by using your client's," he looked at Vance, "company name to ensure the plan would happen. Then Gory Trust got a heads up and Carmichael was alerted. We knew that by using the involvement of Johnson Everdeen's name, we would secure the funds we needed. But you," he looks at Vance again, "and your client kept stirring things up. So, we went and got a messenger to go to Johnson Everdeen to deliver a warning of a counter suit. After that didn't work, it was weeks later when I went to my father's company to look for barriers against you. I ended up overhearing his publicist have it out with ~" Cadrin's heart sunk, she thought he was going to say he heard her and Vance alone in the conference room. Vance kept staring at Quinton, "Tim Davenport over the phone in her office. We needed you and Carmichael to back off," he pauses to catch more of the breath he'd lost, "then I heard her on the phone with him," he looks at Vance.

"Keep going," Creighton rolled his hand round about the wind.

Quinton angrily stares at the detective.

"I told Davenport the two of them are seeing each other."

"What else do you have to tell us?"

Quinton looks at the angry faces before him.

"Tim Davenport assured me he would fly someone out from Kentucky to back up what I'd told him."

"Well guess what genius? You ended up in the photos as well."

Having no idea who Quinton is, the photographer for The Weekly Chronicles ended up with snapshots of Quinton who had silently refused to stay out of the way. He'd wanted to keep an eye on Vance and Cadrin. If the pair had decided to leave the jazz club to go elsewhere – with the close eye he kept on them - he would have been able to immediately assist The Weekly Chronicles in keeping up with the pair. The slick photographer who was dressed in a tan trench coat had obtained all the snap shots she needed before heading back to Kentucky. Vance was right all along, there was no way Jim Grainger could be of a vindictive character.

Quinton lowers his vision to the ground.

"And the money?" said Creighton.

"We never got our hands on it because it became frozen between two secret accounts that my father obviously has forgotten he has a hold of."

And since the letter did fail them, Quinton thought he'd show up to Stone and Nichols. On more than one occasion he'd done so and had left with two pieces of information which holds enough power to damage two thriving careers.

"I believe we are done here," Creighton said looking at one of his detectives, except there's one more thing, Mr. Grainger.
Who else came to your father's event with you? This evening you will tell me the name or names of everyone who are involved in all of this," Creighton finished.

Creighton hailed a cab to take himself and Quinton back to the event for charity. Vance hailed a second cab for Cadrin's transportation; he protectively walks her over to the waiting cab. Before they could climb in, the glass behind the windowsill where Quinton had sat before being repeatedly shoved against it had given way, falling out of its pane. Vance feels incredibly bad for the situation he'd placed the store's owner into.

Vance saw Cadrin to the front seat of the cab. He closed the door then entered the jewelry store to offer the funds needed to replace the window as it was. Before he left the premises, he offered his apology for the mess he helped sweep up.

Vance along with two of Creighton's detectives decided to walk back to the puzzled crowd at the hotel. Vance needed some time to clear his head of all which had taken place. What he also needs right now is to hold Cadrin in his arms and whisper in her ear,

"*Everything is okay now.*"

And everything is better than just okay, no one else would make his and Cadrin's like for each other their business.

Vance and the detectives arrived back at the hotel to see the swirling emergency lights of authority vehicles and those of an ambulance; Maureen ended up twisting her ankle running behind Jim. From afar, Vance also sees Creighton. The detective is standing next to a police car scribbling down some information onto a small notepad as he speaks with one of the officers there. They will soon be on their way to apprehend Claude. And poor Jim, he's leaning an arm on the open door of the police car his son occupies as he holds his head down in embarrassment of his son's actions against him.

Cadrin did what she could do in helping the paramedics and Maureen's husband get her onto the ambulance. Right behind the last police car a limo pulled up. The driver exited the vehicle and waited there for Carmichael who had been watching everything going on around him. He was even more puzzled when he got an apology from Jim as the disappointed father had gone down the steps on his way to the policeman's car. On the way back to the venue, Creighton obtained Jim's cell number from Quinton. Because Quinton didn't have the courage to speak to his father, it was the detective who told Jim of everything that had transpired.

Vance had gotten much closer to the event's aftermath. Cadrin sees him walking towards her. He looks highly aggravated yet relieved, even tired. Looking around at the chaos, she feels his disarray. No one seems to be paying the two any attention. Sure enough, Vance's stare reaches out to her, her body's language is giving in to him. Cadrin raises her hands then hopelessly drops them to the side of her hips. She looks at Vance with the warmest smile he's ever seen. As soon as Vance reached her, Carmichael got out of the limo to try and talk with Vance about everything he'd seen, even him chasing that guy out of the dining room. Carmichael even heard the detective as he'd discussed the close of Jim's legal matters with Johnson Everdeen. Then it happened. Flash. Carmichael saw the light in Cadrin's eyes as she looks up at Vance. Easing back into the limo, Carmichael relaxed and closed the door with a smile as wide as the one he will wear days from now when Gory Trust will learn in more detail about his noninvolvement regarding the scandal. Naturally, he immediately began thinking about the unscheduled stop he'd made at the corporate apartment. He could do nothing other than smile once more.

A few weeks later, Gory Trust placed their offer back on the table. The offer is up for grabs again and Johnson Everdeen is again their number one prospect.

The pending lawsuit was dropped. And neither party had time to focus on anybody's romantic involvement.

Jim is too hurt and embarrassed to bring it up, and of course Carmichael regained Gory Trust's interest. Lynn Fields? She had nothing to do with this one. And the photos? Tim didn't publish them.

The limo took off leaving Vance holding Cadrin against every beat of his heart. He whispered in her ear then he let her go, well he tried to. He kissed her lips like the lover he is to her and plans to be for however long cupid will look out for them.

"I'm going to drop by the hospital to check on Maureen, you want to come with me?" she spoke with her arms still wrapped around Vance.

"She wants to meet you, remember?" she said while smiling up at him.

"Yes, I remember," he kisses her.

"Um, Vance, tell me something…you never believed Jim was guilty, did you?"

He smiles back at her.

"No, I didn't. Not for one second. Well, maybe two," he grins.

Cadrin gently rubs the back of his hand.

"After we make sure Maureen is going to be okay, how about I help you pack then you help me pack and we both can head off to Maryland, then Fort Lauderdale. So, what do you have to say to that Ms. Porter?" he gently strokes the side of her face.

"That sounds good to me too, Vance."

Hold on girl, here he comes again!

Self-Publisher: Author, Lawana Dinkins
Order Your Copy of Burgundy & Brown's
The Executives via Amazon.com

Have any comments about Vance's & Cadrin's story? If so, share your thoughts with the author by clicking the Comments tab when you visit www.burgundyandbrownportfolio.com ****

www.ingramcontent.com/pod-product-compliance
Lightning Source LLC
LaVergne TN
LVHW091035080826
845145LV00002B/501

* 9 7 8 0 5 7 8 8 8 2 5 1 2 *